"You ever kill anybody?"

Mitch looked at the kid who had asked the question. *How do I answer that one? Yes, but not as a cop.* "I pass," he replied, grateful for the rule that said he didn't have to answer any question that was too personal.

"How old are you?" a girl near the door asked.

"Forty-six."

"That's old. How come you still a cop?"

What else would I do? "I like it. But I wanted a change of pace so I left the New York police force to come here."

"Why?"

"Because it's a slower pace." He smiled. "Because I'm old."

The kids laughed. "Why here?" the same girl asked.

"Because your chief of police is an old friend of mine." *Who tricked me into working with you kids.*

And he'd had to be tricked into this. But he didn't want to let these kids get closer. He didn't want to care. He couldn't afford to care.

He'd cared once and it had ripped him apart.

ABOUT THE AUTHOR

Cop of the Year is Kathryn Shay's fifth Superromance novel. And its theme—teaching kids—is very close to her heart. Kathryn has been teaching high school students for twenty-seven years and still gets a thrill helping kids grow, change and make good decisions about their futures.

Much like Cassie in this book, Kathryn has taught reluctant learners, kids who are as tough as Johnny (also in this book) and just as angry at the world. Some have gone on to be successful; some haven't. But as a teacher, she never gives up hope, never stops trying to make a difference in the lives of her students.

Kathryn lives in Rochester, New York, with her husband and their teenage son and daughter. She loves to hear from readers. You can reach her at: P.O. Box 24288, Rochester, New York 14624-0288.

COP OF THE YEAR
Kathryn Shay

Harlequin Books

TORONTO • NEW YORK • LONDON
AMSTERDAM • PARIS • SYDNEY • HAMBURG
STOCKHOLM • ATHENS • TOKYO • MILAN
MADRID • WARSAW • BUDAPEST • AUCKLAND

ISBN 0-373-70774-6

COP OF THE YEAR

Copyright © 1998 by Mary Catherine Schaefer.

This edition published by arrangement with Harlequin Books S.A.

® and TM are trademarks of the publisher. Trademarks indicated with ® are registered in the United States Patent and Trademark Office, the Canadian Trade Marks Office and in other countries.

Printed in U.S.A.

To my best friends, Mary Jane Brooke, Mary Gerhard and Candy Carlo, the three women I started teaching English with over twenty-five years ago. Thanks for always being there—both in school and out.

CHAPTER ONE

"AM I UNDER ARREST?"

Mitch glanced at the kid draped on the wooden bench in the squad room. "What did the officer who brought you in say?"

"Can't you just answer a freakin' question?"

Mitch sighed. *Insolent punk.*

"No, you're not under arrest. But if you don't keep your mouth shut, I could probably find a reason to keep you here."

Burning brown eyes held his. "Yeah, well you've already done enough damage. What's a little more?"

"A record of arrests doesn't look good, Battaglia."

The boy settled down, and Mitch finished typing his report into the computer. When he was done, he set it to print and leaned back. Linking his hands behind his neck, he stared at the young man who was headed for trouble. Mitch had seen too many others in New York City, and in Long Island suburbs like this one. "Who do you think took the scalpels? Since you contend you didn't."

Battaglia raked a shock of thick black hair off his brow. "I don't know. There were lots of people in the operating room. Other orderlies, janitors, the guy to pick up the anesthesia stuff. Hell, maybe some nurse on crack took them to sell.''

Mitch eyed the kid's jacket, lying on the bench next to him. The Blisters was printed in large capital letters on the back, surrounded by exploding fireworks in vivid red. Blood red. ''You sure you didn't take them? For the next street fight? I hear scalpels are the newest weapons of choice.''

''I don't fight.''

''No, you go to tea parties with your gang buddies.''

''Listen, man, if I'm not under arrest, why do I have to stay here?''

''Because you're under eighteen. Our town ordinance says an adult has to sign you out if you're picked up by the cops for any reason.''

''I'll be eighteen in a few months.''

''Should have waited until then to get into trouble.'' Mitch rose to remove the paper from the printer.

The boy stood, almost matching Mitch's height. ''I didn't do anything.''

''Sit down, Battaglia.'' He sat. ''Did you call someone?''

Eyes full of resentment stared back at him. They were dark and hostile.

''Johnny, what happened?'' a deep female voice called from behind Mitch.

He turned to see a woman in the doorway. *This* was the kid's mother? God help him. She couldn't be more than thirty. His policeman's mind cataloged her features. About five-seven, tall for a woman. Her carriage was an odd combination of athletic grace and streetwise toughness. She had delicate bone structure, big gray-blue eyes and strawberry-blond hair that hung in careless waves on her shoulders.

"Johnny?"

Battaglia stood again. "Sorry to get you up, Cassie. I...didn't know who else to call."

Battaglia leveled a venomous gaze on Mitch. "This pig said I need an adult to get me out of here."

Ignoring his slur, the woman circled to face Mitch. "What happened?"

Mitch noted she didn't ask what the kid had done. Interesting.

"Some scalpels were stolen from Bayview Heights General Hospital. Originally we thought Mr. Battaglia had taken them."

Outrage made her eyes mostly blue. "And why is that?"

"He was the last one in the operating room."

"He didn't take the scalpels."

"How do you know that?"

"He loves his job as an orderly. He'd never do anything to jeopardize it. He wants to be a doctor."

Remorse flickered through Mitch. "We're not arresting him. We just brought him in for questioning."

"Because of his jacket."

Mitch rammed his hand through his hair. "No, because he was the last one seen in the operating room." He glanced at the jacket in question. "Though I hate seeing any gang paraphernalia in Bayview Heights."

"He didn't do it."

"Probably not. We searched him and checked his locker."

"And found nothing."

Battaglia picked up his jacket and crossed to the woman, touching her arm gently. "It doesn't matter, Cassie. I lost the job, anyway. They told me not to come back."

Too late, Mitch tried to stop his reaction to the boy's obvious pain, but he wasn't fast enough to short-circuit it. Damn, he hated dealing with kids.

"Oh, Johnny," she said, placing her arm around him. "I'm so sorry."

The kid leaned into her for a minute, then whispered, "Get me out of here."

Cassie turned to Mitch. "What do I have to do?"

"Go pick up your stuff in the outer office, Battaglia." After Johnny left, Mitch retrieved a form from his desk.

"Sign here."

When she handed it back to him, he scanned it, then said, "You need to fill in the relationship. Who are you?"

"His English teacher."

Mitch stepped back. "His English teacher? Over at the high school?" He looked down at the signature. "Smith. You're Cassandra Smith?"

She frowned. "Do we know each other?"

Mitch gave in to the urge to laugh. "Not yet, Ms. Smith."

"What do you mean?"

"On Monday, I'll be part of your class for the next ten weeks."

"You're joking."

"I wish I were. You can blame the Resiliency Program cooked up by the school board and the town officials. They seem to think schools working with the police force will help make kids more resilient in dealing with today's pressures.''

"I'll never allow you in my classroom," she said implacably.

"I never thought I'd come."

CASSIE SMITH SLAPPED her hand down on the desk. "I won't do it, Seth."

"You don't have any choice." Her principal, Seth Taylor, was clearly choosing his words carefully; he wasn't just pushing her buttons. He'd never do that, anyway. Not this man who'd saved her life, not this man who was responsible for her becoming the person—and the teacher—she was. "Now, sit down, take a deep breath and listen to what I have to say."

She dropped into a chair. "I'm sorry. But a cop? You know how I feel about cops. This one has a history with my students already, and he's only been in Bayview Heights a few months."

"Cassie, your feelings about policemen come from things that happened eighteen years ago. You've gotten beyond everything else, why not this?"

Before she could respond, his phone buzzed. The principal sighed. "Do you mind if I take this? I'm expecting a call from the superintendent and I've had trouble reaching him."

Cassie shook her head. "No, of course not. Do you want me to leave?"

"That's not necessary."

While he took his call, Cassie stood and wandered around the spacious office, comforted by the mahogany furniture and subtly striped wallpaper. On the side table was a picture of Seth's son, Joey. After his wife died, Seth had raised the boy alone, and they were very close. Above the photo, plaques were proudly displayed on the wall: Outstanding Teacher of the Year, Civic Leader Award, Crime Prevention Scholar. Next to those was a framed inscription Cassie herself had given Seth when she graduated from high school and was on her way to college. It read "One good teacher can change a delinquent into a solid citizen."

During his years as an English teacher at Bayview Heights High School, Seth Taylor had been the best. Once he'd become principal, he'd started an innovative At-Risk Program, where four teachers worked with the forty least motivated students in the school. Five years ago, he'd convinced Cassie to come back to her alma mater to teach one of the controversial classes. She'd bet her Grateful Dead T-shirt that if the program had been in place when she'd been here as a student, it would have kept her out of trouble.

Instead, she'd had too many run-ins with the Bayview Heights Police Department. She shuddered just thinking about them. *Why* was a cop coming to participate in her classroom program? And why this particular cop?

"Sorry." Seth's voice drew her away from the past. "Now, where were we?"

"You were about to try to convince me that this cop thing is going to fly." When he started to speak, she held up her hand, palm outward. "No, wait. I know the routine. 'Cassie, it's best for the kids. Cassie, think of what it will mean to the program. Cassie, you've got to get past your personal bias to make this an experience that will save lives.'"

At forty-five, Taylor had flecks of gray in his dark

blond hair and he was a little heavier than when he'd been her English teacher, but his deep blue eyes still twinkled back at her. "Am I that transparent?"

"Yes. It's how you got me back to Bayview Heights, after all."

"Lucky for us that I did."

Cassie blew errant bangs out of her eyes. "Oh, God, I can't believe this. Me and a cop working together."

"It might be nice if you called him a police officer. He *is* a captain, you know."

"Oh, yes, I know. He's so by-the-book it's scary. I saw his attitude toward Johnny firsthand. And then he testified against Amit—who's barely staying in school—on the dealing charge."

"As I recall, he saved Amit's neck by recommending a community service punishment, instead of juvenile detention, so he *could* stay here as a student."

Cassie sighed and sank into the chair. "Yeah, that's true. But he's just so stiff, so formal. Rules, rules, rules. Do you know how my class will appear to him?"

"You have rules, Cassie."

"Yeah. Try telling that to Jerry Bosco. He thinks we run a zoo down in hall 400."

Seth frowned at the mention of the veteran teacher who had vehemently opposed the At-Risk Program. Cassie knew Seth had had run-ins with the man, too, some of them very serious and long-standing. "Bosco's just jealous of all the money that's been funneled there."

"No. He thinks advanced placement kids are the

only ones deserving computers, field trips and special programs.''

"Which is what Mitch Lansing is, Cass. Part of a special program. Just like the ones we brought in from business and social services.''

"Why can't he work with Ross's math class? Or Jack's social studies class?''

"You know he can't. Ross and Jack have done their stints. You and Zoe get to participate this half of the year. And Zoe's got the artists.''

"Why don't I have the arts? I use art in English class more than she does in a science class.''

"Because the arts, writing and reading are part of every curriculum, not just language arts.''

Cassie smiled as she listened to Seth expound on his favorite topic. One of the first things he'd done when he became principal at Bayview Heights High School ten years ago was to erase as many lines as he could between the disciplines. Because of him, research papers became the requirement of all subjects, even math; reading and writing were heavily emphasized in each course; and physics teachers participated in the dance workshops and the improvisational theater specials. Seth Taylor had truly helped make Bayview Heights High School an innovative school.

"Then shorten the time. Every day for ten weeks is too much.''

Seth just stared at her.

"All right,'' Cassie said with exasperation. "He doesn't really start today, though, does he? I've got to prepare the kids.''

"Yes, he does. We knew something like this was in the works, but I just got word Friday afternoon exactly what kind of program it would be and when it would start. And I didn't want to ruin your weekend." He glanced at his watch. "But I'll stall him here for half of your class. We'll discuss the program, and I'll get to know him a little. You can use the first part of that two-hour-block schedule you talked me into to prepare the kids."

"All right."

"I'm counting on you, Cass."

For a minute, Cassie was transported back nineteen years. Seth had stood at her desk after one of his English classes and said those exact words to her. He'd known she was going to take off for good that night, to escape the seediness of the one-room apartment where she lived, the derogatory names people called her and her mother, the consistent failure in school.

She'd been sixteen.

And the man before her had encouraged her to stay, to keep a journal about her life, and he'd insisted she talk to him about everything. Finally he'd arranged legal and professional help for her. Cassie shuddered when she thought about where she'd be if it wasn't for him.

Glancing down her leg, she caught sight of the small rose tattoo at her ankle. She'd had it done in a grungy tattoo parlor in Greenwich Village when she was fifteen; she kept it as a reminder of what it was like to be one of the kids she now taught.

"Cassie?" Seth's question brought her back to the present.

"Yeah, I know you're counting on me. Just like I know that *you* know exactly what you're doing when you say that to me, Mr. T." She used the old name intentionally, and it brought a smile to his face.

"Now go," he said gruffly. "Unless you want to bump into Lansing."

Cassie stood and hurried out of the office. She didn't want to bump into Lansing now, or ever. But damn, she'd do anything for these kids, even it meant letting a cop—correction, a police officer—into her classroom.

MITCH LANSING WAS NOT a happy man. As he strode down the hallway with the principal of Bayview Heights High School, he cursed the fates that had brought him to this point in his life. How the hell had he ended up here?

When they reached the east wing of the school, the first thing he noticed was the low hum of student voices. There was occasional laughter punctuated by adult comments.

"Here we are." Taylor knocked on the open door of 401.

Mitch looked around for Ms. Cassie Smith. Had she left the kids alone? They were all in a group in the far left-hand corner of the room. But they weren't at desks. Some were on couches, some sat on the floor, one perched on top of a table. The area was plushly carpeted and brightly lit by the sun slanting in from uncovered windows behind them. He scanned the walls, taking in some of the posters: "School might be hard, but it's better than growing up... The thing we call failure is not falling down but staying down... It's what you learn after you know it all that counts." He smiled at the sentiments.

Someone unfolded from a zebra-print stuffed chair and came toward them. Mitch's smile disappeared when he realized who it was. She looked even younger today, probably because of the way she was dressed. Her clothes were casual—checked shorts that looked like a skirt and a long-sleeved wine-colored sweater. He tugged at his tie.

When she reached them, she held out her hand and smiled. Plastic. He knew it matched the one on his face.

"Hello, Captain Lansing."

"Ms. Smith."

Taylor stepped farther into the room. Mitch noticed that the kids had continued with whatever they'd been doing when he and the principal had come to the door.

"Silent sharing time?" Taylor asked.

She nodded.

"Can I go over?"

"You can go, but they probably won't let you see their writing today." She looked at Mitch. "No offense, Captain, but they aren't too happy about having a stranger invade their turf. However, they've agreed to be civil, and it will work out, I'm sure."

She didn't sound sure, Mitch thought. Well, hell, neither was he.

As Taylor crossed to the far corner, the kids glanced up at him. Most greeted him congenially. He spoke to the girl sitting on the desk, and she smiled. He ruffled the hair of two boys who sat on the floor. A kid on the couch tipped his baseball cap to him.

"They're allowed to wear hats in class?" Mitch asked.

Ms. Smith closed her eyes briefly. When she opened them, they reminded him of an overcast sky in January. "This isn't a church, Captain."

"No, but kids should show respect for their school."

"And taking off your hat shows respect? Not in here. Read the poster over my desk. We have our own definition of respect."

Mitch scanned the room. "Where's your desk?"

She pointed to an area to the left. A big gray metal desk sat unobtrusively in the corner. It was covered with folders and papers. Next to it was a tall bookshelf that housed books, picture frames, more folders. Sure enough, on the wall behind her desk was a big poster—beautifully scripted by someone with artistic talent. The word *respect* was printed vertically, and each letter spun off horizontally into a statement. "R—Rules are for a reason, obey them; E—Expect and return common courtesies; S—Show others you care; P—Put a lid on negative comments, even if you have them; E—Exhibit pride in yourself and let others have theirs; C—Consider the effect your words and actions have on others; T—Take what you need but give what others have to have, too.

After he'd read it, Mitch turned back to the hostile Ms. Smith. Her face was smug. He was about to comment on the definition, when Taylor returned. "Where's Johnny?"

Ms. Smith threw Mitch a scathing glance. When she looked at Taylor, though, her face showed very real concern and a surprising vulnerability. "No one knows. When we called home, his mother said she hadn't seen him in three days."

"Since Friday?"

"Yes."

"Did you have any contact with him over the weekend?"

"No." She bit her lip and something inside of Mitch shifted. "I'm worried."

Taylor reached out and squeezed her shoulder. Not a smart move in these days of sexual harassment cases, Mitch thought.

"I'll see what I can find out," the principal told her.

"Thanks."

As he walked to the door, Taylor said, "Good luck, Mitch. Stop and see me when you're finished here."

Mitch nodded, and Taylor left. Casually, Mitch stuck his hands in the pockets of his suit pants pockets and looked at Cassie. "I'm sorry the boy is missing," he said simply.

"Are you?"

"Yes." When she said nothing more, he asked, "Well, how do we start?"

Silently, she folded her arms over her chest and leveled wary eyes on him. "With the kids, of course. After all, that's why you're here. Come on, I'll introduce you." She looked him up and down. "I realize you've come to help educate these students, Captain, but you can't be in class without participating in the activities. Participation is required from everyone."

He hadn't planned on that. The idea was mildly alarming. He thought he'd just be an observer on the days he didn't have to present material. "That was never discussed."

"Well, it's a rule in this classroom, Captain. Everyone participates, including the adults. You like rules, don't you?"

She was toying with him, and *that* he didn't like.

"I'll see what I can do," he said sarcastically.

Accompanying her across the room, he could feel his heartbeat accelerate as he approached the teenagers. Damn, this was hard.

"Okay, everyone," Ms. Smith said. "This is Captain Lansing from the Bayview Heights Police Department." Indicating the chair she'd vacated, Cassie said, "Sit here, Captain."

He sat. As he did, he saw two boys watch his every move with suspicious eyes. Three kids totally ignored him. One girl whispered to another next to her, and they both giggled.

The teacher addressed him. "I've told everyone about your stint with us. They have a lot of questions, but I thought we should start by getting acquainted." She glanced at the clock. "We have an hour left. Let's play the name game." When most of them groaned—good naturedly but expressing their reluctance, nonetheless—she made eye contact with each student and got their assent. Then she met his gaze. Hers was direct, no nonsense, confident.

Mitch felt as if he had no choice but to nod, too. "Could you fill me in on the *rules* first?"

"Each person tells his or her name and shares one significant personal thing with the group. It helps us get to know one another and also will help you learn their names."

At least he would be all right there. He had a photographic memory. Unfortunately. There were a lot of things he'd give his soul to forget. As he looked around, he squelched the inner warning that working with these teenagers was going to bring back those images. That was why he'd stayed away from adolescents for twenty-five years. That was why he didn't want to be here now.

"Who would like to start?" Cassie asked, interrupting his reflection. When no one volunteered, she dropped to the floor, clasped her hands in her lap and looked at them. A long, uncomfortable thirty seconds passed before a young girl raised her eyes to the ceiling and said, "Oh, all right. I'll start." Cassie gave her a million-dollar smile, which the girl returned. "I'm Jen Diaz."

"And? One significant thing about yourself?"

Again, the rolled eyes, the stock-in-trade teenage show of disgust. "I, um, just got a new stepfather."

They went around the room—slowly, some begrudgingly.

"Austyn Jones," a young black student said. He pulled at the lapels of his sport coat. "And I'm into rags."

"Clothes," Cassie said to Mitch.

"I know," Mitch responded dryly.

"Nikki Parelli," a sweet-looking redhead volunteered. "And I like to write."

"Nikki won first place in the literary magazine's poetry contest last year," her teacher said proudly.

"Brenda Uter," a dark-eyed girl said when it was her turn. "And I'm popular." Everybody laughed, but no one made a smart remark as Mitch expected.

They proceeded like that—Som Choumpa, a young girl from Vietnam who loved clothes and had the same eyes as those that haunted Mitch's dreams; Amy Anderson, who had a two-year-old child; Joe

DeFazio, who took mechanics in a special afternoon program; the sports star Don Peterson; Tara Romig, a dancer; Amit Arga, whom he'd met in court. Two kids were absent, Mike Youngblood and Johnny Battaglia, bringing the total to twelve—an even dirty dozen.

"Your turn, Ms. S.," Jones said. "And don't give him nothing stupid. Like you're a teacher."

She smiled. "Okay, okay. Let's see. My name is Cassie Smith," she began, but Jen Diaz interrupted, "Cassandra…named after the Greek woman who could foretell the future."

Cassie chuckled. "And I like to play softball."

"Yeah, she teaches our spring phys ed unit," Arga told him.

"Are you certified to do that?" Mitch asked.

She gave him a disgusted look. "The law says you can teach one course out of your certification. Now, how about you, Captain?"

He squared his shoulders and struggled not to wipe his sweaty palms on his pants. How long since he'd been forced into such uncomfortable disclosure? "I'm Captain Lansing."

"Captain your first name?" the young Italian boy—DeFazio—asked.

Unnerved, Mitch shot back, "No. It's Mitchell. Mitch Lansing," he corrected himself, feeling foolish. "And I…" Suddenly he was at a loss. What did he tell these kids? Who was he, really? His family came to mind—what was left of it after his parents had died within six months of each other. "I have a brother Kurt. He's…important to me."

Revealing anything about himself was tough, but the soft approval in Cassie Smith's eyes made him even more uneasy. He didn't expect her good favor, didn't want it.

"Can we ask him some questions now?" Nikki directed the question to her teacher.

Cassie looked to Mitch. "It's up to him."

He scanned the kids. How hard could this be? "Sure."

"You can pass on some if you want," the young girl told him helpfully.

He gave her a small smile. He was going to like Nikki Parelli. "Fair enough."

"You the one who arrested Johnny?" Arga asked.

"I didn't arrest him. I had him brought in for questioning."

"He lost his job."

"I was sorry to hear that."

"Why you here?" the boy continued.

"Because the Bayview Heights Police Department decided it would be good business for the law enforcement agencies to work with the schools. Remember the DARE program when you were younger?" Mitch asked, referring to the statewide anti-drug program the police conducted in the lower grades. Arga nodded. "This is an extension of that. They believe it will help crime prevention and establish better relations between the school and the police department."

"They?" This was from Peterson, the sports star.

Mitch ducked his head. These kids were quick. "I just came to Bayview Heights six months ago. I guess I'm not fully acclimated."

"What's that mean, Ms. S?" Peterson asked.

"He's not used to being in Bayview Heights yet."

"Will you be teachin' us anything?" DeFazio asked.

"Yes. There's a curriculum of ten lessons, one a week, that I'll be delivering."

"On what?" several asked at once.

"Drugs, weapons, juvenile crime, vandalism, addiction, violence prevention, theft."

Their teacher added, "It's a lot like the other people who came into your science, math and social studies classes. We're trying to integrate the community into this program and use their expertise to help you."

"Yeah, I liked that social worker broad," Peterson said. "She was great lookin'."

"I liked her because she helped me out...you know, at home," Som Choumpa said.

"And the business guy, he got me the job at the garage." This from DeFazio.

"See," Cassie said. "Some good things came out of those programs. Captain Lansing has a lot to offer, I'm sure."

The lady doth protest too much, Mitch thought. He seemed to be the only one to catch the note of uncertainty in her voice.

"Where were you before, if you just came to Bayview Heights?" popular Brenda asked.

"I worked in New York City. On their police force."

A few of the kids whistled. "Yeah? You ever kill anybody?" Jones asked.

Not as a cop. "I pass."

Out of the corner of his eye, he saw Cassie studying him critically.

"What did you do in the city?"

"I worked in vice. Then, for several years, in the narcotics unit."

"Hey, DeFazio, you better watch out."

He saw Cassie stiffen and quell the kids with just one look. Amused in spite of himself, Mitch thought he'd shut up, too, if she looked at him like that.

"How old are you?" Amy asked.

"Forty-six."

"That's old. Even Mr. T ain't that old," Arga teased. "Why you still a cop?"

What else would I do? "I like it. But I wanted a change, so I left my job in the city and decided to come out here."

"Why?"

"Because it's a slower pace." He smiled. "Because I'm old."

They laughed. "Why here?" Jen asked.

"Because your chief of police is a long-time friend of mine." *Who tricked me into working with you kids.*

And he had to be tricked into this. Interacting with these teenagers had already caused a little bit of the wall around his heart to crack. He didn't want to care. He couldn't afford to care.

He'd cared once and it had ripped him apart.

CASSIE WATCHED MITCH straighten his paisley tie, pull up the legs of his trousers and sit down on a straight chair. He was armored with his suit, tie and wing tips again today. She was only partly amused by his stuffed-shirt demeanor. Mostly, it raised her old fears.

They'd had an inauspicious beginning with Johnny's visit to the police station Friday night and then with Lansing's attitude yesterday—they wear hats? for God's sake—but she'd hoped today would be better. If this program was going to work, she had to readjust her attitude.

And he had to participate. She insisted he do the activities right along with the kids. He'd looked displeased, almost fearful, but he'd done them. Right now, his green eyes were as cool as dewy summer grass, watching her intently.

She addressed the class from where she sat on top of a desk. "It's time to start, everyone. May I have your attention, please." On the signal, the kids quieted down. "The quote's on the board. Write." She walked over and handed Mitch Lansing a black notebook and pen. "This is a journal. It's a very important tool in language arts instruction. We begin every class by writing. You can use the quote on the board, relate it to what you're feeling, or you can write about anything that's on your mind." She smiled, trying to make it a pleasant one. "Then we share, so don't write something you don't want anyone else to see." That had been the biggest source of resistance she'd had with the kids. That they had to share with a stranger and a police officer.

"No passing today?" he asked.

"You can always pass, but it's not a good example to set for the students."

His chagrin made her bite her lip to hold back the mirth. She wasn't here to rile him, even though she really wanted to. His uptight attire, his proclivity for rules, his staid manner just begged to be taunted.

Which was why she'd chosen the quote for the day. "Rules were not made to be broken. But they need to be examined carefully."

Lansing reached into his pocket, drew out a pair of glasses and settled them on his nose. He looked nice in them—scholarly. He had a honed body, big and powerful, and she imagined he used his strength and muscle skillfully.

She sat down on the floor next to Brenda to write. Yesterday, all the girls had been abuzz over Captain Lansing's physical attributes. "Hunk...stud...totally rad..."

Reluctantly, Cassie admitted that his perfectly cut dark hair, sprinkled with gray, the cleft in his chin and those chiseled features *were* appealing—in a Pierce Brosnan kind of way.

Forcing herself to stop thinking about him, she began to write, analyzing why she balked so much at rules. Why she felt such a need to buck the system. Wondering how, at thirty-five, she could still be such a misfit. As usual, putting things in words clarified and released her feelings. Ten minutes passed, then the door opened.

Johnny Battaglia sauntered in. If Cassie didn't know the kid so well, she'd be tempted to take him down a peg or two. If she didn't care so much, she'd scold him for being late. But she was lucky he was here at all, and she knew it. At seventeen, he'd already dropped out once.

And she was going to save him if it was her last act on this earth.

Johnny closed the door quietly and headed straight for her. Cassie smiled at him, though it was hard. The boy's face was drawn, lines of fatigue marring his youthful brow, bracketing his sulking mouth. His shoulders sloped with weariness. When he met her eyes, he gave her a weak grin. And she knew in her gut that the last few days had been hell for him.

According to procedure, he put the late pass in the envelope on the wall behind her, signed in, then settled onto the floor. She handed him his journal. As he opened it, he glanced around.

And spotted Mitch Lansing.

Johnny's entire body tensed. Reaching out, Cassie touched his arm and squeezed it. He looked over at her, the sudden flare of anger in his eyes making her heart stutter. She watched him warily.

She could see him struggling with himself.

So she stood, inclined her head to a little alcove designed for private consultations, and drew him over to it while the others kept writing.

"What the hell is he doing here?" Johnny asked in a whisper.

She cocked her head at his language. All the teachers insisted on no cursing or obscenities in front of them, or in class.

"Sorry," Johnny said.

"If you'd been here yesterday, you'd have heard the entire explanation. I'll give you a shortened version."

When she was done, his dark brown eyes were even more tumultuous. "You gotta be kidding me." His voice rose, and everyone looked over. Cassie moved in between the other students and Johnny.

"I'm not working with any cops. Especially not him." He looked around the room, his eyes bleak. "Especially not here." Then he focused on her. "Why, Ms. S? Why here? This is the only place I feel…" He stopped, but Cassie knew what he was going to say. This was the only place he felt accepted, comfortable, different from being on the street. It was, really, his only chance to go straight. Cassie knew personally, and from having read the statistics, that success outside of the home—and it usually meant doing well and fitting in at school— was one of the most important factors in at-risk kids graduating from high school and becoming productive members of the community.

"Johnny, we don't have any say. The school board decided to implement this program. He'll only be in language arts class for the next ten weeks."

"Then I won't be."

"What?" Cassie gripped his arm.

Roughly, Johnny shrugged it off. "You heard me. I won't be." He stepped out from behind her and faced the now avidly attentive group. His cold stare zeroed in on Mitch Lansing. "If he stays, I'm gone."

With that, Johnny Battaglia strode out of the room.

CHAPTER TWO

JOHNNY CHALKED THE POOL cue and bent over the battered table. His eyes were gritty, and he had a pain between his shoulder blades that wouldn't quit. "My break," he said without inflection. He had long ago perfected the art of not letting anybody know what he was really thinking.

Except Cassie. Damn her. He'd let her in, and she'd gone and blown it. Well, no more.

Sure. Who are you kidding, Battaglia? He'd tried a thousand times to get the woman out of his life and nothing had worked. Now that he'd had time to cool off, he didn't really expect that one lousy pig would affect his and Cassie's friendship.

As he broke the stack and took the shots, he thought about Cassie.

He only called her that in private. In public, it was Ms. Smith, Ms. S., or affectionately, "Teach." At one time, his feelings for her had been all mixed up with male-female stuff. But that had stopped once he started dating girls his own age. Plus, despite her warmth, Cassie had always played the grown-up; that had helped keep things clear in his mind. Now he saw her as his friend first, teacher second, and sometimes...dangerously...his savior.

Damn, why had she done this? As he banked a shot off the side, he let his mind form vile obscenities, just because she wouldn't allow them around her or in school. *Why* had she done this?

We don't have any choice, Johnny. The school board insisted.

Yeah, well, people always had a choice. Hadn't that been what she'd drilled into their dumb-ass little heads since ninth grade? *You choose whether you win or lose in life, you decide how addicted you get to the bad stuff, you pick how you handle the lemons fate throws your way.*

Eventually, he'd begun to believe her. It took him a whole year, but he'd learned to trust her.

Except when he'd dropped out for six months.

Johnny shivered just thinking about it. That had been the worst time in his life. So he pushed it—and Cassie Smith—out of his mind.

"Six ball in the far left corner," he called, and proceeded to demolish his opponent, a scruffy little man who worked the night shift at the electronics plant down the road. Johnny bested him for ten bucks, and the guy wasn't too happy.

So, join the club, buddy.

"Battaglia, phone call for you." Pepper stood by the wall phone, holding out the receiver to him. The guy was the oldest man Johnny knew, with more wrinkles on his face than in his clothes.

Johnny tried to quell the spurt of hope that it might be Cassie on the line. "A chick?" he asked casually.

"Nope, it's your pal, Zorro. He asked for Tonto." Pepper gave him a dirty look. Cassie had gotten to Pepper, too. They were all watching out for him, trying to keep him from hooking up with the Blisters again, now that he'd moved out here from the city with his mother on the advice of some starry-eyed social workers. Probably that's what this Lansing guy was supposed to do, too. Make sure Johnny didn't get into any trouble. He smiled. Cassie hadn't seemed too pleased that the cop had been in their class, either. Johnny could tell by the way her shoulders got real stiff and her mouth got those lines around it like it did when she was mad about something.

Reluctantly, he walked to the phone. "Yeah?" he said simply.

"Tonto, my man. How's it goin'?"

"Just peachy, Zorro. What you want?"

"How come you ain't in school?"

"How come you call here if you think I was?" Johnny fell back into the street talk whenever he was with these guys. Sometimes he hated it, but it comforted him today.

"Got a line on Fish," Zorro said, all serious.

"Yeah. How?"

"I got my sources. We gonna go lookin' for him tonight. Wanna come?"

"I gotta work from three to eleven."

"Thought you lost that crummy job at the hospital."

Johnny tensed. It still hurt. "I got a new one at the garage." Changing oil and pumping gas instead of learning how to save lives. Shit.

"After eleven, then."

Soft gray eyes appeared before Johnny. *Please, don't do this,* she'd said the last time he'd gone to his old neighborhood in the pit of the city to hunt with the gang.

Then he remembered the freakin' cop, sitting

stiffly in a chair, looking at the students as if they were cockroaches, butting in on the only thing that was good in Johnny's life.

"I'll think about it," he told Zorro.

"HOW DID IT GO with the cop?" Zoe Caufield asked from the doorway. Cassie looked up from the student portfolios she was reading. Zoe was her co-worker and best friend, but they couldn't be any more different. At thirty-eight, Zoe was short, petite, dark-haired and dark-eyed, and bought her clothes at Lord & Taylor. She'd grown up with the proverbial silver spoon in her mouth and had married a rich doctor. Divorced, she now lived in a pricey condo on the bay. The only thing she'd ever done out of sync was to become a science teacher—and work with the At-Risk kids.

"It went as well as can be expected," Cassie answered.

"He's a doll."

Cassie rolled her eyes. "Not you, too. The girls are driving me nuts. They actually like those suits he wears and that noose around his neck."

"Mmm. Me, too."

"You would."

"So how are the kids taking to him?"

Cassie sighed. "I got them to keep an open mind—mostly through bribery and some threats. I agreed to shorten their research project by four pages if they'd give him a break."

Zoe came into the room and perched on the edge of her desk. "What happened with Johnny?"

Taking in a deep breath, Cassie tried to quell her fear. "Johnny walked out."

"What?"

"You know he wasn't in school yesterday." Zoe nodded. "Well, he missed the prep I gave the other kids. It would have been a push, anyway, getting him to accept Lansing. He doesn't relate well to men in general, he hates cops and he already had that run-in with the good captain Friday night. But I was hoping he'd cooperate. He wouldn't."

"If anyone could have gotten Johnny to work with Lansing, it would have been you. He worships you."

"We're kindred spirits."

Zoe smiled. "I know. So what happened?"

Briefly, Cassie described Johnny's reaction. "I'm going to find him after school, if I can."

"Too bad he lost his job at Bayview General."

"Yeah. He loved it."

"Thanks to you."

"Why?"

"Because you flirted shamelessly with the director to get him in there."

Cassie shrugged. "Whatever works…"

"Hey, maybe you could use your charms on Captain Lansing. Get him to give up his stint here."

"Are you kidding? That guy's got ice in his veins. I pity the woman who tries to thaw him."

Zoe's exotic eyes took on a dreamy quality. "I wouldn't mind trying. Take a good look next time, Smith. He's definitely hunk material."

After Zoe left, Cassie sat back, thinking about Mitch Lansing. Hunk material?

Well, maybe. He did have a great body. And she'd bet those green eyes could melt a girl just as quickly as they could freeze her out. For a minute,

Cassie wondered what it would be like to have him touch her. It had been a long time since she'd fantasized about a man. Though she dated, she hadn't had a serious relationship since her marriage broke up six years ago.

I can't compete with them, Cass. You're too absorbed in your job. Those damn kids are more important than me.

Paul just hadn't understood. No one outside of education really did. No one felt the compelling need, the driving force to make a difference in kids' lives like Seth Taylor had made in hers.

You've got a savior complex, Paul had told her. *I want a real woman in my life.*

She'd been hurt, and disappointed in herself that she couldn't give him more. Her self-confidence as a woman had been shaken. But she'd let Paul leave, and experienced some measure of relief that she didn't have to defend her actions anymore.

But she missed the closeness, and the sex.

A picture of Mitch Lansing came to her again, and before she could think about him in a sexual way, she banished the image. Luckily, the kids were coming back from lunch, so she didn't have to analyze her reaction.

Two hours later, she swung open the battered front door of Pepper's. The owner of the pool hall-cum-diner was at the counter, wiping up after the last of the regular lunch crowd. "Ah, my favorite teacher."

"Hi, Pepper." She looked at him expectantly.

"He's in the back," the old man told her. "Been here since eleven."

"Thanks."

Cassie found Johnny slouched in the corner, pool cue in his hand, feet stretched out, eyes closed. The picture he created tugged at her heart. He looked so *alone.* She crossed the room to him. "What are you doing sleeping in a pool hall like some bum?" she asked lightly.

He opened one eye. "I am a bum."

Serious now, she said, "No, Johnny, you're not."

"Better watch it, Teach, the school district ain't gonna like you in here with us riffraff."

She plunked down beside him. "I got tenure."

He snorted.

"You been winning?"

"Some."

Silence. She watched the game in progress, scrambling to find some way to reach the boy. Finally, she called to the players, "I've got winners."

Johnny straightened abruptly. "Cassie...this isn't a good idea. You shouldn't be rubbing elbows with these guys."

"I want to play," she said implacably.

His brown eyes lit on her. "All right, spit it out."

"Play me. If I win, you come back to school and try to accept Lansing. If I lose, I'll leave you alone."

Pure panic flitted across the boy's face. Cassie recognized the emotion. As a kid, she'd relentlessly pushed everyone to give up on her, and when she thought they might, she panicked.

"You're on," Johnny finally said. "But don't blame me if Taylor hauls your...rear in for being down here again."

Cassie stood and picked up a cue. Someday, she'd tell Johnny a few things about Seth Taylor's unorthodox methods all those years ago. But right now, it was better to let him worry about her. As she'd told Zoe, she'd do anything to help these kids. Especially this one.

HAL STONEHOUSE WATCHED Mitch wolf down his roast beef sandwich at Pepper's that afternoon. "How come you eat like a pig and never gain an ounce?"

Mitch smiled, a genuine response, if a rare one. "Just luck, I guess. And I work out every day." His eyes scanned his friend. "You should too, Hal. After what Kurt told you."

"Your brother's a good doctor, but I can't change overnight."

"You're walking daily, aren't you?"

"You know I am. You watch me like a hawk."

"Well, you're the one who lured me to Bayview Heights."

The old man smiled. "Yup, I am."

"Then threw me into the lion's den."

Stonehouse scratched his chin. "Sorry about that. I needed a juvie officer after Gifford…died."

Mitch winced at his friend's tone. "Hal, that wasn't your fault."

"He was inexperienced. I should have…done something different."

"It's in the past. Let it go."

But even as he said the words, Mitch knew all too well that the past could be a living, breathing entity that wouldn't allow you to escape no matter how hard you tried.

Hal looked at him. "Least I don't have to worry about you."

Which is the only reason I agreed to this purga-

tory. To ease the pressure on you. Though Hal Stonehouse had mentored him from the age of twenty, the old man still didn't know why Mitch avoided working with kids. No one did, except Kurt, who knew only sketchy details. When Mitch had come back from Vietnam, he'd refused to talk about his experiences to anybody. All Hal knew was that Mitch had been in Southeast Asia at the very end of the war and had come back with the scars and baggage that many vets had brought home.

"So, how's Smith?" Stonehouse asked. "She's a tough one. Didn't know you'd get assigned to her."

"Oh, she's tough, all right. And sassy. And manipulative. And a regular mother hen with her little chicks."

Hal's white eyebrows rose. "Must've hit a nerve with you. I never heard you go on about anybody that way."

Mitch concentrated on his sandwich. "Don't start, Hal."

"Okay, okay." His moustache twitched when he said, "But you gotta admit, she's a looker."

"She's okay. A little tall for my taste. Lots of angles. I like my women soft."

"Not me. Haddie was as tough as they come. Only kind of woman that could be married to a cop."

Mitch snorted. "Marriage isn't an institution I'm fond of, anyway, so it doesn't matter." He glanced around and his eyes focused on the doorway to the back room, which functioned as a pool hall. He saw a flash of red the same color as the dress Cassie Smith had been wearing today. Mitch started to rise.

"Hold on a second, will you, Hal? I'll be right back."

"Naw, I gotta go, anyway. I'll see you at the station."

After Hal left, Mitch stood and checked the clock. Two-thirty. He and Hal were having a late lunch. Could school be out already?

Straightening his suit coat and buttoning the front for good measure, he walked to the back room.

And couldn't believe his eyes. Bent over the pool table, with her back to him, was the illustrious Ms. Cassie Smith. Her dress—which he'd thought too short for school, anyway—was creeping up her thighs. He had to tear his eyes away from the generous length of leg exposed by her position. Across the table, Bad News Battaglia, as the department had dubbed him, was grinning at her. Neither spotted Mitch, so he eased back into the doorway to remain undetected.

"This is your last chance, Teach. If you don't bag this one, I'm off scot-free."

"Can it, Battaglia. You're just trying to break my concentration."

Confidently, she took an impossible shot off the side, banking it right into the pocket. "Yes!" she said as she stood, raising her right fist into the air. "I won."

Battaglia mumbled something under his breath. She giggled girlishly, then circled the table and hugged the boy. Mitch was discomfited by the gesture.

"Don't worry, kiddo, it's only for ten weeks," she said, ruffling his hair. "You can handle Captain Lansing that long."

Though Battaglia tried to look disgusted, his body language indicated relief. It took a minute for Mitch to realize what had happened here. But he must be wrong. This teacher couldn't really have *bet* a kid on a pool game to get him back to school.

"Um... Teach," Battaglia said as his eyes met Mitch's. "Don't say any more."

Cassie looked at Battaglia, then turned to track his gaze. "Oh," she said when she saw Mitch. Her eyes wide, she bit her bottom lip; she looked like a little girl caught doing something naughty. But she wasn't a little girl. She was a teacher and supposedly a role model, and this wasn't a very healthy example to set.

She nodded, lifting her chin in unmistakable challenge. "Captain. What brings you here?"

"Ms. Smith. Do you think I could see you alone for a minute?"

Before Cassie could answer, Battaglia stepped aggressively in front of her. "Why?"

"Johnny," Cassie said as she walked around the boy and stared him down. "I can take care of this." She turned to Mitch. "You can buy me a soda out in the diner, if you like." She faced Johnny again. "You better get going. You'll be late for work."

After giving Mitch a purposeful stare, the kid turned to Cassie and said, "Okay."

"See you tomorrow."

This time his look *was* disgusted. He said, "Don't rub it in, Teach," and hustled out of the diner.

Cassie approached Mitch, the jersey material of her dress swaying above her knees, resting against her full breasts. Her eyes were alight with...mischief. "Now, what can I do for you, Captain?"

Out of nowhere, he thought of a dark bedroom and satin sheets. And Cassie Smith. Mitch's whole body tightened.

"Ah, we need to talk, Ms. Smith."

WITH A CHERRY SODA in front of her, Cassie sat across from Mitch in one of the vinyl booths. He sipped his coffee as she toyed with her straw. "Answer the question," he said.

She looked up at him, her eyes flaring. "This isn't an interrogation, Lansing. I agreed to discuss Johnny with you because I'm stuck with you in my class, but I won't be pushed."

Hal was right, she was a tough one. Reluctant admiration joined the irritation he felt every time he was with her. "You know," he said idly, "sometimes you talk and act just like those kids you teach."

"*Those* kids? I should have known."

"Known what?"

"You're pretty obvious, Captain."

"What the hell do you mean by that?"

She scanned his hair, then gave his clothes the once-over. "That meticulous haircut and those suits of armor you wear give you away before you even open your mouth."

"And then?"

"Then you say things like, 'Hats in the classroom?' 'Are you qualified to teach phys ed?' I gotta tell you, you're going to have a tough time these ten weeks."

"I'm beginning to see that."

"And my guess is you couldn't care less about

one lonely teenager.''

Big black eyes with hair to match flashed before Mitch, almost taking his breath away. She couldn't be more wrong. ''Now who's being biased?''

''What do you mean?''

''I mean, you accuse me, based on my appearance, of having a prejudice against *your* kids, then you turn around and stereotype me.''

''You just beg to be stereotyped.''

He arched an eyebrow.

Her face flushed—very appealingly—and it made him mad that he noticed. ''Oh, all right. I guess I'm stereotyping you.'' She stirred her drink, then looked up at him. ''These kids are my hot button.''

''No kidding.'' When she just stared at him, he saw a fleeting vulnerability in her face. It led him to ask, ''Why?''

She cocked her head, probably assessing the sincerity of his question. Again, it reminded him of one of her students.

''You might as well know,'' she said finally. ''I was just like them when I was in high school.''

''You were in an alternative program?''

Cassie shook her head, sending thick, unruly strawberry-blond locks over her shoulders. ''No, there weren't any At-Risk programs at Bayview Heights then.''

''Bayview Heights?''

''I was a student there eighteen years ago.''

He stared at her, searching for the girl she must have been. Then he whistled. ''You must have been a handful. Your lucky teachers.''

That brought a smile to her face. "Some of them are still there."

He grinned. "Oh, they must love you."

Cassie laughed, not the girlish laughter he'd heard in the pool hall, but a sultry, all-woman sound. He shifted uneasily in his seat.

"We do have some run-ins," she told him. "But Taylor's on the program's side, so we get what we need despite the stick-in-the-muds who should have retired years ago."

"What happened to you?"

Cassie watched him carefully, and he wondered if she'd tell him the truth. "A teacher helped me see what I *could* be instead of what I *was*. It changed my whole life."

"And now you want to change others."

"Of course." She raised her chin again. "It can be done."

His heart constricted. "Not always."

"What do you mean?"

"Sometimes, despite your best efforts, you lose them."

She opened her mouth to protest, then her gaze turned thoughtful. "Are you speaking from experience?"

"Only from what I've seen on the force," he said quickly.

"Well, I'm going to win."

"Especially with Battaglia."

"With them all."

"By betting their attendance on a game of pool?"

Cassie shook her head. "I might have known that would stick in your craw." She studied him for a minute. "Don't you ever think with your heart instead of your head?"

"What do you mean?"

"Well, like in *Wuthering Heights*. The kids and I discuss acting with your head or your heart."

"You teach *Wuthering Heights* to *those* kids?"

"*You've* read *Wuthering Heights?*"

For a moment, they stared at each other. Then they laughed simultaneously.

"I guess we're both guilty of stereotyping," he said.

"I guess," she confirmed. "Anyway, it's not healthy to always act with your head. You lose out."

"Well, Heathcliff wasn't such a winner. And he was all heart."

"No, but Hareton made it."

"Hareton operated with both his head and his heart."

Cassie gazed at him, surprised, and pleased, by his insight. "You know the book pretty well."

"I like the classics. And other kinds of fiction."

"What kinds?"

"Mysteries. Westerns. Bestsellers."

"Oh, good, bring one to class tomorrow. We have SSR for two hours."

"SSR?"

"Sustained Silent Reading."

"You let them just read in English class? What about the curriculum?"

At the perennial question about innovative language arts techniques, Cassie felt her pulse accelerate. It was a challenge she loved to meet. "What do kids do in typing class, Captain?"

"Type?"

"In art class?"

"Draw?"

"In technology class?"

"What's that?"

"Shop," she answered with a grin.

"Cut boards?"

"So, in English class, we read and write."

"Makes sense. I guess."

Impressed by his surrender—and not pleased by her reaction to it—she said, "Good, then maybe you'll learn something this rotation, too."

She didn't like the way his eyes trapped her. It made her think of the girls' and Zoe's comments about him. "Oh, I believe I will," he said.

Nervous, she started to rise. "Well, I've got some errands to run," she said a little breathlessly.

He grabbed her wrist. His hand was big, strong and powerfully male. She didn't feel threatened—but his touch made her weak.

"Wait a minute, we still haven't settled the issue of the bet," he said.

Tugging her arm away, she sat down fast. "There's nothing to settle. My methods may be un-orthodox, and I may not be everybody's favorite. But get one thing clear, Captain. I'll do anything to keep those kids in school and to help them suc-ceed."

"Anything—even accepting me into your class-room?"

"Anything," she said, standing. "Even that."

CHAPTER THREE

THE TEACHERS' CAFETERIA was crowded during sixth period, but Cassie and her principal managed to find a table in the corner to share lunch. Cassie wanted to give him a progress report on Lansing. She knew Seth was going to keep close tabs on this phase of the program, partially because his job demanded he know everything that was going on in the school, and partially because he knew she wasn't pleased about hosting the law enforcement stint.

Absently spreading her bagel with cream cheese, she watched Seth settle in.

"So, how was the first week?" he asked.

Cassie smiled. "Not as bad as I thought it would be."

He raised his eyebrows. "You mean I was right? If so, I'd like to hear those words come out of your mouth."

"It's too soon for such a sweeping statement. I only meant that it wasn't as bad as I thought."

With mock exasperation, Seth said, "I should have known." As he bit into one of his two hamburgers, he said, "So tell me."

Before she could respond, they were interrupted. "Seth, a kid is smoking out by the bus to the training center." Both of them looked up to find Jerry Bosco staring down at them. He was in his fifties and so out of shape his face flushed with any exertion. He jammed his hands into his pockets to deliver the last blow. "One of yours, Cassie. A ninth-grader."

She started to rise. Seth stopped her. "I'll handle it."

As he left, she glared at Bosco. Besides disagreeing with his approach to teaching, Cassie disliked Jerry Bosco because he'd spearheaded a committee three years ago that had recommended some school policies that had eventually hurt the kids. After a trial period, Seth had abolished all but one of the new rules. "You know, Jerry, Seth does have to eat. You could have followed procedure and brought the kid to one of the vice principals. Carolyn Spearman or Alex Ransom could have handled it."

"The contract says when we feel threatened, we're to find an administrator immediately."

"Convenient for you, isn't it, Jerry? You never have to get your hands dirty." She glared at him. "Who is it?"

"Baker."

"You felt threatened by Baker? He's a pip-squeak."

Before the argument could escalate, Seth was back. He took his seat and started into his second hamburger.

"What did you do?" Bosco asked.

Seth looked up at him. Outwardly calm, Cassie could tell he was not happy by the firm set of his jaw. She also knew Seth had reason to doubt Bosco's word from some ambiguous situations in the past. "Nothing. He didn't have a cigarette by the time I got out there."

"I saw it."

"Then you should have taken him to the office at the time of the violation and written a referral."

"He should be suspended."

"He would have been if you'd followed procedure."

With a disgusted look, Bosco turned and left.

"Talk to Baker, Cassie," Seth said sternly.

"I will."

"Now, tell me about Lansing."

"Well, he seems as inflexible as Bosco."

"Tell me some good things."

Cassie took a bite of her food, choosing her points carefully. "He's written with us every day, reluctantly, and shared a few of his thoughts on the book he brought in to read. But it's been like pulling teeth. He offered to help Nikki brainstorm for her research paper. Then he almost flipped when he found out they could research any person they wanted and she'd picked Madonna."

Seth shook his head. "Who cares what they research, as long as they get the skills?"

"That's what Nikki told him."

Cassie smiled, thinking about the young girl who had a big crush on Captain Lansing. "You should have seen him, in his Brooks Brothers suit scrunched in the corner with Nikki in her black Def Leppard T-shirt and pierced eyebrow. I could almost see him counting the number of piercings. Her mouth really got to him."

"Her mouth? She has her mouth pierced?"

"Well, more precisely, her tongue."

"Oh, Lord."

"And then today, when he saw me in this—" she

plucked at her red T-shirt with Bayview Heights emblazoned on the back "—he couldn't believe the teachers and students wear them every Friday."

The principal shook his head. "Not my idea of appropriate dress, either," he said, glancing down his chest at the red shirt peeking out from under his suit.

"Yes, but you gave your approval."

"After the faculty advisory board voted ten to two to buy them and wear them for school morale."

"You were pretty good about going along with us. Too bad the ten or so teachers who disagreed aren't as gracious about wearing them. Like Bosco."

"You'll never win 'em all, Cass."

"Maybe."

Seth chuckled. "I think…"

"Phone call, Seth." The message came from the other side of the room.

"Don't take it," Cassie said. "You have to eat."

Giving her an I-have-no-choice look, he rose and made his way to the phone.

As she watched him abandon his meal for a second time, she wondered why anyone would want to be a principal. She'd much rather be in the trenches.

Cassie pulled a book out of her bag and nibbled on her bagel. She thought again of Lansing. He'd brought in a novel the day after the pool hall incident. As usual, Cassie covered the room to check on what each student was reading. They were sprawled on the couches, lying on the floor, sitting on tables propped up against the wall. Lansing had looked horrified, but he'd said nothing, taken a seat at a desk and opened… *Wuthering Heights*. She'd smiled when she saw it, and he'd looked up at her with challenge. Cassie had noticed for the first time how thickly lashed his eyes were. They were deep green that day, and intense. Then he'd smiled, and her pulse speeded up. Uncomfortable with her decidedly feminine reaction, she'd turned away.

She had herself under control by the time they shared their reading. Lansing hadn't volunteered to discuss his book, but Johnny had pointedly asked what he was reading and why. Lansing had held Johnny's gaze steadily....

"*Wuthering Heights*. I read it when I was your age, but people see books differently years later."

"We read it," Johnny said defensively.

"Yeah? What did you think of Heathcliff?"

"I thought he was a jerk. He should have ditched Catherine when she married the other guy and found a new squeeze." Johnny angled his chin. "What did you think?"

Mitch said, "I agree. She wasn't worth all his suffering...."

"Sorry," Seth said as he came back to a now-cold lunch. "That was Hal Stonehouse. I asked to be notified right away if any of the kids were in trouble. Did you hear what happened with Young-blood last night?"

Cassie shook her head.

"The captain found him about midnight curled up in a warehouse sound asleep."

"What did Lansing do?"

"Took him out for breakfast."

"*What?*"

"Apparently, he took the boy out for breakfast, then brought him back to the group home. Mitch insisted the proprietors punish Youngblood for breaking curfew, but the kid was pretty amenable after his talk with Lansing."

Cassie's mouth dropped. "No one said anything today." She was torn between pleasure at Lansing's response to a very troubled boy and annoyance that he didn't tell her about this.

"Looks like this thing is working, Cass. Getting to know the cops, seeing them as adults who can help, rather than the enemy."

"Yeah, I guess."

"When does Lansing get to do his part in the program?"

"Next week. He teaches his first lesson on Friday."

"What's he starting with?"

"Violence prevention."

"I was thinking of asking him to do a presentation for all staff on how to break up a fight."

"Sounds good to me."

"Cass, it's helping. I can feel it. This could really be an asset for Bayview Heights."

"Yeah. Okay. You're probably right. I'm reserving judgment, though."

Taylor smiled at her. "So, what else is new? You're always the last one to concede on anything."

"Are you calling me stubborn?"

"Only when it comes to what's best for the kids."

DAMN. THEY WERE ONLY KIDS. There were only twelve of them. Mitch had faced a gang of more than this number on the streets once, and his palms hadn't been this sweaty. More so, he'd been in a brutal war and confronted death head-on. How hard could it be to teach a class, for God's sake?

Ms. Smith sat in the back, hands folded, eyes on him. He recognized the look. She expected him to fall flat on his face.

It gave him courage.

"All right, let's begin," he said, passing out the papers. At least he'd gotten them all into desks. They'd be easier to control that way.

It took a long minute for the papers to get to the back; by that time, two kids had started to talk.

"No talking, please," he said in his best police officer voice.

"I was just askin' him for a pen," Arga said.

"I got one," Som volunteered. She took a ballpoint out of her purse.

"Don't throw..." Mitch began just as the instrument sailed across two aisles.

"All right. Calm down, now. What we're going to talk about today is violence prevention. How you can keep your world orderly and safe."

Snickers rumbled through the group. He saw Battaglia slouch down in the chair, fold his arms over his chest and close his eyes. "Mr. Battaglia. Are you with us?"

"Nope."

"May I ask why?"

"You can ask."

"Why?"

"I pass."

Palms even more clammy, Mitch said, "Straighten up and stay alert."

Johnny opened his eyes but didn't sit up.

Mitch turned to the rest of the class. "All right.

On these five pages, there are several situations or circumstances you might find yourselves in. Then there are choices for you to make at the end of each question. Please do all twenty.''

That ought to keep them busy for a while. Five students picked up their pens and looked down at the paper. Two made faces at each other. One was staring out into space. Battaglia put his head down.

Mitch started to walk back to him when Nikki Parelli raised her hand. He went over to the girl. ''I don't understand what this word means, Captain.''

Mitch explained the meaning of *contention,* baffled that such an easy word could cause a high schooler problems.

As he returned to the front of the room, a paper airplane landed on the floor. He bent down and picked it up. It was page five. Everyone was looking at him. He knew he could go through each row, find out who didn't have page five, but he sensed it was the wrong thing to do. He folded his arms over his chest and told them all to get to work.

He walked to the back of the room. ''Mr. Battaglia?'' The boy raised insolent eyes to him. ''You're not doing the assignment. Why?''

''I'm tired. I worked till midnight last night.''

''Answer the questions on the sheets.''

After a long, hard stare at Mitch, Battaglia picked up his pen. He circled an answer for each question without reading them. Then he looked up at Mitch again. ''Done.''

Mitch was about to respond when he heard a student say, ''Quit kickin' me, man.''

''I ain't.''

''You just did.''

"Shut up, Youngblood."

"You tellin' *me* to shut up?"

Mitch hustled to the front of the room. "All right, you guys, knock it off."

"He started it," Arga said.

"This isn't a first-grade classroom, gentlemen," Mitch scolded.

DeFazio looked around. "It ain't? You could have fooled me."

Everyone laughed, and Mitch knew he was losing control. Rules. They needed rules. "I want everyone to be quiet and finish this assignment."

They settled down somewhat. Intermittently, someone would stretch and everyone would turn to look at him. One student burped and they all laughed. Two kids tapped their pens on their desks. Mitch stopped that by standing close to them. In fifteen minutes, half the class was done. The other half, Mitch noted, were in different phases of completion. As he looked at them, he realized he had no idea what to do with those who had finished.

Someone snapped gum loudly. Mitch's head jerked up. "Whoever did that, throw the gum out."

Twelve angelic faces stared at him wide-eyed. His hand fisted at his side. He glanced at the clock. He couldn't possibly have sixty more minutes of this chaos to deal with.

He caught Cassie's eye. She wasn't smiling. She looked...sad.

As he tried to discuss the material, he got more of the same antics from the kids. The remaining hour crawled by. Inch by inch, Mitch lost control. Finally, Cassie announced it was time to leave. The kids rose. There was some conversation as they picked up their gear. They all said goodbye to her. As they walked by him, Nikki smiled at him. "Bye, Captain." He was grateful for that. When they were gone, he realized they'd left their papers on the desks. Solemnly, he collected them.

Cassie leaned against the wall and watched him. His body language was a study in frustration. His shoulders were stiff, every muscle taut. Absurdly, she felt sorry for him. When he'd retrieved all the papers and returned to the front of the room, she looked at him somberly. "It didn't go so well."

Placing the pile on a desk, he scrubbed his hands over his face. "No, it didn't. Is teaching always like this?"

"It can be."

"I had no idea."

"Most people don't. They think anybody can be a teacher. You just stand up in front of the kids and deliver the material."

"Yeah, but no one listens. Even if they do, they don't always get it, do they?"

"No, they don't."

He shoved his hands in his pockets and faced her squarely. "I...need some help."

Cassie knew that cost him. She understood intuitively that Mitch Lansing rarely said those words to anyone. Neither did she.

"I'd...like to help."

"I don't like failure. I don't want to experience it again."

Giving him a quick smile, she said, "I appreciate your honesty." She perched on the edge of her desk. "You sure you want this?"

He nodded.

"Okay." She held up her index finger. "Rule number one—kids learn by doing." A second finger joined it. "Rule number two—they learn if you can make it relevant."

Mitch watched her for a minute, then said, "So how do you get content across?"

She picked up the packet he handed out. "I looked through your material. It's good stuff but should be used as reinforcement of the ideas, not to teach them."

"How do you teach ideas, then?"

"Tell me what you want them to learn."

"Alternatives to violent behavior."

"All right, then ask them first for their own input. What alternatives can they come up with? Then maybe ask them for situations where they've been involved in violent behavior, and how they could have chosen something different."

"But that would take so long. I'd never get through all the material."

"No, but they'd be thinking, coming up with their own conclusions. And they'd be with you every minute."

"What about the rest of the content?"

Cassie sighed and stared over his shoulder at the window. Then she looked back at him. "Let me tell you a story. One of my favorite workshop presenters told us this once. There was this guy, Ted, who was supposed to give his friend Bill a ride to the airport. But Bill had to tie up some things before he left. Ted went to pick up Bill and waited in the living room while Bill made phone calls. It was getting later and later. Ted kept prodding Bill, but Bill kept calling people, and he hadn't started to pack. The plane was leaving at three. At two-thirty, Bill still wasn't ready. So Ted left for the airport without him.''

Mitch nodded. "Okay. I see what you're getting at. A teacher can't leave the kids home and make the trip to the airport by himself.''

"Bingo!''

"So you deliver no content?''

Cassie's temper flared; this accusation was a sore spot with her. "No, I deliver content. Sometimes not as much as I'd like, but enough.'' She looked down at the packet of papers she held. "From what I can tell, this last page with the alternatives is what you want them to know. You could finish getting all their input, then go to this sheet and see how many of these points they covered. For those they missed, you could start a discussion about how they apply and how they might be relevant in different situations. Then you could ask for examples.''

"Makes sense,'' Mitch said. "Even if it does go against my grain.''

Cassie's gaze swept over him. She hadn't expected this openmindedness. "I wonder, Captain, underneath that suit, what grain really exists.''

CASSIE STARED OUT the window of the glassed-in porch of Zoe's huge condominium on the bay. The water lapped lazily, though the temperature this January afternoon edged around freezing. She pressed her face to the cold glass, hoping the sting would encourage her to go inside and socialize. Behind her, music from the sixties combined with the din of conversation—teachers letting down after a tough week.

Usually she loved these gatherings, where she shared her joys and frustrations with her colleagues.

"Hey, kid, what are you doing out here by yourself?"

Cassie turned to Zoe, who'd changed into a Japanese-print caftan to play hostess as she often did on a Friday night.

"Thinking."

"About?"

"What else?"

"School. Honestly, Cass, you're a hopeless case. You need a man in your life to distract you."

Unbidden, a vision of Mitch Lansing came to mind. She wondered what he'd look like out of that damn suit...in a dark green T-shirt that accentuated his eyes. "Yeah, maybe you're right." If she was having these thoughts about Lansing, she definitely needed something.

"Did you see the hunk Susie brought? He's a vice president down at the electronics plant."

"No, I didn't notice."

"You must be dead, girl, not to have noticed."

No, she wasn't dead, Cassie thought. She'd noticed some things...the way Mitch's face had hardened with determination when the kids were brushing him off...how the cleft in his chin deepened when he was frustrated...how his smile was warm and reassuring to Nikki when the girl couldn't quite master the language of his worksheet.

"Zoe, someone's at the door," one of the teachers called from the other room.

Zoe gave Cassie a strange look, then turned to go to meet her new guest. Cassie faced the bay again. She shouldn't be noticing anything about Mitch

Lansing. But she knew why she was. His wit, intelligence and determination were traits that appealed to her. She liked the fact that he enjoyed reading. Thank God he'd blown it with the kids today. She stilled the little voice inside her that reminded her he'd wanted her input after class and had accepted her suggestions. God help her if he got good with them. She was a real sucker for men who worked well with kids.

Cassie turned when Zoe came back into the room. With her was Mitch Lansing. "Cass, look who's here."

Cassie bit her lip to keep her jaw from dropping. "Captain. What a surprise."

"I invited Mitch to our get-together tonight. I'm glad you came, Mitch. What can I get you?" As always, Zoe was a perfect hostess.

Mitch glanced at his watch. To make sure he was off duty, no doubt. "I'll have a beer."

"Cass?"

Cassie sipped the bottle of Michelob. "No, thanks. I'm nursing this one."

When Zoe left, Mitch faced her. His hair was a little mussed, but his white shirt was as crisp as it had been this morning. A faint growth of beard shadowed his face, and she had a sudden urge to touch him.

He watched her closely. "I get the impression you're not glad to see me."

"No, no, I'm just surprised."

His grin was little-boyish; the switch from cynical cop threw her. "Truthfully, so am I."

"Why? That Zoe would ask you, or that you'd come?"

Green eyes sparkled. "Both, I guess."

"Well, Captain, if nothing else, you're honest."

"No, not always."

Before Cassie could respond, Zoe returned with a frosted glass of beer for Mitch. She chatted for a minute then left to see to the food.

Cassie lifted her beer. "Toast, Captain?"

"To?"

"To a better lesson next time?"

He smiled broadly and Cassie's stomach contracted. "Let's hope so. Nothing could be worse than today." He looked down at her. "Thanks for your help."

Cassie smiled up at him and clinked his glass.

He said, "To a successful collaboration." His husky tone made her shiver. "Are you cold?" he asked.

Oh, God, had she really shivered?

"Ah, a little. This porch isn't heated well enough for January."

Before she realized his intent, he set his beer down, removed his suit coat and placed it on her shoulders. His hands lingered there for a minute; they felt solid and firm and made her wonder briefly if his fingertips would be callused. As if he read her thoughts, he removed his hands abruptly and looked away, out to the ocean.

Released from his touch, she steadied herself—until his scent surrounded her. It was so male, so potent that for a minute she had to stop breathing, had to stop the bombardment of her senses. The jacket was heavy and huge on her.

Mitch said nothing, just stared at the waves lapping against the shore. Cassie watched his throat as he swallowed a swig of beer. It was an oddly erotic sight, and she turned to look out at the bay, too. Lost in their own thoughts, they were both silent.

"You don't like me much, do you," he finally said.

She shook her head. "It's not that. We're just very different."

Still facing away from her, he said, "Yes, we are. Then we had that problem with Johnny." She just nodded. "And I know you don't like cops."

"How do you know that?"

His grin was wry. "You're a pretty easy book to read, Ms. Smith." She smiled. "Why?"

Distracted by his sexy stare, she asked, "Why what?"

"Why don't you like cops?"

To Cassie's surprise, the words just spilled out. "When I was eleven, I got caught by a cop for shoplifting a candy bar from Miller's Groceries. At thirteen, I was nabbed by one for spray-painting graffiti on the outside of the middle school. A patrolman picked me up drunk on the reservoir once when I was fifteen. And a year later, I was found with marijuana at school in a surprise search conducted by the local officials."

He was so still, it was eerie. His eyes studied her face. "That's not all of it, is it?"

"What do you mean?"

"All those cops were just doing their jobs. You're a fair person. Something else happened with the police force, didn't it."

"Yes."

"What?"

"It wasn't anything traumatic. But there are bad cops out there."

"What do you mean?"

"I don't really want to talk about it." She looked up at him, his chiseled features standing out against the backdrop of the bay. "Can I ask *you* something?"

"You can ask."

"I get the impression you don't really want to be working with my class. Why are you?"

Mitch shifted uneasily. This woman knew how to keep him off balance. It was bad enough that she'd felt good in his hands when he'd given her his jacket, that she looked utterly lovely with her hair peeking out of her braid and her gray-blue eyes shining. Then she'd shared a confidence that she could have kept to herself. Now she was asking him to share his feelings—why he was working with kids. "Because I owe Hal Stonehouse. I was sick of the city, and when he asked me to come out here, I came on a lateral transfer."

"You agreed to work in the school?"

"No, I thought I'd be doing other things. Do you remember when the young police officer got caught in a random drive-by shooting?"

"Yes."

"Well, he was the one assigned to do this job. Hal felt responsible for what happened to Gifford. Then when there was no one to fill this position, I agreed to do it." He turned to face her, not sure why he was sharing so much. Maybe because she had. The twilight from outside was filtering into the dim room, softening her features. He didn't see the angles today. Just the curves. The feminine curves that were too well outlined in that damn red T-shirt and those jeans that made her legs look a mile long.

"You don't enjoy working with the kids, though, do you, Captain?"

He looked down at her. When she'd turned, a lock of hair had fallen on her cheek. He raised his hand to tuck it behind her ear. He said, "My name's Mitch."

"What?" Cassie had gone very still.

"My name is Mitch," he repeated. "Say it. Just once." His voice, usually so controlled and some-what harsh, sounded like a stranger's—soft, in-bed coaxing.

"Mitch."

He didn't take his hand away. Instead, he rested it briefly on her neck. "That wasn't so hard, now, was it Cassandra?"

Her eyes widened at his use of her full name. This close, he could see a few freckles on the bridge of her nose. It gave her an unexpected vulnerability again. Some primitive male instinct yearned to protect her. Because Mitch knew the raw danger of those instincts, he removed his hand and turned away.

She said nothing for a minute, then asked again, "The kids, Mitch. Why don't you like working with them?"

He thought of Som Choumpa. She reminded him of the Vietnamese civilians he'd encountered. Damn, he didn't want to remember this. He'd been pretty successful at keeping the war memories at bay. But tonight he recalled too much. Vietnam—a beautiful country. A deadly one. He remembered vividly both sides of it. The earthy smell of the lush jungle, as well as the stench of burning flesh. And—for the first time in his life—he wished he could share his memories with someone. With someone who understood pain and loss and helplessness. He glanced over at Cassie Smith, standing there wrapped up in his jacket, invitation and something else in her sultry eyes. Did she know those grim, lonely feelings that ambushed you when you least expected them?

"Excuse me," Zoe said from behind them. She held a cordless phone in her hand. "It's for you, Mitch. It's the department."

Glad for the reprieve, Mitch took the phone from Zoe. "Lansing."

"Mitch, it's Hal. We've got a couple of your kids down here."

"Who?"

"DeFazio and Battaglia."

Mitch looked at the woman next to him. She watched him expectantly, and again, he wanted to protect her. Especially from this. "What happened?"

"There was some kind of altercation at Pepper's. We're still trying to get to the bottom of it."

"I'll be right there." Clicking off the phone, he said to Cassie, "DeFazio and Battaglia were just picked up for fighting at Pepper's."

Her face drained of color, and she gripped the bottle with both hands.

Mitch set down his beer. "I've got to go."

"I'm coming with you."

"No, you're not."

"You can't stop me, Captain." Her voice was steely and her eyes challenged him.

He picked up the gauntlet. "I can stop you from seeing him."

"Why would you want to do that?"

"It's the rules, Cassie."

Slowly, she put down her beer, removed his jacket from her shoulders and stuffed it into his hands. "Screw the rules, Captain," she snapped. "I'll see you at the station."

CHAPTER FOUR

THE TWO INTERVIEW rooms at Bayview Heights Police Department were particularly drab with their
gray walls, absence of windows, straight chairs and
hardwood furniture. Right now, Joe DeFazio was
slumped over one of the tables, pillowing his head
on his arms.

"Sit up," Mitch snapped. Towering above the
boy, he struggled to keep his temper intact.

DeFazio lifted his head sluggishly. Glassy-eyed,
he moistened his lips. "Can I have some water?"
His words were slurred.

"As soon as you tell me how much you used."

"Didn't do nothin' illegal."

Mitch glanced over at the ten aerosol cans of
whipped cream on the shelf behind the boy. They'd
been recovered from the alley behind Pepper's.

"How much did you use?" Mitch enunciated
each word. All ten canisters were empty of gases
but full of cream.

"Dunno what you mean." DeFazio's head
drooped toward his arms again.

"I said, sit up," Mitch barked. "I know you
didn't inhale all the gas in those canisters or you'd
be dead. But how many did you use?"

DeFazio stared at him vacantly.

Remembering the hurt in Cassie's eyes, knowing

she was waiting in the small outer area for this punk—and Battaglia, who was cooling his heels in the other interview room—Mitch reached over and yanked DeFazio up by the collar. If he didn't already know the boy had been doing inhalants, the distinct gaseous smell wafting from his jacket would have confirmed it. "You stupid punk. Do you have any idea how dangerous inhalants are?" Mitch angled his head to the row of cans commonly called whippets. One of the newer drugs to hit the suburbs, inhalants were becoming more and more prevalent because of their availability.

"They said it was just some dumb gas," DeFazio argued.

"Let me tell you what it really is, tough guy." He let go of the boy, who sank groggily onto the chair. "The vapors enter your bloodstream faster than any other drug because they bypass your liver. That means you get a double dose. They depress all your major organs. If you're lucky, you just get irritated eyes and severe headaches. If you're unlucky, you could end up with permanent brain damage." Mitch leaned over, bracing his arms on the table. "But want to know the worst-case scenario? Last year, I saw three boys die from inhaling aerosol fumes. They drank vodka beforehand. Two bagged the gas—used it with their heads covered by a plastic bag so they'd get a bigger rush. They suffocated. The other one was surprised by the cops, and the sudden adrenaline flow combined with the depressant caused cardiac arrest." Mitch forced himself to straighten and beat back the image of the young hollow faces that still haunted him. "They were all thirteen."

DeFazio's eyes closed.

"Oh, hell, why am I even—"

A knock on the door cut off his comment. One of the other police officers poked his head in. "Mitch, DeFazio's father is here. He's raising hell in the waiting area."

Where Cassie is. "Bring him in here," Mitch said.

In minutes, a larger version of the kid who was slumped before Mitch stalked into the room. Dressed in battered jeans, a hunting jacket and thick army boots, the guy was slightly overweight and red-faced. He was breathing heavily.

"What the hell's going on here?" the elder DeFazio asked.

"Your kid is stoned," Mitch said.

"He been drinkin'?"

"No, he's been doing drugs."

"My kid ain't no druggie."

Patiently, Mitch explained the abuse of inhalants to the man.

"You gotta be kiddin' me. You arrested him because he's been sniffin' somethin'? Shit, I did that with airplane glue when I was his age. Ain't no harm in it."

"We didn't arrest him. But there *is* harm in it. Even though he didn't inhale all these cans alone, he still endangered himself." Parental acceptance of kids' habits was the biggest factor in the rise of adolescent drug use.

"You didn't arrest him? Then why's he here?"

"He got into a fight playing pool at Pepper's. I think it's because he was high."

"Sniffin' stuff ain't illegal."

"No, but it's deadly."

DeFazio turned to his kid and shook his arm roughly. "Get up. We're gettin' out of here." He looked at Mitch. "Next time you pick on my kid, I'm gonna charge you with harassment. They got lawyers now who'll take a case for a piece of the action. My brother-in-law told me."

"Get out of here," Mitch said, white-knuckling the table. "Before you have something more to charge me with."

After the DeFazios left, Mitch took several deep breaths then left the first interview room and headed for the next. Inside it, he found Battaglia standing erect, studying the Wanted posters on the wall.

"You could be one of those guys some day, Battaglia."

The boy spun around. In stark contrast to DeFazio, Battaglia's eyes were clear, though they were burning with anger. His coordination when Mitch surprised him had been normal.

Slamming the door, Mitch said, "Well, did you just have a smaller dose than DeFazio or are you too smart to mess with the newest drug of choice?"

"Don't know what you're talking about." Insolently, the boy slipped his hands into his jeans pockets and leaned against the wall.

Mitch felt his insides knot at the intentionally smug posture. "Do you know your English teacher is here?" he said unkindly.

Johnny straightened. "Cassie?" Then his face flushed and his hands came out of his pockets and curled into angry fists at his sides. "You son of a bitch. Why'd you call her?"

"I didn't. She was with me when I was notified about the fight."

Shock widened Johnny's eyes. He glanced at the clock behind Mitch. "Why was she with you at seven o'clock at night?"

Mitch attacked, sensing the advantage he'd gotten with that bit of news. "Why do you put her through this?"

Johnny's eyes changed. A look of profound remorse muddied the clear, almost black of his irises. The boy said nothing, just stared at Mitch. The forced-air central heating started up, and a muted phone rang somewhere in an outer office.

"Sit down, Battaglia," Mitch said, breaking the charged silence.

The boy's posture became even stiffer.

"I said, sit down."

Johnny kicked out a straight chair, circled it around, then straddled it.

"Your friends were there."

Again, the sullen quiet.

"We were told your buddies from the city paid Pepper's a visit."

"So what?" Johnny finally said.

"Your pals give the inhalants to DeFazio?"

With faked nonchalance, Johnny examined his fingernails. "What're inhalants?"

Switching tactics, Mitch said, "I understand you want to be a doctor."

Johnny's head snapped up. "Who told you that?"

Again ignoring his question, Mitch went on, "You know physically what can happen when you use these things?"

Pride reared its ugly head in the boy. "I'm not stupid. That shit fries your brains."

"Then how come you let your pals give it to DeFazio?"

Silence again, but a flicker of unease crossed the kid's face and his shoulders sagged in guilt.

"Let me tell you something, Battaglia. I'm not going to let your gang buddies recruit anyone from Bayview Heights. It might be too late for you, but you're it, kid. If I see any evidence of gang activity—colors, paraphernalia, hand signals—at the high school, I'll take you down so fast, you won't have time to blink." Mitch sighed and ran a frustrated hand through his hair. "Now, get out of here." Then he surprised himself by adding, "And try to reassure Ms. Smith you were clean tonight."

Opening the door, Mitch preceded Johnny out and stalked to his office, carefully avoiding the waiting area, where he knew that soft gray eyes would stare at him accusingly and slender shoulders were about to take on more of the world's problems.

JOHNNY WATCHED THE WIPERS make a slow descent to the bottom of the windshield as Cassie shut off the engine and turned toward him. Then he focused on the bumper sticker she'd stuck on the dash. Be Someone Special. Be a Teacher. He was trying to avoid her eyes. He knew what he'd see there—the same disappointment and hurt he'd glimpsed as she whisked him out of the police station and into her car without a word and driven to his seedy apartment complex.

"Want to tell me what happened?"

Tugging the nylon collar of his jacket up around

his neck, Johnny stared ahead. When he didn't answer, she waited. "I was playing pool with DeFazio at Pepper's," he finally said. "Zorro came in about six, looking for me."

"Oh, Johnny." Cassie's disillusioned tone matched the look he'd seen earlier.

"I didn't plan it, Cassie."

"You've got to break off with them for good. One foot in the gang, one foot out, isn't going to cut it much longer."

Johnny remembered the six months he'd dropped out of school. "You don't understand, Cassie."

"Then tell me."

"They're my family."

"No, they're not. They're a bunch of selfish, brutal punks."

Which is why I haven't officially gone back. "What's going on with you and Lansing?" he asked.

"We were talking about the gang."

"Look, I'm not a real member anymore. When me and my mother moved out here, I left the gang. I see Zorro now because he's been my buddy since day one. I won't abandon him."

Cassie sighed. "You think they've let you go, but they haven't. They're trying to suck you back in, and Zorro will go to any lengths to get to you." She hesitated, then added, "I know."

"He never bothered you after that first time, did he?" Johnny remembered how Zorro had paid Cassie a visit when he realized he was losing Johnny because of Cassie's influence. Johnny had found out and had beaten the shit out of Zorro. Then they'd talked. Zorro convinced Johnny he was sorry and wouldn't do it again.

"No, he didn't. But I see what he's doing to get you back. My guess is he'll go after DeFazio now."

Lansing's words echoed in Johnny's head. *I'm not going to let your buddies recruit anyone from Bayview Heights.* "What's going on with you and Lansing?" Johnny repeated his question.

He couldn't see her clearly in the dim light of the car, but he could feel her tension. "What do you mean?"

"He said you were with him tonight when he got called about the fight."

Cassie cleared her throat. "We were at the same party."

"Party?"

"A teacher get-together at Zoe's."

"Oh, sounds like fun." Johnny's sarcasm lightened the mood. "I hope Bosco wasn't there, at least."

"Bosco doesn't socialize."

Johnny studied her. "You should have somebody in your life, Cassie. Just not Lansing."

"My social life isn't the issue here. Your future is."

God, he hated it when she pulled the teacher routine on him. "Oh, excuse me. I forget. You're the teacher, I'm the kid." He reached for the door handle. She grabbed his arm. Her grip was firm, but it wasn't what held him back. Her emotional pull on him always kept him from fleeing from her.

"Johnny."

He waited.

"I am your teacher, and I have a right to guide you, to try to help you."

Staring ahead, he willed himself not to be grateful that she felt responsible for him. Not to count on it.

"But I care about you as a person, too. As your friend. You know how much you mean to me."

He slumped against the front seat, feeling like he was ten again.

"Please," she begged. "Don't shut me out. I can't bear the thought of you going back to the gang."

In spite of his resolve, the words tumbled out of Johnny's mouth. "I...I feel good at school. It's the *only* place I feel good anymore after losing my job at the hospital. Lansing took that away and now he's taking school away." He willed back the moisture from his eyes and turned to look at her. Her face was drawn tight with worry. "And tonight...made me think...maybe he could take you away, too. You know, turn you against me. All I'd have left then is Zorro and the Blisters."

She reached over and hugged him. It was a sisterly gesture, one she did infrequently, but it felt so good he wanted to lean into it. For a minute, he did.

"I won't let anyone turn me against you, Johnny. I promise. But I'm afraid you'll let the gang turn you against me. And everything else that's good in your life."

He drew strength from her closeness, then pulled back. "That won't happen."

"Promise?"

"I promise."

"Okay. Go get some sleep."

He looked at her, cursing the fact that he needed her—wanted her—to help him.

And thanking God that she, at least, was there for him.

CASSIE LAY BACK against the cast iron of the old claw-footed tub and submerged her head under the water. Soothing heat took away the January chill. Surfacing, she slicked back her hair and closed her eyes. *What a night.* First, all that stuff with Lansing. Then Johnny.

Shivering at the thought that the Blisters had come to Pepper's, she reached for the hot water faucet in an attempt to escape the icy fear that gripped her at the thought of the gang on Johnny's turf.

Needing diversion, she tried to clear her mind and think about school. It didn't work. Instead, she saw Mitch Lansing's green eyes, full of wary need as he confided in her at Zoe's party. She felt again the rough touch of his hand when he tucked her hair behind her ear, the weight of his jacket on her shoulders, the smell of him enveloping her.

"Damn," she muttered, and dunked her head back under. It didn't stop the images. She still felt that helpless reaction of her body to his...maleness.

Well, maybe it was a good thing he'd pulled his Dr. Jekyll and Mr. Hyde routine when the call came from the station. He had an effect on her that she hadn't expected and therefore hadn't resisted strongly enough. It wasn't all physical, either, though that was a good part of it.

The ringing phone interrupted her reflection. She wouldn't answer it. She didn't want to talk to anyone. The machine could pick it up. Despite her lecture to herself, she climbed out of the tub, grabbed a thick towel from the rack and a terry robe from the hook on the back of the door and padded to her bedroom without drying off. She wrapped her hair in the towel on the way and hastily donned the robe, then she picked up the receiver.

"Cassie? This is Seth."

He'd heard already. "Hi. Who called you?"

"Hal Stonehouse. He didn't have all the details, though. What happened?"

Closing her eyes, she repeated the story to her principal.

"Hal said they weren't arrested."

"That's right. The fight was provoked by the townies that they beat at pool. Apparently, the cops hauled in the kids because they were underage and because he suspected some drug abuse."

"Were they using?"

"Johnny wasn't. I didn't get to see DeFazio. Why don't you call Lansing, since you were so hot on having him work in our building." She regretted her words almost immediately. "I'm sorry, Seth. I didn't mean to attack you. This thing with Lansing has been tough."

"I know, Cass. I wish I could make it better."

She chuckled. "You used to say that to me when I was in your class."

He laughed.

"You do, you know."

"I do what?"

"Make it better."

"Yeah, well, only you can cooperate with Captain Lansing to make it really better."

"Oh, Seth. I don't know. After tonight..." *Especially after tonight.*

"Try." He hesitated, and she knew what was coming. He rarely asked for anything. "I want you to try, as a favor to me."

"You're so transparent sometimes," she said with long-standing affection. The doorbell rang. "Listen, someone's at the door. I've got to answer it."

"Cassie?"

"All right. I'll try harder with Lansing."

"Thanks. And check to see who's at the door before you open it."

"Yes, Mr. T. I'll see you Monday."

As she headed downstairs, Cassie thought it was probably Zoe spontaneously visiting her. She did that once in a while, and Cassie was grateful for the company.

But through the peephole she saw massive shoulders encased in dark wool. And the unmistakable frame of Mitch Lansing.

Opening the door, she shivered with the blast of frigid air.

Her physical discomfort diluted her surprise. "What do you want?"

He scanned her from head to toe, his eyes turning as dark as the forest at midnight. "I want to talk to you. Let me in before you freeze to death."

She was about to object to his peremptory tone when she remembered her promise to Seth just minutes ago. She said nothing until he was inside and the door was closed. To get a grip on her irritation, she excused herself to dress and flew up the stairs. As she donned an old mismatched sweatshirt

and pants, she tried to quell her reaction to having
him in her house.

Filling the doorway, he'd looked powerful in the
navy wool coat that covered his suit. Geez, didn't
the guy ever change into something casual? Of
course, when you looked that good in...

Stop it, she told herself. He's not your type.

Not quite true. She took a deep breath. All right,
so she found him attractive. So what? It didn't mean
anything. God, she didn't even like the guy.

Pulling on socks, she admitted to herself how
she'd begun to gravitate toward him earlier...until
he'd gotten the call about Johnny.

Johnny...

He won't turn me against you. The promise gave
her perspective. She couldn't afford to fall victim to
Lansing's charm. Too much was at stake here. She
might have to let him into her classroom, but she
sure as hell didn't have to let him into her life. Heading to the closet for her sneakers, she unwrapped her
hair and towel-dried it quickly. She was in control
now, just as she'd been since she left this godfor-
saken town eighteen years ago.

Mitch paced her living room, taking note of the
eclectic decor. Framed posters of art shows from
New York City galleries covered the walls. An en-
larged photo of a pair of ballet shoes advertised the
Bolshoi Ballet. Another contradiction—Cassandra
Smith loved the arts. Taking stock of the rest of the
room, he noted her sofas and chairs were sturdy and
slightly worn, but looked comfortable. The two
sofas flanked an old stone fireplace on the far wall.
Crossing to it, he studied the rows of books on either
side, struggling to keep himself from thinking about

how she'd looked when she answered the door, wet from a shower or bath. *The Complete Works of Shakespeare*. A bath, he'd bet. *A Room of One's Own* by Virginia Woolf. Her high cheekbones were accented by the towel around her head. Grisham's *The Pelican Brief* and *The Firm*. Her gray eyes were tumultuous. Lawrence's *Lady Chatterly's Lover*. Against his will, he remembered how her breasts thrust against the terry cloth; when the blast of cold air hit her, it had made her nipples pout visibly.

Warm—too warm—he turned from the bookcase, shrugged off his coat and adjusted his trousers. He shouldn't be thinking about her this way. He *wouldn't* think about her this way. He had to prepare for the battle that he knew was coming.

"Captain."

He pivoted to face her. She looked only slightly less tempting in plain sweats. But her hair was still damp and it gave him a jolt as he pictured her under the water...as it sluiced over... "Ms. Smith."

"Sit down." She studied him for a minute, and the conflicting emotions on her face were like a neon sign. "I've got coffee," she finally said with a touch of resignation in her tone.

"Are we going to be civilized about this?"

"About this we are," she said. "Would you like some?"

He nodded. While she was gone, he dropped onto the cushiony sofa and stared at the dead coals in the fireplace. The grate look well used. When she returned, she handed him a mug. He took it and read its lettering. "Those who can, do. Those who can't, teach." But the saying was crossed off in bold red lines and replaced by "Those who can, teach others how."

He smiled.

"I guessed you like it black."

"How did you know?"

"You're a tough guy."

"I am." He glanced at her cup. "Yours is black, too, right?"

"Yup." She sipped. "Why are you here?"

Sighing, he sank back onto the couch and crossed his left ankle over his knee. He silenced his first response, *I was worried about you.* Instead, he gave her the second reason he'd come. "I wanted to talk to you about the lesson I'm supposed to teach on Monday."

"We already discussed this last week." She eyed him warily. "Why do I have the feeling I'm not going to like this?"

"I want to change the lesson plan, but I didn't want to surprise you. It's supposed to be on drug usage—the law, the penalties, some of the more severe consequences."

"I know. We went over all this. What do you want to change it to?"

"Inhalants. What they are, why they're dangerous."

Cassie drew in a deep breath. Consciously trying to relax—Mitch was astute in reading body language—she sipped her coffee but held his gaze. Finally she said, "Some people think that kind of information encourages kids to experiment."

"Do you?"

"No, I think it informs them of the dangers, especially if it isn't instructive in the methods of doing drugs.''

''Well, national research bears you out.'' He sipped his coffee, too, noting absently that she was one of the few people who made it strong enough for him. ''I have a movie that explains the physical effects. It's interspersed with kids talking about their use and what it did to them.''

''It sounds good.''

Mitch shifted in his seat. ''I'd need help again—planning the lesson, until I get the hang of it myself.''

The corners of her mouth turned up, making him feel like one of the students who had pleased her. ''All right. I'd like to see the movie first, anyway. Why don't we put your lesson off until Tuesday, then if you're free, we can work together after school Monday on a lesson design.''

Mitch set his cup on the table. ''Why are you being so cooperative? I thought you'd be furious at me.''

Cassie sat back and tucked her feet under her. Her face was clean of makeup and still flushed from the heat of her bath. ''I'm not mad you brought the kids in. They deserved it, especially DeFazio.''

''But...''

''But I am mad that you seem to think you have to keep me out of all of this.''

''It wasn't your place to be there tonight.''

''And just who are you to decide that?''

He thought about that and decided to pick his battles. ''You're right.''

She cocked her head. ''Why do I have the feeling I'm being mollified?''

"No wonder the kids can't pull anything over on you."

Chuckling, she gave him an easy smile that made him uncomfortable.

Linking his hands between his knees, he said, "I've got another lesson I want to add to my list. As a matter of fact, I'm thinking of approaching Seth Taylor about doing this for the whole school." He held her gaze unflinchingly. "On gang prevention."

Cassie lurched forward. "No!" The action splattered coffee all over her shirt. Luckily, it had cooled somewhat so she wasn't burned, but it got her sopping wet. Mitch reached into his back pocket and pulled out a handkerchief. Rising, he crossed the two feet between them and hunched down in front of her as she set the cup on the end table.

Give her the cloth. Don't touch her.

"Here." He passed her his handkerchief. She took it and pressed it to her chest. He watched her for a few seconds, then started to stand. She grabbed his wrist, keeping him where he was, down on one knee in front of her. Close enough to smell the soap from her bath. Near enough to see the smattering of freckles on her nose.

"You can't do this, Mitch. Please, listen to me."

There was so much emotion in her voice, he was distracted from the effect of her nearness.

"Why?"

"Because of Johnny, of course."

"He's in a gang."

"Not exactly." Mitch arched a brow. "Johnny was in the Blisters when he lived in New York City. On the advice of some social workers, his mother moved out here when he was in ninth grade. He'd already been in the gang for two years.''

Mitch swore vilely. "God, that young."

Cassie continued, "Apparently the gang let him go because he moved. He only kept in touch with Zorro, his buddy from childhood, who was still in the gang."

Mitch was skeptical. It wasn't that easy to get out of a gang.

"But when they moved here, his mother couldn't support herself very well and could only get a part-time job as a maid at the local motel. Now she drinks most of the time." Mitch remained silent. "Johnny helps support her. They get along on that and the social security from his father's death. But really he has nobody."

"That's why you've taken such an interest in him?"

"Among other reasons. I'm the only adult in his life who cares."

"Aren't you assuming a lot of responsibility for this kid?" Mitch asked, immediately feeling hypocritical when he thought of a similar responsibility he'd sought to assume a lifetime ago. Pain needled him, exposing the memory he could usually suppress.

Cassie shook her head. "Maybe. But kids need a strong adult role model in their lives if they're going to be resilient to the pressures of today."

Listening to her passionate response, Mitch asked, "Are we still talking about Johnny?"

She blushed. "Of course." The pressure of her hand on his wrist increased. It was surprisingly strong. "The point *is* that Johnny was almost completely out of the gang, but then eighteen months ago, Zorro took over as head of the Blisters. Gradually, he's tried to get Johnny back, telling him he could be a long-distance member. Even choose what things to get involved in. Set his own standards.''

"Gangs don't operate with part-time members, Cassie.''

"I know. But it seems this one is bending the rules because Zorro's their leader. And Johnny flirts with the idea of going back, especially when things get rough—like at school. Or when he's afraid.'' She raised her chin a notch. "I've managed to keep him out of most of their doings, though.''

"While Zorro's trying to lure him back in.''

Cassie nodded.

"Does he spend time with them?''

"Some. I can't stop it completely. He's got this bond with Zorro. Like he's family.''

"Gangs function as family to kids like Battaglia.''

"They're not his family.''

Neither are you. "He's walking too fine a line, Cassie. He'll never make it.''

"I don't believe that.''

Sighing, Mitch backed away from her, stood up and began to pace. He felt like he was picking his way through a mine field.

She was blind to what was really going on because she cared about the kid too much. He tried a different tack. "The gang is encroaching out here. You know how urban gangs infiltrate the suburbs?''

She shook her head.

"From transfer students.''

Bolting off the chair, she stood, too, and grasped his arm. "No, not Johnny. He's not doing that.''

Mitch spun around to face her. "Maybe not. Battaglia seems pretty strong. But DeFazio isn't. They got to him tonight through the drugs. Next, they'll suck him into the gang. It's contagious. Your whole school is in danger."

Cassie drew in a deep breath and released his arm. "But if you go into this gang prevention stuff now, I'll lose Johnny for good. He'll never sit through lessons. He'll never take this from you. He already resents you." When Mitch didn't respond, Cassie added, "A couple of years ago, some teachers wanted to establish a policy that kids couldn't get early dismissals from school to work. They felt outside employment interfered with the learning process. Some of us, including Seth, didn't think that we should make a cut-and-dried policy, but he agreed to try it. Johnny was only sixteen, but he was working hard to help support his mother. He got so angry at the administrative inflexibility, he quit school for six months. Eventually, it became clear that we needed to make some exceptions, and I got Johnny to enroll again."

Mitch bit back a retort about sacrificing one kid for the good of the whole school. He said instead, "I can't just let this go."

"Don't you see?" Cassie pointed out. "This could do the same thing to him. It could make him quit if he feels he's being personally attacked. It will kick into old resentments."

His better judgment told him to turn her down flat. All his police instincts said the gang issue had to be addressed right away.

"Please, Mitch, don't do this. Not now, at least."

He blew out a heavy breath. "All right. I'll hold

off a little while. But I'm not promising to let it go. And if I see any evidence of gang activity, I'm stepping in."

She closed her eyes in relief. That small gesture swept through him, bathing him in strong emotion that was completely separate from the physical attraction he felt for her.

And it scared the hell out of him.

CHAPTER FIVE

"STAYIN' LATE AGAIN, Cassie?" The wizened janitor smiled at her from the door of her classroom. *Phantom of the Opera* blared from his radio, making her smile.

"Yeah, Hank. Got a meeting with the cop. Come on in. You can sweep and do the boards before he gets here."

The old man trudged in, the bottles on his big cart clanking, the smell of disinfectant stinging Cassie's nostrils. They talked as he wielded the broom up and down the rows of desks.

"The kids say he's tough."

"Lansing?"

"Uh-huh."

"Oh, he's tough, all right."

I'm not promising to let it go. If I see any evidence of gang activity…

Frustrated, trying to change the subject, Cassie angled her head toward the radio. "You looking forward to seeing that?"

A youthful grin claimed his tired features. "Three weeks." His eyes misted. "Can't believe you all got those tickets for me."

"Believe it, Hank. The kids love you."

As part of their yearly Christmas projects, the student body did something nice for those within their school, as well as helping the needy. This year, they'd raised money to buy their favorite custodian a gift—and managed to get him tickets for *Phantom* at the end of January.

Hank snorted. "Nah, it's you they love."

"Am I interrupting?"

Cassie looked over to the door and into the inscrutable face of Mitch Lansing. As he loomed at the entrance, his broad shoulders spanned the doorway and, as usual, he dwarfed the large classroom when he stepped into it.

Hank headed for the door. "Nope. Just finished in here. See you, Cassie." Slowly, he wheeled the cart out, nodded to Mitch and disappeared down the hall, humming "The Music of the Night."

Mitch ambled farther into the room and leaned against the edge of one of the desks. His hair was tousled from the January wind and snowflakes dotted his wool coat, underneath which he still wore the gray pin-striped suit, light gray shirt and striped tie that he'd had on that morning.

Not that I noticed, Cassie told herself.

"At the risk of stereotyping again," Mitch said, the corners of his mouth turning up just a bit, "your janitor listens to Broadway music?"

In response, Cassie smiled, too. "Schools are full of odd people. I could tell you stories you wouldn't believe about some of the personnel here."

Mitch's green eyes focused on her with intensity. "Tell me one about you."

Cassie stood. She picked up some folders and crossed to him. "You know all about me."

He scanned her and scowled. "Not all. *What* are you wearing?"

Looking down at her clothes, Cassie took in her bright purple leggings that ended at the knees and white, oversize T-shirt displaying a purple-and-yellow butterfly and the saying "The Wonder Of Teaching Is Watching The Caterpillars Turn Into Butterflies."

"Volleyball clothes." Mitch's eyes stayed on her legs a few seconds too long, she thought. When he lifted them, the look in them made her shiver.

"Volleyball?"

"Yeah. I play with a team from school on Monday nights at Hotshots." At his puzzled look, she said, "You know, that warehouse on Glide Street that they turned into a bar with the courts in the back."

He glanced at the clock. "What time?"

"Seven." When he said nothing, she continued, "Well, we'd better get going." She crossed to a table where she'd left the material for their lesson and he followed her.

He cleared his throat. "Aren't you cold?"

The look in his eyes made her want to perch on the edge of the table, cross her legs and let him stare all he wanted. To stifle the urge, she retrieved a sweatshirt from her gym bag, tugged it over her head and sat down in a chair.

"Better?"

He nodded, removed his overcoat and took a seat next to her. He was only about a foot away. He smelled like cold air and some woodsy cologne that reminded her of sex.

"Um, here's the blank lesson plan form that we've been using. We should probably start with that."

He reached inside his suit coat and drew out his glasses. Settling them on his nose, he picked up the paper and scanned it. Onyx cuff links glimmered at his big wrists. "All right—a focus. That's what we start with, right?"

"Yes."

"One that's relevant to their lives."

"Uh-huh."

"Well, I obviously can't use the incident Friday night."

"No, but you might use your experience in New York City—a vivid story that will grab their attention."

Mitch's face muscles tightened as he told her about the three thirteen-year-olds who had died from inhalants right before his eyes.

"How do you do it?" Cassie asked when he finished.

"Do what?"

"See so many horrible things and still function?"

"Sometimes I don't."

She cocked her head.

"There've been times in my life when I haven't been able to function because of what I've seen."

Cassie touched his hand impulsively. It was still a little cold. "Want to talk about it?"

He shook his head, but his eyes contradicted the gesture.

"Do you talk about it to anyone?"

Mitch swallowed hard. "To Kurt, once and a while."

"Your brother?"

"He got divorced recently, so we spend more time together now. He's a doctor in the city."

"Johnny wants to be a doctor."

Mitch just stared at her.

"You don't think he'll make it, do you."

"Let's just say the odds are against it."

She angled her chin. "They were against me, too."

Unexpectedly, he reached over and tucked a strand of hair behind her ear, the same way he'd done that night at Zoe's. The feelings she'd experienced then returned in full force.

"Yeah, well, you're pretty special." His voice was deep and low and curled inside Cassie, making the shirt she'd just donned feel like a thermal blanket. Heat rose to her cheeks.

Coughing, she dropped her gaze down to the papers, then back up to his face. "We should, um, do this. I have to leave..."

He stared at her a minute then drew back. "So do I. I have to be in town court at six."

"Well, then, let's get this lesson planned."

Sixty minutes passed. Mitch was a fast learner—he'd already internalized what she'd told him before about planning a lesson. He had good ideas, was flexible when she told him some wouldn't work, and his wry sense of humor slipped out more than once. By the time they were ready to preview the movie, Cassie's emotions were churning. The close proximity, his intelligence and surprising sensitivity were impossible to resist.

Which was why, after she got up to start the video, she pulled out a chair on the other side of the table, farther away from him.

Mitch didn't miss the distancing gesture, and he was grateful for it. She'd been so close he could smell her—something light and fresh, shampoo or lotion she'd probably put on that morning. Had she rubbed it over her legs, now encased in those damn leg-things that he had trouble keeping his eyes off? God, did she put that outfit on to torture him? He laughed at himself. That wasn't Cassie's style. She was no femme fatale. She didn't even wear makeup and obviously spent little time on her hair in the morning. As the tape began, he wondered idly when the clean, fresh-scrubbed look had started to appeal to him.

Through sheer force of will—something he had perfected to an art—Mitch kept his mind on the somber video. He watched kids tell heartbreaking stories about using inhalants because they thought they weren't dangerous, because they were legal, because they kicked you up so fast you got a great buzz quickly and cheaply. Though he'd heard them before, the stories wound their way into his heart; he tried to suppress the emotions, but he couldn't.

The last kid was Vietnamese. Mitch leaned back as he watched the boy, about the age Tam had been, recount how being a minority in a white culture had driven him to drugs. Would Tam have done that? Would Mitch have been able to preclude the loneliness and isolation that the young man on the screen so wrenchingly articulated? He could still see Tam's sad black eyes stare at him from across the compound, could still remember the laughter bubbling out of him when Mitch gave him the little portable radio that Kurt had sent. Suddenly, superimposed over the images was a blinding flash...and screams. Terror gripped Mitch....

"Mitch?" Cassie's voice penetrated the dark reminiscence. She'd gotten up and moved back to the seat next to him. Her hand clutched his arm. "Mitch, are you all right?"

Focusing on her face, he consciously slowed his rapid breathing. "I'm fine." His words were clipped. He looked down to see both hands fisted. He immediately unclenched them.

Gently, Cassie rubbed his sleeve with her fingertips. It felt good and helped settle his heartbeat.

"What happened?"

More in control, he looked at her. Concern had darkened the color of her eyes to warm steel. "Nothing. I'm fine."

"You don't look fine. You look—"

Scraping his chair back, he shook her off and stood. "I said I was fine." Jamming his hands in his pockets, he walked over to the TV. "The waste I see upsets me sometimes." He knew *she knew* he was lying. He ignored it and angled his head to the video. "I told you this was good. It will affect the kids, too. Let's talk about some points to discuss after the movie's over."

Watching him for a minute, Cassie finally nodded. "Sure."

Fifteen minutes later, Mitch rose and picked up his coat. "It's almost six. I've got to go."

Cassie stood. "Okay." She smiled. "We've got a pretty dynamite lesson, don't you think?"

"Yeah." His shoulder muscles were tense, and his back felt as if he'd been carrying an eighty pound knapsack down a jungle trail. He shrugged into his coat and briefly massaged his neck.

"You seem tense."

"It's been a long day." *And I didn't get a lot of*

sleep last night. I kept dreaming about a wet body encased in white terry cloth.

"Exercise can help."

"I work out every day."

Cassie's eyes roamed over his shoulders and chest. "I believe that." He felt her appreciation deep in his gut—and lower. Damn.

"Ever play volleyball?" she asked.

He remembered the pickup games in Nam. "Once or twice."

"After your court appearance, you could come to Hotshots. We can always use new team members."

More than anything he'd wanted in years, Mitch longed to accept the invitation and all that it implied. But getting close to this woman, becoming a real part of the school, was not in the cards for him. He couldn't risk the emotional involvement.

"I don't think so," he said coldly.

For a minute, she looked as if she was going to argue. Then she shrugged, and he got a glimpse of what she must have been like as a student at this school. Pretending she didn't care. Taking the blows to her pride with feigned nonchalance. "Suit yourself." She walked over to her desk and sat down.

He scowled. "What are you doing?"

"I'm going to read some of the kids' journals."

He glanced at the clock. "Why don't you take them home?"

"I'm not going home," she said without looking at him. She picked up one of the notebooks. "I'm going to work here until it's time to go to the game."

"Here?"

"Yes, of course, here."

He glanced at the windows, glazed with January frost. Through them, the school grounds were dark and deserted. "It's pretty late to be here alone at night."

"I'm not alone. The janitors are here. And there's a wrestling match at the gym tonight. The school's open to walkers, too."

After a moment, Mitch crossed to the doorway and inspected the hall. It was dim—and completely empty. "You're far away from all that action. You can't even hear it. And no one would hear *you* if something happened."

Cassie looked up at him and gave him an indulgent smile. "Mitch, I walked the streets of Greenwich Village alone when I was fifteen." Her smile faltered. "And worse."

"What's that got to do with this?"

Purposefully, she looked at the clock. "It's five of six, Captain. You're due in court."

He didn't like this, but there wasn't anything he could do about it. And he *was* running late. "All right." He glanced down at her legs in the form-fitting pants. "At least put the bottoms of that sweatsuit on so you don't catch cold."

Her laughter followed him out of the room.

It irritated him. He was feeling a lot of things right now, but mirth had nothing to do with any of them.

"DAMN IT!" CASSIE SWORE as she stuffed her legs into her purple sweatpants. *Aren't you cold?... Put the bottoms of that sweatsuit on... It's pretty late to be here alone at night.* Who did he think he was, Sir Galahad?

She plunked down on her desk chair and flipped open a journal. Though reading about her students' daily thoughts and feelings was a favorite part of her paper load, her mind wasn't on Nikki Parelli's latest poem.

Admit it, Cassie. You liked his concern.

"All right," she said aloud. "I liked it." Disgusted with herself, she reached for the cup of coffee on her desk. After Mitch left, she'd taken out the light snack she'd brought and eaten half of it. She fingered the lettering on the coffee cup. It read, "Experience is the toughest teacher. It offers the test first, and the lesson after."

Cassie's experience had taught her well. It wasn't safe to depend on anyone. For thirty-five years, she'd only trusted herself—with the exception of Seth Taylor and maybe Lacey Cartwright, the one student at Bayview Heights who had befriended her. But no one else.

And your lack of trust ended your marriage.

Still, she wouldn't be sucked in by an enigmatic man with green eyes that hid painful memories. Something had happened to him while they were watching the movie. She hadn't a clue what, and he wasn't about to tell her.

She respected that. A private person herself, she didn't expect everybody to spill their guts to her.

Johnny would call her a liar—tell her she was always trying to get all of the students in her class to open up. She leaned over and dug through the pile of notebooks until she found his. In today's entry, she saw at the top Johnny's precise, controlled handwriting. "Not private. Read this."

Breathing a sigh of relief—she let the kids pick

what they wanted to share and never violated that trust—Cassie scanned Johnny's entry. "I'm okay, Cassie. Don't worry about the gang. I know you don't think I know what I'm doing, but I do. I'm in control, and I'm going to be all right. I hate working with Lansing, though. He's an SOB, and he thinks he's so tough...."

Just like you, Johnny. He's so much like you. The thought came out of nowhere and stopped her short.

It bore some consideration, but not tonight. She tossed the journal down on the desk. Restless, she got up, adjusted the blinds and tidied the reading area. She was passing the doorway when she felt a chilling gust of air—as if someone had left the outer door open. Peeking into the corridor, she saw the door down at the end of the hall was closed. Puzzled she went back into her room and decided that she was not going to make much headway with the journals tonight. Maybe she could work on a new bulletin board. Yanking open her middle desk drawer, she pulled out the key to the storage area that connected her room with Zoe's. She crossed to the back of the room and jabbed the key in the lock, leaving it there so she didn't lose it. The kids teased her all the time about losing her keys.

As she switched on the storeroom light, she blinked. The fluorescent bulb flickered briefly before it lit to full capacity. Then it dimmed. Cassie hated the light in here. It was unpredictable and gave off an eerie glow. Stepping farther into the narrow, twelve-by-five area, stacked on each side with shelves, she reached up to the top one for the construction paper. Unable to grasp it, she dragged a low stool over and had just gotten hold of her material when the door to the storeroom slammed shut. Cassie came down off the stool and grabbed the door handle. She twisted it. Nothing happened. Levering her body, she shoved at the door with all her weight behind her. It didn't budge.

Oh, great. She tried to visualize what she'd done with the key. Had she relocked the door after she'd opened it? Damn. She and Zoe had talked about the problem of this room locking so that you couldn't get out from the inside, but they hadn't filled out a work order to have it changed.

Cassie began to pound on the solid-core wooden door. "Hank...somebody...I'm in here! Hey... *somebody!*" After a few minutes, the palms of her hands stung and they were red. She slid down to the linoleum floor and sat with a thunk. Her knees propped up, the toes of her sneakers hitting the opposite row of shelves, she leaned back. The air was heavy, and the light above hummed. It flickered and dimmed again.

Taking a deep breath, she thought of all the work sitting on her desk that she could be completing. She pictured the mounds of laundry in the corner of her bedroom. And she visualized the volleyball game beginning without her. Cassie hated wasting time. It almost killed her to sit through repetitive faculty meetings and unproductive committee meetings.

It's pretty late to be here alone... You're far away from all that action... You can't even hear it... And no one would hear you if something happened.

Suddenly she felt chilled, though the storeroom was easily ten degrees hotter than her classroom tonight, and getting warmer by the minute. No, her imagination was playing tricks on her. Mitch had spooked her, was all.

Mitch. For a brief minute, Cassie let herself imagine being trapped inside here with him. Closing her eyes, she could feel his hands at her waist—squeezing gently at first, then grasping tighter as his lips came closer to hers. Maybe he'd ease her down to the floor. What would his body feel like covering hers? If she thought really hard, remembered really well, she could almost conjure the smell of him tonight—the utter masculine, alluring scent that was his.

Damn. It was going to be a long night.

DAMN. IT HAD BEEN a long night. The court appearance had dragged on, then Mitch had stopped at the station to get his messages. He should go home, relax and go to bed. From his car, he stared at the pink neon sign. Hotshots. What the hell was he doing here?

We can always use more team members.

He closed his eyes, telling himself he should simply drive away from the old converted warehouse. But the image of clinging purple spandex pants kept him from leaving. He could still feel the grip of her strong fingers on his arm. And he could still hear her slightly husky voice asking if he was all right.

Restless, he'd tried to call Kurt earlier, but his brother was unavailable. And Mitch was tired of being alone, tired of being on the outside, tired of *not* being like everyone else.

So he'd come to Hotshots.

He hadn't changed his clothes, though. He had no

intention of actually playing. No, he'd just order a beer, sit on the sidelines and enjoy the game.

Mitch climbed out of his car and made his way inside. The volleyball courts were in the back, so he stopped at the bar, got a draft beer and walked slowly to the rear.

Scanning the teams on the court, he recognized a lot of the people. Some of the older teachers, mostly the new ones. A couple of administrators. Idly—or so he told himself—he perused the group for sassy purple pants and an even sassier... He cut off the thought but continued to look for her.

She wasn't there. Methodically, he went back and checked out each person. Cassie was not among them.

The game ended and a beer break was called. Mitch waited as Zoe wandered off the court with Ross Martin, one of the other At-Risk teachers, and the young vice principal, Alex Ransom. When Zoe spotted Mitch, she smiled warmly. "Hi, did you bring Cassie?"

His heart stumbled. "No. Isn't she here?"

Zoe shook her head, her eyes narrowing. "She was supposed to meet us at seven. She never showed."

"We thought maybe she was with you," Ross added. "We knew you two had a meeting."

Plunking the glass down on the table to his right, Mitch fished in his pocket for his keys as he said, "I left her at school at exactly six o'clock." He found his keys and looked up at Cassie's three colleagues. "Did you call her house?"

"Yes, of course," Zoe told him.

"School?"

"You can't call school at night, Mitch," Ransom said.

"Does she have a cell phone?"

"No."

Abruptly, Mitch turned to go, but pivoted back for a minute and touched Zoe's arm. "It's probably all right. I'll go by the school and call you here when I find her."

If I find her.

The thought echoed in his mind and bounced off the interior of his car for the entire twelve-minute trip back to Bayview Heights High School. He made it in seven, thanks to his portable flashing red light and siren. Once at the complex, he drove right up the bus loop and left the door open and the engine on as he ran to the front of the school. As he'd feared, the outside door was locked.

He gunned the engine over to the gym entrance. His long legs eating up the distance into school, he reached the east corridor, only to find the double fire doors locked.

Damn.

"I-am-the-Phantom-of-the-Ope-ra." The lyrics were being belted out from somewhere on his left. Spotting the janitor, Mitch called out, "Hank, over here. Unlock this for me."

The old man came down the hall at what seemed a snail's pace. "Everything okay, Captain?"

Mitch remembered the tender look on the guy's face when he talked to Cassie. "Yeah, I think so. I just need to see Cassie again. Thanks." He took off down the dark, deserted corridor.

Cassie's door was wide open. Inside, he could hear the faint rock music coming from her radio.

The middle drawer of her desk was ajar, and a napkin lay wadded up by a cup of coffee. He touched the mug. It was cold.

"Cassie?" he called.

No answer.

"Cassie?"

Silence.

He raised his voice. *"Cassie?"*

Then he heard it. The pounding from the back of the room. Coming from behind a door. He strode to it and yanked on the knob. It didn't budge. Glancing down, he saw the key and twisted it viciously. He pulled open the door.

Cassie was standing on the other side, her face flushed. She'd removed both the sweatshirt and pants, but still her hair was damp and there were beads of perspiration on her brow. Roughly he grabbed her arms.

"Are you all right?"

"Yes." She looked at him quizzically. "What are you doing here?"

"What happened?"

"I got locked inside the storage closet."

"How?" When she didn't answer right away, his hands tightened on her shoulders. *"How?"*

"I'm not exactly sure. Look, I'd like to get out of here...."

Reluctantly, he stepped back and withdrew his hands. He didn't know what he'd expected—certainly not that she'd throw herself into his arms in a terrified storm of weeping. But also not this cool, collected response to being locked up for hours.

He watched as she walked over to the desk,

looked down at it, then turned to face him, her arms crossed over her chest. "Why did you come back?"

He explained his impulsive trip to Hotshots. The smile that lit her face was hard to ignore. So he forced himself to play the cop. "Cassie, sit down and tell me exactly how this happened."

She blew her bangs out of her face and shivered. Returning to the storeroom, he picked up her sweat suit and gave it to her. It was a little damp. "Put this on."

"Haven't we already been through this tonight?" she said lightly as she leaned against the edge of the desk.

"This is no joking matter. Somebody locked you in this closet."

"What makes you think that?"

"What other explanation is there?"

"I left the key in the door. I could have relocked it."

"And who closed it, the Opera Ghost?"

Cassie smiled. "Very quick, Captain."

"Cassie?"

"All right. Earlier, I felt a draft from the hall, like someone had opened the door. The wind could have blown the storeroom door closed."

"The outside door is locked."

"Now. Maybe not—" She looked at the clock. "Wow, I've been in there two hours?"

"Someone could have come in and trapped you in there."

She frowned. "One of the kids?" Her expression turned into a scowl. "I'll kill them if they pulled a prank like this on me."

"Maybe it isn't a prank."

"Why wouldn't it be?"

"Would anyone want to hurt you? Scare you?"

"No one."

"Are you telling me the truth?"

She angled her chin. "Why would I lie?"

"To protect someone?"

"Who?"

"You tell me."

"Look, Captain, I'm not in the mood for guessing games. If you have something to say, say it. Otherwise, I'm going home."

Suddenly, anger, mixed with the anxiety Mitch had felt since he discovered she'd never made it to Hotshots, was ignited by a fierce blast of desire. He grabbed her shoulders again and gave her a not-very-gentle shake. "Damn you, I was worried."

Her eyes deepened to charcoal, and her lips parted slightly. Her breathing speeded up, making his own breath catch in his throat. "You were?"

He yanked her to him. She was tall, and as he locked his hand at her neck, he could feel how perfectly each soft curve of her body fit against the hard planes of his. He pressed her face into his chest and threaded his hand in her hair, then he buried his lips in it. "Yes," he whispered hoarsely. "I was."

He felt her relax against him, and allowed himself to enjoy the sensation of holding her close.

"Hey, what are you doin' down here?" The voice from the hall was raised and irritated.

Mitch stiffened. He glanced toward the door and saw someone whiz past it, heading down the corridor to the front of the school.

In seconds, Mitch set Cassie aside and bolted for the door. The intruder was six feet away from the outside exit when Mitch tackled him. He slammed the guy facedown, jammed his knee in the man's spine and yanked his arm behind his back.

From behind him, Cassie asked, "What's going on?"

Then the janitor said, "I saw this guy—"

"Let me up, you bastard." The voice was familiar enough, but when Mitch heard Cassie's gasp, he knew who his victim was. Jerking the kid's head to the side, Mitch could clearly see Johnny Battaglia's profile.

CHAPTER SIX

JOHNNY KICKED the loose gravel with the toe of his boot as he made his way up the alley that led to Zorro's tenement house. The midnight wind whipped his Blisters jacket open, sending a chill skittering through him. The nylon coat wasn't warm enough for the end of January, but after the scene at school, Johnny had purposefully gone home and exchanged his heavy parka for his gang jacket. He tried not to think about what had happened, but he couldn't stop remembering....

"Let me up, you bastard," he'd said to Lansing after he'd been tackled like some featherweight. He hadn't realized the cop was so big.

"Not until I get some answers."

"Mitch, what are you doing?" It was Cassie, standing behind them.

Thank God, Johnny had thought. She'd call off this watchdog.

"Let him up. Right now."

Reluctantly, Lansing had let go, and Johnny scrambled to his feet.

"I've caught our prankster," Lansing said when Johnny faced him. "Get a kick out of locking your teacher in the storeroom? Out of scaring Ms. Smith?"

Johnny remembered his confusion. Until he

looked at Cassie. She'd stood there with accusation in her eyes, written all over her disappointed face.

It was only for a second. But it was enough.

"You believe him." It wasn't a question.

She'd shaken off the doubt, almost visibly. But it had been there. Briefly, Johnny explained that he'd been on his way to catch the end of the wrestling match after work and seen her room lights on from the parking lot. He was stopping by to say hello. In truth, he was going to tell her she shouldn't have been at school so late, all alone, but he hadn't revealed that. He'd listened while Lansing told him what had happened, but he didn't look again at Cassie.

After the explanation, she'd insisted Johnny didn't do it, that Lansing let him go. When the cop agreed, she asked to talk to Johnny alone.

"We got nothin' to say to each other," he'd said callously, and stalked out of the building....

And ended up here, for more than one reason. Hunching against the cold, he headed to the front door, carefully picking his way around broken glass and scattered two-by-fours. He entered through a thin, creaky door, turned right and strode down the first-floor hallway. A naked bulb burned above, illuminating the colorless walls. Water stains ran down in tiny rivulets, and there was a new hole in the plaster about the size of a man's fist.

Johnny rapped hard on the door to apartment 112, stinging his knuckles.

"Enter."

Inside, he found Zorro staring at a black-and-white TV, its volume so muted Johnny could barely hear it. When Zorro glanced up, his ebony eyes lit from within. "Tonto, my man."

For a moment, Johnny glimpsed the boy he loved behind the facade of a man he no longer respected. Walking to the rumpled bed, Johnny leaned over and grabbed Zorro by the collar of his faded flannel shirt. He yanked hard.

Zorro's head snapped back and his chin bobbed. "What the f—"

"Saw your car at school an hour ago."

Zorro stared at him. "No, man. I been here all night."

"I saw it. I was on my way to the wrestling match."

"What you doin' at a wrestlin' match?"

"Don't change the subject."

"I ain't."

Johnny studied Zorro's face. His eyes were smudged underneath with faint purple rings. The two-inch scar on his cheek—earned in a knife fight at fourteen—had faded over the years, but still marred his olive skin. A trademark of the Blisters, his hair was shaved on each side and shaggy on top. It was the exact texture and color of Johnny's own hair, which was now cropped short. They'd pretended for years they were brothers. Hell—they *were* brothers in all the important ways.

For a moment, Johnny was transported back to the old neighborhood. He'd been seven when his father first hit him. Johnny had staggered out of the apartment right into his best buddy....

"What happen to your face?" Zorro had asked.

"Nothin'."

Zorro, a year older and quite a bit bigger, had

grabbed Johnny's shoulder and inspected his cheek. "You got hit."

Mortified, Johnny shook his head. But he couldn't quell the tears filling his eyes.

Zorro had dragged him down the hallway into his own seedy three-room place. "My old man hits me," Zorro said, snagging some ice, popping it into a bag and scrunching it into Johnny's face. "Lemme tell ya what I do...."

The memory increased Johnny's need to believe his friend. He let go of Zorro's shirt and dropped down on the chair next to the bed. "Aw, hell, I thought it was your car. Maybe not."

"Why you think I was at your stupid school?"

"Somebody locked Cassie in the storeroom. I thought you'd paid her another visit."

Zorro's eyes turned February frigid. He swore vilely.

Johnny glared at him. "Don't say nothin' about her."

Like quicksilver, Zorro came off the bed. He kicked a wastebasket, sending the contents flying. "What's with you and that broad, man? You sure you ain't gettin' it on with her?"

Johnny closed his eyes. God, he was tired of this. Zorro just couldn't understand how he felt about Cassie. It wasn't sexual. It was sisterly and maternal and friendship all mixed together. "Let's drop it."

Zorro's eyes flamed at him for a few seconds, reminding Johnny why his friend had been sought out to head the Sixth Street gang. As one of the toughest fighters in lower Manhattan, Zorro held grudges that would shame the Mafia. He was also the best with a blade—hence his name—and dangerously reckless when he used it.

"Fine, I'll forget it if you come with me tonight," Zorro said.

"Where?"

Zorro's smile was silky. "An initiation."

Johnny sighed and checked his watch, stalling for time. He remembered his own jumping in. He could almost feel again the punches jabbing him in the gut, at the temples. He could hear the crack of bone that led him to wonder if his jaw was broken. He'd been sick to his stomach for an hour after. Zorro had held his head until he was finished. Johnny had been thirteen.

"Tonto?"

Johnny stared at his buddy. Why the hell not? he thought as he stood and zipped up his jacket. He wasn't going near school tomorrow. Not after the bastard accused *him* of locking her up. Not after the look in Cassie's eyes said she'd believed the cop—if only for a few seconds. *Any doubt* about something like that was enough.

God, he'd almost begged her in the car that night not to let Lansing turn her against him. *And tonight...made me think...maybe he could take you away, too. You know, turn you against me. All I'd have left then is Zorro and the Blisters.* How humiliating. Well, never again. He faced his buddy. "What you takin'?" he asked Zorro.

His best friend in the world slapped him on the back and crossed to the scarred dresser in the corner. He pulled open the bottom drawer. Johnny followed him and glanced down at the chains, clubs and even some old-fashioned brass knuckles Zorro had found at a pawn shop in Times Square. Bending over, Johnny picked up a chain. The once-familiar weight was heavy in his hand.

But he hadn't forgotten how to wrap it around his fingers. When he did, it felt more comfortable.

It felt right.

FROM THE DOORWAY of the office at the Forty-second Street Clinic, Mitch watched his brother Kurt close his eyes, lean back on a chair, link his hands behind his head and prop his feet up on the desk. His sagging posture testified to his fatigue. Operating an independent clinic in the heart of New York City was tough, even if Kurt did have the help of two partners. His brother's desire to do humanitarian work, like running this clinic, rather than earning money as a hotshot doctor on Park Avenue, had cost him his marriage.

Mitch slouched against the door frame. "When are you going to get some more help around here?"

Kurt's eyes opened and a smile spread across his face. "You volunteering?"

"Nope, I shoot them. You patch 'em up."

The old joke between brothers widened Kurt's grin. Mitch sauntered farther into the small office. Dropping onto a faded chair facing the desk, Mitch's smile quickly transformed into a worried scowl. Kurt's eyes were bloodshot, and there were deep lines around his mouth.

"Seriously," Mitch said. "I thought you were going to hire some help."

"I did. Five premed students from Columbia University. One lasted a week, one ten days. The jury's still out on the others. Real life in the city is too much for them.''

Mitch rolled his eyes.

"You wouldn't know anybody interested in medicine who can handle what goes on in the trenches, would you?"

An image of hostile black eyes and a sneering mouth popped into Mitch's head. *Johnny wants to be a doctor... He didn't take the scalpels... He loves his job... He'd never do anything to jeopardize it.*

"*Do* you know someone?"

"Yeah, but it's complicated. Let me think about it."

"Fine. It's nice to see you." Kurt peered at his brother intently. "Something's wrong."

Without warning, Mitch felt his heartbeat quicken with the familiar welling of panic he experienced every time he considered opening up. "Not wrong, exactly."

Kurt unlocked his hands from behind his neck, dragged his feet off the desk and rose. He went to the small utility table, poured coffee for them both, gave Mitch a mug and sat down in the chair opposite him. And waited.

Looking into the cup, Mitch took a couple of sips before he said, "I've met someone."

Coffee sputtered from Kurt's mouth. Laughing, he wiped his face and said, "Sorry. But, my God, are we talking about a woman?"

"I do occasionally spend time with them, you know."

"Yeah, but you've never come in here wound tight as a spring and told me you cared about one.

I couldn't be happier. It's about time some female penetrated that wall you've built around yourself.''

"I never said I cared about her.''

His brother sat back, still smiling. "Okay, who is this woman you don't care about?''

"A teacher at the school.''

Kurt sobered. "Is it still hard for you? Being there?''

Mitch was tempted to brush off his brother's concern, but he needed help tonight and Kurt was the only person in the world he could be honest with.

"Yeah.'' Mitch dragged his hand through his hair. "It is hard. But I like it, too. I like the students. Cassie has a saying on her wall, 'Teachers change the world, one kid at a time.' I can help do that and it feels…good.''

"Is Cassie this *someone* you've met?''

Mitch nodded.

"What's she like?''

Blowing out an exasperated breath, Mitch stood and paced. "She's opinionated, obstinate, feisty and mostly a real pain in the butt.''

"Oh.''

"She's also loyal and brave and almost as concerned about helping others as you are.''

Kurt smiled. "My kind of woman.''

"Well, she isn't mine.'' Mitch paced to the other side of the room.

"So I can see.''

Mitch let out a string of colorful obscenities— which made Kurt laugh again. When Mitch glared at him, Kurt said, "You obviously like this woman. Let yourself seek a little human comfort.''

"It's not comfort I want from her.''

"Oh. You can barely talk about her and it's all sex? What is she, a Cindy Crawford lookalike?"

Mitch stopped in his tracks. "No, not at all. She's pretty enough—she doesn't wear any goop on her face." He hesitated. "She's wholesome-looking, I guess. Except for the tattoo on her ankle."

"The what?"

"It's a long story."

Kurt glanced at his watch. "Well, my partner should be here in ten minutes. I'll buy you a beer and you can tell me about this plain-Jane."

"All right." He glanced around. "And maybe we can discuss getting another helper around here."

"It's a deal, buddy."

"THIS WAS THE THIRD DAY he was out of school. No one answers his phone or doorbell." Cassie, perched on top of a ladder, looked over at Zoe, who was across the room on a makeshift scaffold. They were stenciling the walls of Zoe's bedroom.

Zoe said, "I know, Cass."

"I can still see his face. In that split second when I doubted him...." She swallowed hard and blinked. "He'll never forgive me for that."

"I think Johnny Battaglia is a bigger person than that."

"Maybe. Maybe not."

Zoe turned back to the painting job. The design was of abstract birds in various tones of silver. "Johnny's got a lot of depth and sensitivity. Especially when it comes to you."

"Maybe too much. How *could* I have believed—even for a moment—that Johnny would lock me in the storage closet? Lansing's accusation was totally unfounded.''

"Oh, now it's Lansing. Not Mitch or even Captain.''

"Don't start." Zoe was quiet. Cassie continued with painstakingly small brush strokes. "I'm sorry.''

"That's okay. Obviously it's a sore spot with you.''

It was still hard, after all these years, to talk about her feelings. Even with Zoe, who was a wonderful, loyal friend. But damn it, Cassie needed to get some of this out or she'd go nuts. "Actually, it's more than that.''

Much more. Cassie could vividly remember the feel of Mitch Lansing's chest against her cheek, the steady thud of his heart beneath her ear, the all-consuming, potent smell of him.

Zoe didn't answer.

"I'm having some unexpected feelings for him.''

"Honey, every female at Bayview Heights High School except you has been having those feelings for him." Zoe got down from her ladder and set the brush in its can. "Let's take a break. I'll get us coffee.''

Cassie was sitting on a drop cloth when her friend returned. Zoe sank onto the floor, handed her a mug and faced her squarely. "Talk to me.''

"You've got paint on your face.''

"And your feelings are written all over yours. Even if you can't express them.''

"I express my feelings all the time at school. Much to the dismay of people like Jerry Bosco.''

Zoe reached over and squeezed Cassie's arm.

"Feelings about school and the students. Cassie, the kids aren't enough."

"I'm scared," Cassie finally admitted.

"You're also lonely and ready for more in your life."

"But why did I have to pick *him*? Why couldn't this be easier?"

"I doubt if you've ever done anything the easy way in your whole life."

Cassie's shoulders sagged. "Damn. This isn't fair."

"Honey, you always tell the kids that nothing's fair. Griping about it won't change that. Do what you always tell them to do."

"And what's that?"

"Go after what you want, no matter what the risk."

"How do I know what I want?"

Zoe chuckled. "As I said, it's written all over your face."

FEBRUARY SLUSH had turned the small lawn in front of Battaglia's apartment house into mud. Mitch pulled over in front of the Franklin Street address, mentally kicking himself for getting involved. He didn't want to get close to any of these kids, especially not this one. But all week Cassie had been so sad that Mitch couldn't take it anymore.

Angry at himself as well as Battaglia, he stormed out of the car and up the small walkway. He stumbled once on the cracked cement, but righted himself with the agility of a trained soldier.

Battaglia would love it if I fell on my face at his doorstep.

The notion made him madder. He found the number of the kid's unit on the mailboxes and proceeded in. When he was just about to knock, the door opened.

The oldest eyes he'd ever seen looked up at him. They belonged to a small-framed woman with mousy brown hair and pasty skin. "Oh, Captain Lansing."

Mitch cocked his head. "Do we know each other?"

Her thin hands fluttered to her neck. "No, no, we don't. I'm Betty Battaglia. I've seen you at the diner where I fill in on the night shift." He nodded, then her face crumpled. "Oh, no, it's Johnny, isn't it? He's in trouble."

"He's been truant from school for the last four days." Mrs. Battaglia's shoulders sagged in relief. "Do you know where he is?"

"Why, yes. He's in bed."

"Here?"

"Yes." She checked her watch. "But I...I'm late as it is. I don't have..."

"It's all right. You go ahead. I'll wake him up myself."

After a hesitant look, Betty Battaglia's eyes filled with resignation and she left. Inside, Mitch closed the door and looked around. The living room was about ten by fourteen, with a sagging sofa covered by a throw, and two chairs with springs sticking out of them. A heavily draped picture window took up part of one wall. Faded pictures hung tipsily on the others. There were stacks of magazines by the couch, and a forgotten breakfast lay half eaten on the coffee table. A fine layer of dust covered everything.

He spotted a hallway leading to the bedrooms and followed it. Only one door was closed. He opened it slowly. The morning light peeked through half-closed venetian blinds, letting in a fair amount of light. Johnny lay asleep on the bed, his face buried in a pillow he grasped with his left hand. There was a stark white bandage across his knuckles.

Mitch studied the room. Unlike the living room, not a thing was out of place. The closet and drawers were closed. Posters on the walls were arranged artistically. A bureau top was clear, sporting only a lamp and some keys. Mitch walked over to the desk. Johnny's books were neatly stacked with pens and pencils propped in a cup. He noticed a frame that had been turned facedown and picked it up. It was a picture of Cassie. She was sitting at her desk, flashing a smile that both scolded and laughed. It was black and white, probably taken for a yearbook. Mitch set it down carefully.

As he turned, his foot connected with something on the floor. Leaning over, he picked up an empty bottle. The label read 110-Proof Vodka.

Sensing he was being watched, Mitch looked across the room.

"I call this trespassing," Battaglia said from the bed. He was sitting up now. He wore only a pair of ragged sweatpants. The sunlight angled on his face, showing the beard of a man and the eyes of a street kid.

Mitch held up the vodka bottle. "I call this stupid."

"Who gives a shit?"

Without hesitation, Mitch answered, "Cassie does."

Johnny sucked in his breath, then sagged back on the pillow and closed his eyes. "Sure she does."

"I just left school. Remember how she looked that day when Brenda told her she had an abortion?"

Johnny tried to ignore him, but Mitch could see him swallow hard.

"That's how she's looked all week."

"Somebody else get knocked up?"

"No, but somebody else let her down."

Johnny sat up so fast Mitch stepped back. "Yeah, well she let me down, too."

"I imagine she did." Mitch chose his words carefully. Lying to this one would never work. "You never make a mistake, Battaglia? You never jump to a stupid conclusion or say something dumb that makes you wish you could bite your tongue off?"

Again, the maddening teenage silence.

Wanting to strangle the kid, Mitch battled back his temper. He'd come here with a purpose. "Well, I have. And it tastes bitter." He jerked a piece of paper out of his suit pocket. Walking closer to the bed, he tossed it to Battaglia. "My brother's a doctor. He runs a clinic in a dirt poor section of the city. He's looking for some people interested in medicine who can handle the street stuff they'd see."

Johnny stared at him unblinkingly. "So?"

"So, you've got an appointment with him today at four o'clock for an interview. If you can clean yourself up, sell yourself to him, you've got yourself a job." Mitch gave him a meaningful stare. "Like the one I helped you lose." Straightening to what he hoped was an imposing height, Mitch finished, "The catch is, you gotta stay in school and not cut out when you get pissed off at somebody." Then he turned and walked to the door.

Just as he reached it, Mitch called out. "Lansing?"

"What?"

"You doing this because you feel guilty?"

Mitch shook his head. His back to the boy, he pulled open the door and stepped out. While he was still within earshot, he mumbled, "No, I'm doing this because I'm crazy."

ON MONDAY MORNING, Cassie faced her class, trying to ignore the fact that Johnny was not there for the beginning of another week. Mitch Lansing sat in the back watching her.

"Aw, we gonna do this again?" Austyn Jones threw down the packet Cassie had just given him, his beringed hands raised in disgust. He rolled his eyes. God, Cassie hated that gesture.

"Yes, Austyn, we are. We can use some vocabulary drill."

"But Ms. S., when are we gonna use words like *contingency?*"

"Never, if you don't know what they mean."

"That's a teacher answer," Mike Youngblood said, drumming his fingers on the desk, then tapping his foot. His hyperactivity, usually routine for Cassie to deal with, was getting on her nerves today.

"I'm a teacher," Cassie said, trying to stifle a flush that crept up her neck. Her exasperation had little to do with contrary kids.

"Leave her alone," Nikki Parelli put in. "She's upset about Johnny."

The kids became quiet immediately.

"I am upset about Johnny," Cassie told them, scanning the whole room. "But we're still going to do this lesson." She glanced at the clock. "I'll make you a deal. If I can't tell you when you could use each of these words in your own life by the time class is over, I'll cancel tonight's homework."

"All right."

"Totally rad."

"Mucho grande."

"With one *contingency*," she added. Everybody laughed. "On one condition."

"No, that ain't fair," Don Peterson said, his team jacket draping his big shoulders.

Cassie nailed him with what educators called "the look." All teachers had one; it was their greatest weapon. "Afraid, Don?"

"Me? Never."

Jones stood, kicked out his new alligator boots and crossed his ankles. "What's the *contingency?*"

"That Captain Lansing help me."

"Not a chance," Tara Romig said. "He's got a photographic memory."

Cassie eyed the girl. "How do you know that, Tara?"

"He wrote about it one day."

Cassie said, "Still, he'll have to think on his feet." She turned to Mitch. "Game, Captain?"

His smile was slow and sexy, setting her pulse spinning. "Game, Ms. Smith."

It was fun. They all sat on the floor—even Mitch. First, the kids got together in a group and studied the words so they'd know if he and Cassie got them right.

As they concentrated hard, Mitch leaned over to her and said, "Did you plan this?"

"No, it's what educational jargon terms a *teachable moment.*"

When the kids were ready, DeFazio stood and took the lead, probably to get Mitch back for the inhalant lesson, which had gone over surprisingly well.

"Okay—the first one's *dispirited.*"

Cassie said right away, "Joe, you'd be dispirited if your girlfriend dropped you for another guy."

Mitch added, "Or, you'll be dispirited if you fail the test."

Nikki took a turn. *"Laconic."*

Jen Diaz piped up. "Mr. Bosco is so laconic he almost puts us to sleep."

Jones yelled, "Diaz, whose side are you on?"

"Sorry," she said, grinning. "It was just too perfect to let pass."

"Try another, guys," Mitch challenged, sitting back and bracing his arms on the floor. His shirt pulled tightly across his chest.

"Virile."

Cassie wanted to moan. Instead, she tore her eyes away from Mitch and said, "In order for you guys to be virile, you have to have more than muscles and brawn. A real man is sensitive and talks about his feelings."

The boys coughed and pretended to gag themselves.

The girls rolled their eyes. "Sensitive? Fat chance."

Five more words brought them to the end of the lesson. So far, Cassie and Mitch hadn't been stumped.

"The last one is *prodigal*," Jen yelled out.

Before anyone could answer, the door to the classroom flew open. Johnny Battaglia stood in the threshold, his hair cut, his jeans pressed and his cheeks ruddy. "Uh, sorry I'm late," he said, looking sheepishly toward Cassie. "I had some things to do."

The room was ghostly still. Cassie stared at Johnny.

Mitch grinned. "The prodigal son returns."

CHAPTER SEVEN

CASSIE TOSSED the volleyball over her head, drew her arm back and smacked it with her fisted hand. It was a good, low serve. The ball sailed over the net and plopped down in the middle of the opposite court, as three players from Bayview hospital failed to reach it.

Ross Martin said, "Hey, you guys. Need glasses? You could probably get them cheap at the hospital."

"Naw," retorted one of the technicians Cassie dated occasionally. "*We* work till five, and it takes us a while to get in the groove. You all had time for a nap after school."

The hospital's team laughed at the friendly jab while the educators booed.

"Yeah, sure," Cassie called to the accuser. "We're short two players tonight because they're home finishing up the scan sheets. Grades are due tomorrow."

Before anyone could offer a comeback, Cassie shouted, "Thirteen serving ten," and sent the ball flying over the net with a hard punch. The other team returned it. Zoe set up the shot with Ross. The ball came back to the gym teacher—Bill Carlson—who slammed it over the net right into the chest of a guy in the fourth row. Bill turned and raised his hand, giving Cassie a high five. "One more, Cassie baby. Come on, we're depending on you.''

Cassie smiled. Catching the ball, she jogged back into position. As she turned, she caught a glimpse of someone in her peripheral vision. And stopped dead in her tracks. On the sidelines was Mitch Lansing. He leaned against a table, a beer in his hand, watching her.

He was dressed in a forest green sweat suit. It outlined his muscular torso—which she studied carefully. It took her a minute to realize people were yelling at her. She couldn't drag her eyes away from Mitch until Zoe blocked her view. Her friend was chuckling as she whispered, ''Close your mouth, girl. You're making a spectacle of yourself.''

In a hushed voice, Cassie said, ''Did you see him?''

''*Everyone's* seen him now. Get a grip, Cass. You can look your fill after this point.''

Zoe's words finally sunk in. Horrified at her public display, Cassie stepped back and managed to get into serving position. ''Game point.'' She threw up the ball and served—straight into the net.

Groaning, she accepted the teasing and tried to focus on the game. The teachers finally won, seventeen to fifteen, no thanks to Cassie. As she participated in the hugs and banter afterward, she saw Mitch smile and stare at her. When the players finally came off the court, she headed right for him.

''Hi,'' she said. Up close, he was even more mesmerizing. The color of his sweat suit deepened his eyes to a dark and dangerous green. The material looked soft and inviting. She was tempted to run her hands over those shoulders that were a mile wide.

"Hi. You looked good out there."

"Oh, please. I blew my serve."

He sipped his beer. "Yeah, I noticed. What happened?"

She watched him for signs of sarcasm and saw the teasing glint in his eyes. Damn it, he knew.

Well, two could play this game. She looked him up and down. "I couldn't believe my eyes, Captain. I didn't think you owned any clothes other than those suits of armor you wear."

Slowly, he reached over and tucked behind her ear the wayward strand of hair that seemed to fascinate him. "There's a lot you don't know about me, Ms. Smith." His voice was like warm honey.

Zoe and Ross joined them before she could respond. "Here, Cass," Zoe said, handing her a beer. "Hi, Mitch."

Pleasantries were exchanged, then talk about the game predominated until it was time to start the second round of the match.

"We're short two people," Ross told Mitch. "You wanna fill in?"

"I'd like that," Mitch replied. "Is it within the rules?"

"We're pretty informal here. And since you've been working in the high school for a month, you qualify."

The players returned to the court, and Cassie took her position in the back before she let herself search for Mitch. She groaned again when she glimpsed him in the front line, studying the net and the other players. He'd removed his sweats, and the fantasies Cassie had had of what he'd look like out of his suit became reality. He wore khaki athletic shorts that hit him mid-thigh. His legs were roped with the muscles of an athlete. A navy blue T-shirt was tucked into his washboard-flat waist. When he turned, she saw NYPD sprawled across an Arnold Schwarzenegger chest. Cassie sighed and forced herself to look away. It was going to be a long game.

Mitch was aware of Cassie watching him. Her obvious appreciation took away some of the nervousness he'd had about coming here, about admitting he wanted to see her, wanted to take their relationship further. He'd accepted that he would let himself get closer to her—to all these people. He was glad he'd come, though he hadn't been on a volleyball court since Nam, where they'd routinely run pickup games.

He played easily at first, careful not to slam the ball into any of the women in the front line, being sure to set it up with another player. The lines rotated several times, until Cassie stood directly behind him. After the hospital team scored a point, she cupped her hands around her mouth and said, "I think you're sandbagging, Captain."

He turned to face her. She was sweaty and flushed. Her eyes were bluer now and they were alight with mischief. The navy shirt emblazoned with Teachers Have Class clung to her curves. Her breasts looked full and heavy, and he wondered what they'd feel like in his hands. "Excuse me?" he said, feigning indignation.

"We, ah, don't go easy on the women here, Lansing," Alex Ransom said from next to her. "You don't have to hold back." Ransom put his arm around Cassie and hugged her. "Our females are tough. God forbid you don't play to your potential."

Cassie added, "Or worse, that you hog the ball. It took us months to train these Neanderthals."

Mitch held up his hands. "Fine. I'm happy to oblige."

"And let yourself go, Captain." She gave him a look that had nothing to do with volleyball. "I'd like to see that."

He arched an eyebrow. "Would you, now?"

The game began again, halting their banter. Mitch tried hard to let go but couldn't quite allow himself to spike on the five-foot-tall nurse who faced him opposite the net, or even the skinny orderly. The teachers won, anyway, so it didn't matter.

Afterward, he joined them at the bar. Cassie sat on a stool, more relaxed than he'd ever seen her. "Buy you a beer, Captain?"

"Sure." He sidled in next to her, and for fifteen minutes, chatted amiably with the players. It felt good to be a part of the group.

At about nine, several of the teachers left to go home and finish up their grades. Cassie and Mitch were alone at the bar. "No grades to do?" he asked her.

"No, I finished them at school before I came here."

He shook his head. "You never learn, do you?"

"What do you mean?"

"You were alone at school again before the game?"

"Don't start," she said, but the sting wasn't in her voice. Underlying her tone was something he couldn't put his finger on—maybe didn't want to—but it wasn't anger. Or even irritation.

Her face grew serious. "Mitch, I wanted to thank

you for what you did for Johnny.'' She reached out and squeezed his wrist. Her touch felt so good on his bare skin, he wanted to close his eyes and savor it.

"It wasn't much,'' he managed to say.

"It was.''

"What did he tell you?''

"Not too much. He's as closemouthed as you are sometimes. But it was enough. You got him a job in your brother's clinic, and that gesture of faith turned him around this time.''

"Did he tell you where he'd been all week?''

"No.''

"His hand was bandaged Thursday morning.''

"Mitch, he's going to make it, I know it.'' She smiled. "Some of it's due to you now. How can I thank you for this?''

An image of sweaty sheets wrapped around her flashed into his mind. To banish it, he glanced at the clock. "I know it's late, but let's get something to eat. I'm starved.''

She studied him for a minute, then said, "Me, too. I usually have a light supper after the game.'' Her smile was innocent. "I made minestrone soup. It's waiting in my Crock-Pot at home. Want to join me for some?''

Shaking his head, he knit his brows. "I'd never guess you liked to cook. You're full of surprises, Ms. Smith.''

This time, a Jezebel smile came to her full lips. "You'd better believe it, Captain.''

THE SOUP WAS GREAT, the company even better. They ate in front of the fire Mitch had started while

Cassie dished up their supper. By tacit agreement, they stayed away from subjects that would drive a wedge between them. After the meal, Mitch sat on the floor, his back against the couch, sipping coffee. ''Tell me about how you grew up,'' he said.

She hadn't expected that. Her stomach knotted at the thought of the disclosure. ''You know most of it,'' she said, stalling.

''I know you're from Bayview Heights, you went to the high school here and were a...''

Grinning, she finished the sentence for him. ''I was a brat. I had a real chip on my shoulder that nobody could budge.''

''Someone must have.''

''Yeah.'' She glanced around the room, her eyes finally focusing on the rows of books by the fireplace. ''Seth Taylor did.'' She swallowed. ''He was my English teacher.''

Mitch tracked her gaze. ''He taught you to love literature?''

''He taught me to love myself.'' It just slipped out, past defenses that she hadn't known she was tired of erecting until this one crumbled a little.

''It's hard for an adult to keep a kid straight.''

''Well, after he helped get me on the right track, a very popular student befriended me. She was a real prom queen type, and at first I didn't trust her, didn't believe she wanted to be my friend.''

''Why did she?''

''Lacey had a brother who was always in trouble. None of the so-called good kids wanted anything to do with him. I guess she felt that was unfair.'' Cassie smiled at the memory. ''And she said I added color to her life.'' Sobering again, Cassie said, ''But it was mostly Seth who got me on the right track. I'll never forget it.''

"That explains some things.''

"Like?''

"There's a special bond between you two.''

Cassie smiled again. "There is.''

"It also explains your single-mindedness about the kids.''

"I guess it does. Seth helped me change my life. I want to help my students change theirs.'' Shadows, dark and deep, crossed Mitch's face. Cassie said, "What is it?''

He shook his head.

"Mitch?''

"Helping kids…doesn't always work.''

"Something happened to you, didn't it?''

He nodded.

"Want to talk about it?''

"I can't.''

She was sitting about five feet away from him, leaning against a chair. Rising to her knees, she inched over to him, then sat back on her legs. "I want to know you better. Talk to me.''

This close to him, she could see his throat convulse. He was scared of talking; she recognized the signs. He finally said, "Can we, ah, start with something easier than this?''

"Sure.'' She touched his arm, squeezed and started to remove her hand. He grabbed it and held it tightly. "Where did you grow up?'' she asked.

"In the city.''

"In New York?''

"Yes.''

"Where?''

"On the Upper East Side."

Her brows arched.

"My father was a doctor."

"Wow."

"We had money, advantages."

"Are your parents still alive?"

"No, they died five years ago. Within six months of each other."

"That must have been hard."

"It was."

"You and Kurt are close."

Mitch nodded. "You don't have any brothers or sisters?"

"No, there was just me and my mother."

"Is she alive?"

Cassie shook her head. "She died when I was in college."

"Where'd you go?"

"Geneseo. In Upstate New York. What about you?"

His face shuttered. "Once I decided I wanted to rise in the ranks of the police force, I went to John Jay for criminal justice."

"You didn't go right after high school?" Cassie asked.

"No."

"Why?"

He took in a deep breath. "A lot of reasons." Glancing at the clock on the opposite wall, he said, "Look, it's getting late. School's godawful early...I don't know how you—"

Gently, she placed her fingers over his mouth. "Shh. If you don't want to tell me, you don't have to. Just say so. I know what it's like to need to keep things inside. Under control.''

"It's hard for me to open up.''

Right at that moment, she felt like his soul mate. "I know. Me, too.''

He just stared at her. She didn't look away; she felt his hand squeeze hers tightly. Suddenly, the mood shifted. It had been tense with emotional disclosure. Now it was charged with a different kind of tension. He reached up and grasped the stubborn strand of hair that had escaped from her braid again. "This piece of hair is just like you." He rubbed it between his fingers.

Cassie swallowed but didn't respond. Couldn't respond.

"It's rebellious. It won't stay in its place." He slid his hand around to the back of her head. She felt a tug, then his fingers were loosening her braid. His hands moved rhythmically through her hair until it fell around her shoulders and face. "I like your hair down.''

"You do?''

"Mmm.'' He studied it, caressed it. "It's luscious.''

"Luscious. That's quite a word.''

"Mmm. A new vocabulary word.'' His eyes sparkled with mischief. And seduction. "I can think of lots of vocabulary words that apply to you.''

Cassie cleared her throat, mesmerized, wanting to prolong the flirting. "Tell me.''

He stared into her eyes for interminable seconds, then his hand left her hair and trailed around to her mouth. "Sensuous,'' he said as he brushed her lips with the pad of his thumb. "Soft,'' he told her as his knuckles swept over her cheek. The calloused tips of his fingers moved to her neck and glided up and down. "Sexy..." he whispered.

Tilting her head back, Cassie savored the caress. His grip tightened in her hair; his breath speeded up. His hand followed the zipper of her sweat suit down her chest. She held her breath as he moved his fingers to the left and closed them over her breast. "Supple," he said, his eyes never leaving hers. "So, so supple."

"Oh, God." She closed her eyes and leaned into his touch.

"Look at me, Cassandra."

She did. He flexed his hand, gently squeezed her, massaged her. "Your eyes...they're glowing."

Caught, intoxicated by the things he was saying and doing, she leaned into him further. "More" was all she said.

He lowered his head. His mouth brushed hers, the touch sending currents through her whole body. Back and forth. Slowly. Too slowly. She moaned against his lips.

"More?" he asked.

"Yes. Oh, yes."

Rational thought was slipping away from him. Control, always so important, was fading. The feel of her, full and hot in his hand, was stripping him of the iron will he'd carefully honed over the years.

And right now, he didn't care. All he wanted was to fill his senses with her.

When she swayed toward him, he took advantage of the movement. Grasping her shoulders with both hands, he tugged and she came up to her knees and onto his lap. Settling there, she angled her body to him. One of his arms cradled her back while his other went around her waist. She angled her chin. Again, the clear invitation was impossible to resist. He lowered his mouth.

He took her lips as gently as he could. But when she reached up and circled his neck with her hand, he deepened the kiss. Coaxing her lips open, he tasted her and the last vestige of control snapped. He consumed her, took what she offered with her mouth, her tongue, her teeth. She strained against him. His hand came up to cup her breast again. He heard himself groan. Against her mouth, he said, "Cass, you feel so good."

She squirmed on his lap. "You, too." Inching into him, as if she needed to be closer, she said, "Mitch..." Her mouth left his and went to his neck. Her teeth scraped against his skin and his whole body bucked.

After a few more moments of bliss, he encircled her with both arms and held her close. They stayed that way for a long time, then she drew back. Her eyes were cloudy with desire, her mouth a little swollen. Her cheek was red from his beard, and he frowned when he saw it. The evidence of his lack of control sobered him.

"I should go," he said gruffly.

"Why?"

Tenderly, he brushed the hair out of her eyes. "I knew, if I ever touched you, I'd have trouble controlling myself."

Some women would have been angry. Some would have taken his confession as a challenge. It didn't help his raging libido a bit when he saw understanding in Cassie's eyes. "It's hard for you, isn't it?"

He swallowed and nodded.

"All right. You should go."

"Cassie?"

"Hmm?"

"I'm not sorry."

She smiled. "Oh, good. I wouldn't want you to be sorry."

ON TUESDAY MORNING, Mitch walked into Cassie's classroom twenty minutes early. He hoped to find her alone, anxious to see her. She looked up from her desk when he knocked lightly. Her smile was like the sunrise after a night filled with terrible dreams.

"Hi," he said from the doorway.

"Hi."

"Sleep well?"

She smiled. "As well as can be expected. You?"

"About the same."

"I feel good today, though."

"Mmm...you felt good last—" He broke off the innuendo when Zoe came to the door.

"Cassie?" Zoe glanced at Mitch. "Oh, hi, Mitch. I was wondering which day is your lesson on juvenile crime?" She faced Cassie. "My tenth-graders are coming, right?"

"Tomorrow," Cassie said, her voice husky. "And yes, they're coming."

Then the kids began to straggle in for homeroom, and that was the end of their talk for the day.

It was during class that Mitch noticed Joe De-Fazio's outfit. Black and red. There was some kind of patch on his T-shirt. Mitch wasn't sure why, but the colors and the odd-looking decal bothered him. Halfway through class, he realized it was because DeFazio had been wearing black and red for days now. He filed the information away.

On Wednesday, Mitch taught the lesson on juvenile crime. The sobering statistics had the students hanging on to his words. Having prepared it with Cassie the week before, he was ready for the kids' questions. What he wasn't ready for was Battaglia's support.

"Shut up, you guys," Johnny said when DeFazio and Youngblood made a wisecrack about the information Mitch put on the board.

Mitch listened to see if there was any sarcasm in Battaglia's voice. He heard none.

"Since when you like the cop's lessons?" DeFazio's voice grated on Mitch's nerves.

"You moron," Johnny said. "You're going to be one of those statistics if you don't shape up."

Carefully, Mitch quelled any further hostility by resuming his talk. Afterward, he caught Battaglia by the arm as the kids were moving on to their next class. "How's the job going?" he asked Johnny.

"Great. Your brother—he's really cool." Johnny stuck his hands in his jacket pockets self-consciously. "He...he teaches us things, you know. He doesn't just have us emptying bedpans."

Mitch smiled at the actions of his altruistic brother. "Is that so?"

Johnny watched Mitch. "I, uh, I never thanked you for setting this up for me."

"You can thank me by doing a good job, there

and in school," Mitch said gruffly, more moved by Battaglia's gratitude than he wanted to admit.

"Yeah, right," the kid said, and left.

Mitch turned to find Cassie standing behind him. "What?" he asked, but didn't really need an answer. There was admiration on her face that made him feel so good he wanted to shout with joy. Damn, she was getting to him. They all were.

When he was leaving school that day for the station, he caught sight of Joe DeFazio coming out of the bathroom with two boys. One Mitch didn't recognize. One was Mike Youngblood. A sharp sound startled DeFazio, then he whipped a small square black object out of his coat pocket. A beeper. Mitch stepped behind a post, watched DeFazio walk to a nearby pay phone and make a call. He smiled silkily as he answered the page.

When he was done, he turned back to the two boys. Mitch left his concealed position and approached them. "Good stuff." He heard the comment just before Youngblood spotted Mitch and kicked DeFazio in warning.

"Hello, gentlemen," Mitch said to them.

Three pairs of anxious eyes looked up at him.

"Hand it over, Mr. DeFazio."

"What?"

"The pager. They're banned in school."

Defiance burned in the boy's eyes. "You got a search warrant?"

"I don't need one. Not with probable cause. I saw it and heard it go off. Now, hand it over. You can pick it up in Mr. Taylor's office after school."

DeFazio yanked out the pager, slapped it into Mitch's hand and stalked off. As he stomped down the hall, something about the way he looked raised the hair on the back of Mitch's neck. He stared after DeFazio and the two kids who followed him.

It was their hair. Though there was no set fashion in schools today—football players shaved their heads, the volleyball team dyed theirs blond and several computer hacks had theirs styled in Mohawks—there was something about the way these kids had their hair shaved on the side that set off Mitch's trouble detector.

On Thursday, he stayed at school to have lunch with Cassie. In her room, they shared sandwiches from the cafeteria. "Thanks for inviting me," he said as he bit into ham and cheese.

"I wanted some time with you," she said, sipping sparkling water.

"Any particular reason?"

She smiled. "It's a little awkward, isn't it? Seeing each other after Monday."

He chewed slowly, then said, "A little."

"Still no regrets?"

He shook his head. "You?"

"None."

He thought for a minute, then said, "You busy Friday night?"

"No."

"Cassie, how come there's no man in your life?" The uncensored question surprised them both.

She waited a minute before she answered. "After my marriage ended, I wasn't so anxious to jump back into the fray. I've dated, but nothing serious."

Jealousy snaked inside of him, shocking him with its vehemence. "You were married?"

"Yes. I've been divorced for six years."

"That's a long time to be alone."

She nodded. "As I said, I've dated, but I just haven't been interested much since then." She blushed like a virgin. "What did you have in mind for Friday?"

He didn't dare tell her what was on his mind right at that minute. Instead, he asked her to dinner. He was thinking about where they'd go as he walked down the hall after their lunch.

Again, as yesterday, he happened upon DeFazio. Again, the kid was dressed in a combination of black and red. He met a member of Wednesday's trio, the boy Mitch hadn't recognized, by the john again, glanced around and then stuck out his hand, his palm facing forward. They slapped each other in a high-five gesture, then closed their fists. Knuckles met knuckles, DeFazio's fist topped the other boy's, then they reversed the order and finally splayed their hands, palms facing each other again.

Unnoticed, Mitch sighed and leaned against the wall.

Hand signals.

A distinctive hairstyle.

Black and red colors.

Paged in the middle of the day.

All were clear signs of gang activity.

His own words came back to him. *If I see any evidence of gang activity, I'm stepping in.*

Swearing to himself, Mitch reversed direction and headed toward Seth Taylor's office. Luckily, the principal's meeting was just ending.

Taylor looked up from behind his desk as Mitch came to the doorway. "Hi. What can I do for you?"

"Got a minute?"

Taylor called out, "Sue, do I have a minute?"

The secretary in the outer office called back good-naturedly, "Yeah, you've got forty of them. You need to be at the administration building by two, though."

Mitch stepped into Taylor's office and closed the door. For a few seconds, he studied the principal, the man who had made such a difference in Cassie's life.

"What's up?" Taylor asked

"I..." Mitch looked around, thinking about sad gray eyes.

If you go into this gang prevention stuff now, I'll lose Johnny for good. He'll never take this from you. He already dropped out once....

"We may have a problem."

"We?"

Mitch felt himself redden. Since when had he started thinking of himself as part of Bayview Heights High School? This wasn't good at all.

"Uh, *you* do. At least I think you do." Briefly, Mitch explained what he'd seen. As he talked, Seth's brow furrowed, he shook his head, and his face grew somber.

When Mitch was done, Seth said, "I won't tolerate this. What should I do?"

"Several things. First, is there a written policy anywhere outlining the prohibition of gangs in your school?"

"No."

"You need one."

"It'll have to go through the school board. It'll take some time."

"Initiate it right away. Meanwhile, can you take a stand with the kids without a formal policy?"

"Yes. I have the right to do anything to establish an orderly atmosphere." Seth sat back and steepled his hands. "I'll get on the PA system. We'll have to hold a faculty meeting first, though, to alert the staff."

"They should be told what to look for, how they can help prevent the spread of this at Bayview Heights. The worst thing that can happen is for these kids to think they're getting away with surreptitious gang activity in the school. If they think they're putting something over on you, they'll be hard to stop."

The principal checked his calendar. "I have a faculty meeting scheduled for Monday. Can *you* do the presentation?"

"Yes, I guess so. But you might want to bring in a gang prevention specialist instead."

Seth shook his head. "No, I've had a lot of positive feedback about the material you presented on breaking up a fight. Teachers are notoriously hard to impress. They respect you. They'll listen to what you have to say."

"All right, then." Making a quick decision, Mitch said, "Seth, we've got another problem."

"What?"

"Cassie. She'll have a fit about this."

Sinking back into his chair, Seth ran his hand over his face. "Because of Johnny." Then the principal shook his head. "But he's out of the Blisters. He wasn't with DeFazio, was he?"

"No."

"Do you think he's involved?"

"Truthfully, I don't think so, but I don't know for

sure.'' Quickly, Mitch related the conversation he'd had with Cassie the night the kids were brought in on suspicion of using inhalants.

Taylor's eyes narrowed when Mitch finished. "I don't like having things kept from me. You should have said something then."

"You're probably right."

"Why didn't you?"

"Cassie can be very persuasive."

"Cassie doesn't make these kinds of decisions for the school. I do."

Mitch nodded. "It's my responsibility. I shouldn't have listened to her. Don't lay this on her."

Seth cocked his head. "Defending her now, Captain? When did this start?"

Somewhere after a kiss that knocked my socks off.

Mitch shrugged. "I'm not sure. But I'm worried about her reaction to this."

Seth studied him a minute before he said, "Cassie's got to see that this is bigger than we thought. She'll be reasonable. In any case, I'll handle Cassie. You get the presentation prepared."

Mitch felt the constriction around his heart. Taylor probably could handle Cassie. But Mitch had a bad feeling that she'd never forgive him for going to Seth without talking to her.

Maybe it was for the best, he thought as he left the office and headed out of school. That one kiss, that brief intimacy they'd shared, flooded him with feelings that were too strong for him to control. Best to end things now, before she came to mean too much to him.

Mitch exited the building and strode to his car, an enormous sense of loss threatening to engulf him.

CHAPTER EIGHT

CASSIE LAUGHED OUT LOUD as she hurried down the hall. She was late for a meeting with Seth because she hadn't been able to tear herself away from Johnny. He'd stayed after school to regale her with tales of his experiences at the Forty-second Street Clinic. It had been wonderful to see him animated and excited. He'd even mentioned, twice, a girl from Columbia University premed who was also working with Kurt. It was all so healthy, so good for him.

As she made her way to Seth's office, Cassie had the fleeting thought that, for a change, everything was going right in her life—first Johnny, and to-night, a date with Mitch. She shivered a bit just thinking about last Monday when he'd touched her. She could still feel his hands on her, his lips hard and insistent against her mouth. Though fearful of the closeness, she was ready to spend the evening with him.

"Go on in," Seth's secretary said when Cassie entered the outer office.

"Thanks, Sue."

Breezing through the door, Cassie smiled at Seth and said, "Hi."

"Hi." Seth peered across his desk.

She followed his gaze. On the other side of the room sat Mitch Lansing. For a minute, Cassie was overwhelmed by his raw masculinity, barely concealed by, of course, his navy blue suit. "Hi."

"Hello, Cassie."

She cocked her head. "What are you doing here?"

Mitch gave her an odd look. Before he could answer, Seth said, "I wanted Mitch here while I discuss something with you."

"Something about the Resiliency Program?"

"Sit down, Cass."

His tone made her wary. She sank onto a chair opposite Mitch. "Okay, shoot."

Thoughtfully, Seth leaned over on his desk, bracing himself on his forearms. "Before I do, I want to tell you something. Two things, really. Not many people know that I taught somewhere else for a year before I came to Bayview Heights."

"Really?"

"Yes. I left because I made a bad decision at the other school. I won't go into detail, but basically, I was too caught up in a situation to see it clearly. And there was no one to help me. No experienced teachers or administrators to turn to."

"Is that why you set up a mentoring program here?" Cassie referred to Seth's institution of the controversial program of formally pairing every new teacher with an experienced staff member who helped, guided and was there to give advice.

Seth nodded. "The other thing concerns you. Do you remember when I encouraged the school to file a PINS petition on you?"

"PINS?" Mitch asked.

"Pupils in Need of Supervision," Seth explained. "It's like a legal warrant filed for truancy to get kids the help they need when parents don't—or can't—do their job.''

Cassie nodded. ''I was furious with you.''

''But it was the right thing to do, wasn't it?''

''Yes. My mother couldn't supervise me properly. She needed help.''

''You didn't talk to me for days.''

In a show of disgust, Cassie closed her eyes briefly. ''I was a brat. What's this got to do with now?''

Leaning back in his chair, Seth steepled his hands. ''We need to take some antigang measures at the high school.''

Cassie felt as if she'd been doused with cold water. ''Why?''

Mitch spoke up then. ''I recommended it. I saw some evidence of gang activity yesterday and the day before.''

''From Johnny?''

''No, actually from DeFazio and two other boys, one of whom I didn't know. He isn't in our program.''

''Joe DeFazio? Who was the other?''

Mitch hesitated. ''I'd rather not say till I'm sure he's involved.''

Cassie drew in a deep breath and let it out slowly.

Seth said softly, ''We can't allow this to happen at Bayview.''

''Of course not,'' Cassie agreed. ''DeFazio has to be stopped.''

''I think we need to do more than deal with one student.'' Seth's tone was gentle but firm.

''Like what?''

He glanced at Mitch. ''Mitch recommended we

go public with a full-scale policy. I'm going to start a gang prevention program at Bayview Heights High School.''

"Why?"

Mitch held her gaze as he spoke. "Because talking to DeFazio won't stop it. The kids involved right now will hide their activities for a while, then start again. All the students need to know it's against school rules and will incur disciplinary action. And teachers need to be educated about what to watch for so they can recognize gang activity and help stop it.''

"Is it that widespread?"

Seth said, ''Who knows? Mitch noticed the colors, the hand signals and a distinctive haircut. It sounds organized and serious. If it's burgeoning, I want it stopped now.''

"But what if it's just Joe DeFazio? Won't you give other kids ideas if you meet this head-on?"

Seth looked at Mitch and raised his brows. "Mitch?"

"That's a misconception," Mitch told them. "The first thing a school has to do is admit there's a problem—which I'm convinced there is here at Bayview. Then nothing's secret, everything's out in the open. Limits are set and enforced. Kids don't think they can get away with anything, so they don't even try.''

Slowly, Cassie sank back on the chair, seeing Johnny's laughing face just minutes ago, hearing the subtle traces of hope and expectation in his voice that hadn't ever been there before. Juxtaposed to it, she remembered what he looked like three years ago when he'd dropped out of school and had gone back to the gang for a few months. What would it take to send him back into the hopelessness that had driven him to the Blisters? The strong push of a gang prevention program at Bayview? But she tried to be reasonable. Something had to be done. Quiet nudges worked best in her experience. "I don't think this is the best way to go about it."

"What do you mean?" Seth asked.

"If we have to do something, let's approach it in small groups with the kids. Individual sessions have always worked better here, especially with the At-Risk kids."

Seth said, "Cass, if Johnny didn't have this history with the Blisters, would you be so against this public stand?"

She felt the heat rise to her cheeks. "Are you saying I can't be objective about this?"

"Yes."

"I resent that."

"I'm sorry, but I know what it's like to misconstrue a situation. To let your bias about a student sway you."

"Ah, the story you told." She tried to keep the sarcasm out of her voice, but she could tell from Seth's frown she hadn't been successful.

Mitch stepped in. "Cassie, the other thing is, if we let it spread at the school, Johnny could be lured back easier than if it's kept out of Bayview."

"I'm not saying we should let the gang activity go on. We have a responsibility to the other kids to stop it. I'm disagreeing about how to approach the issue. Your rule-mongering isn't the best way. You don't know what it can do." She turned to Seth. "I'm surprised you don't agree with me. You've always had more of a one-on-one philosophy in dealing with issues. Especially after the fiasco of Bosco's committee recommendation.'' Staring at him hard, she finished, ''You agreed to go along with the no-early-dismissal rule for work and you were wrong. After six months, you changed the policy to judge each case on an individual basis.''

Steepling his hands again, Seth studied her. ''Yes, I was wrong then.'' He turned to Mitch. ''What do you think?''

Without hesitation, Mitch said, ''I think it would be a mistake to hush this up. Both staff and students have to see you're not afraid of confronting the issue. If you go about it the way Cassie wants to, it will look pretty whitewashed.''

Because the charge of being too lax had been leveled against her by Jerry Bosco, Cassie felt her temper rise. She faced Mitch. ''What makes you the expert here? Seth and I have been dealing with kids for years. Our professional opinion is based on experience. We've seen how making global, inflexible rules can really hurt kids.''

Mitch said quietly, ''Your professional opinion is biased because of Johnny. And obviously, because of a bad experience. One mistake doesn't make us wrong this time.''

They both turned to Seth.

''I think Mitch is right,'' he said soberly.

Fighting anger and hurt, she said, ''I can't believe this.''

''I'm sorry if it upsets you. But I'm going ahead with our plan. We'll address the issue with the faculty on Monday and then make a public announcement Tuesday to the student body.''

Cassie stared at him openmouthed. "You had it all planned."

Mitch started to speak, but Seth cut him off again. "I'm principal of this school, Cassie. I make the decisions."

"Not all by yourself, apparently." Staring at Mitch, she remembered the night in her living room when she begged him not to approach Seth. She turned away, her heart pumping fast. Damn him.

"Maybe you should talk to Johnny about this before it hits," Seth suggested. "He might take it better from you."

Cassie said nothing.

"Cass?"

"I'll think about it." Her shoulders stiff, she angled her chin and faced Seth squarely. "Are we through here? I'd like to leave."

"Yes." He looked at Mitch. "I want you to stay, though."

"Fine."

Cassie stood. Woodenly, she made her way to the door, emotions swirling inside her like a summer storm.

From behind her, Seth said, "Cassie?"

She turned around.

"I want you at the faculty meeting Monday."

That did it. Her temper flared. "I always fulfill my teaching responsibilities, Mr. Taylor." She couldn't keep her voice from climbing a notch. "For the record, I find your telling me to be there an insult to my professional integrity." Forcing herself not to slam the door, she stalked out of his office.

MITCH STOOD ON Cassie's front porch for several minutes, trying to summon the courage to ring the doorbell. It had taken the kind of guts it took to face down a street punk with a gun to get him this far. He stared out into the February sky, at the stars twinkling overhead, but he couldn't appreciate the crisp beauty of the evening. He could only see her face this afternoon when she'd looked at him across Taylor's office.

Accusation had been there. He could take that, had been prepared for that. It was the hurt in those misty gray eyes that had sucker-punched him. He'd let her down just as she was beginning to trust him. And trust didn't come easily for her.

Nor did it come easily to him. He paced the ten-foot length of the porch, kicking up the frozen snow with his boot, watching his breath swirl before him in big, fat puffs. He and Cassie were kindred spirits. Both afraid of trusting. Both slowly breaching their wariness these last five weeks. Had it all been aborted on one dreary winter morning by a group of adolescent boys who were biting off more than they could chew—and didn't even know it?

Thoughts of the kids at Bayview Heights High School confirmed his decision. "This is the right thing, damn it," he said aloud. If he lost Cassie in the process, so be it. Sick of quivering on her doorstep like a love-struck boy, he jabbed the bell.

No answer.

He scanned the house. There were several lights on in the living room and a small one burning upstairs. Her car was in the driveway. She was home.

He rang again. And again. Just after he pressed the buzzer insistently for the fourth time, she whipped open the door.

Her face was flushed as if she'd been running. Sweat beaded her face. She was dressed in a ragged white T-shirt and faded red sweatpants.

Guess we're not going to dinner.

He said, "Hi."

Right before his eyes, the surprise left her expressive face and she closed down. Another tactic he knew well. "Mitch."

"May I come in?"

Briefly, her eyes flared with some emotion—anger at his presumptuousness? Surprise at his tenacity? Fear? Well, if it was going to end before it really got started, she'd have to do it right.

"Cassie? I asked if I could come in."

"I heard you." She didn't answer the question but moved aside to allow him into the foyer. Without asking to take his jacket, she led him into the living room. His eyes immediately sought the place on the floor where he'd not only kissed and caressed her, but admitted he'd wanted to take their relationship further. Tonight, it hurt to remember the hope he'd felt then.

There was no fire lit now. Instead, a movie blared from the television, in front of which she'd dragged her exercise bike. She crossed to the TV and lowered the sound but didn't turn it off—a subtle message that he wasn't staying. He saw Sidney Poitier's smiling face and heard the soft notes of *To Sir With Love* humming in the background. Always the teacher, he thought.

"I didn't think you'd come tonight," she said without preamble.

He faced her squarely. "We had a date. For dinner." He scanned her outfit. "You're not ready."

Crossing her hands over her chest, Cassie stared at him. "I just assumed you'd cancel."

He stuck his hands in the pockets of his jacket because they were fisting without his consent. "I didn't." His heart racing, he asked, "Does this mean *you're* canceling?"

The impassivity slipped. For a minute, naked pain claimed her features. He wanted to drag her into his arms and erase it. Before he could, the look was gone. "I'm not going out with you, Mitch."

The rejection hurt more than he'd expected. Because it did, he found the nerve to ask, "Forever, or just tonight?"

Silently, she began to pace. When she faced him again, the mask was firmly back in place. She was so tough. Really tough. And he knew in that instant that he wanted to be the man to soften her. To make her melt both physically and emotionally. To make her moan with pleasure and weep with joy.

"Forever, I think."

He nodded, turned from her and walked to the fireplace. It took all the control he had not to sweep the pretty knickknacks off the mantel. When he faced her again, he saw her bite her lip. The vulnerability of that tiny gesture calmed his violent urge. "Mind telling me why?"

"It won't work, Mitch. We're too different. You're so rule-oriented, and I see things in grays. I can't think like you do, and you'll never understand how my mind works." He watched her closely. "There will be too many opportunities, like this afternoon, to hurt each other."

"If I hurt you today, I'm sorry."

Again the mask slipped. "I was hurt because my

professional opinion and experiences—after fifteen years of teaching—were ignored."

"It wasn't ignored. Seth just disagreed with you."

"Maybe so, but that doesn't alter our differences—yours and mine. The whole incident just confirms how mismatched we are."

Deciding to go for broke, Mitch crossed to her. Softly, he brushed his knuckles down her damp cheek. "I wanted more, Cassie."

Mitch's phrase reminded Cassie of their words four nights ago. *More,* she'd uttered when he kissed her. And later, as he caressed her breast, he'd asked, *More?*

The hot sensuality of the moment zinged through her. For a minute, she couldn't speak. Honesty made her finally say, "I could care about you, Mitch." She'd wanted to tell him *I do care,* but she couldn't get it out.

His eyes burned with intensity. "Me, too, Cass."

Again, the trigger. *You feel so good, Cass.* She wondered if he was doing it on purpose.

No. This hurt him. She could tell by his rigid stance, his clenched jaw. He loomed before her in his worn bomber jacket and forest green sweater underneath. It was thick and...luscious.

She closed her eyes and moaned. Bombarded by reminders of their intimacy, she took a deep breath, turned and stepped away from him. "I can't risk it."

There was silence in the room. For too long. *Please let him leave,* Cassie prayed to a God she'd stopped believing in when she was ten. She held herself still, her arms clasped tightly at her elbows. *Please, please let him leave.*

She felt rather than heard him come up behind her. His touch was tender when his hands closed around her bare upper arms. And Cassie, who hadn't cried since she found out her mother didn't know who her father was, wanted to weep. Slowly, he brushed his fingertips on the tender skin of her inner arms. Goose bumps tingled everywhere he touched. He fitted his big, solid body to her back and tugged her to him. She leaned against him shamelessly. His jacket had retained the cold, and its contrast to the heat coursing through her made her shiver. The reaction increased by volumes when he nuzzled her hair out of the way and pressed his mouth to her neck. She didn't want to do any of this. Her mind raged against the seductive invitation, but her body wasn't listening. She tilted her head to the side to give him better access.

Strong arms encircled her waist. "Reconsider, Cass." When she said nothing, he murmured against her neck, "Please." His voice inflamed her as much as the feel of him, aroused and thick against her bottom. With a slice of blinding desire, she wanted him inside her.

Because the need was so powerful, because raw fear told her if she let him, this man could do anything he wanted with her, to her, she found the sanity to say, "No, Mitch. I won't."

His whole body stiffened. He stepped back and this time, she shivered with the loss of his heat. He stood stock-still, and so did she. The clock on the mantel chimed seven times and neither of them moved.

Then he finally said, "Damn you, Cassie."

She heard his boots clicking against the hardwood

floor in the foyer. The door swished open—cold air swirled at her feet—then it closed with a soft and final snick.

Everything feminine in her screamed to go to him, to stop him from leaving. Instead, she collapsed onto the couch.

But she didn't cry.

Cassie Smith did *not* cry.

JOHNNY GLANCED at the clock. It was 1:10 p.m. He'd have just enough time to meet with Cassie, go home and shower and get to the clinic by four. Though he felt like a sap, he walked around the classroom whistling. He read some of the posters on her wall. "You are the author of your own life story." "Life is not a dress rehearsal." "Once you say you're going to settle for second best, that's what you get." "If you let them, kids have the energy, imagination and intelligence to make a difference." It was sentiments like these that had gotten him through some really tough times. He had this school, this classroom and now the clinic to help him through the rest; he was on his way. As he learned more about medicine in his new job, he became more certain that becoming a doctor was what he wanted to do with his life.

Relaxed, he flung himself down into a desk, stretched out his legs and closed his eyes. Then there was Mary Margaret Mancini. Picturing her sweet face, he smiled again. Those big brown eyes were so gentle, nobody would guess she had a will of steal. The oldest of seven kids from a typical Italian family in the Bronx, she'd overcome all the obstacles to getting into the premed program at Columbia: her traditional family, the Catholic school she'd attended, the general stereotypes of her culture. A sophomore now, she'd told Johnny that she was doing this clinic work against her parents' wishes. He shook his head. She'd go to church and confess her disobedience to the priest, but three times a week she came to Kurt's clinic, anyway. She and Johnny had become friends.

"What's the grin for?" Cassie's voice roused him from the reminiscence.

The smile on his face died when he opened his eyes. Cassie was dressed to kill in a fancy red suit and high heels. But her face was drawn and her eyes shadowed.

He scowled. "I was thinking about the clinic. What's wrong?"

Wringing her hands, she said, "Nothing. I just wanted to talk to you before you left today."

"You look exhausted," he said as she came fully into the room and sank down at a desk next to him.

"I am tired."

He tried to tease her. "Wild weekend?" If possible, the look on her face got even sadder. "Cassie? You okay?"

"I'm fine."

"You're all dressed up today."

"I like this suit."

"You told us once that when you felt your worst, you wore the prettiest clothes you had."

"Did I?"

He nodded.

"All right. I'm a little worried how you're going to take what I'm going to tell you."

Johnny's heart speeded up. "You're not leaving Bayview, are you?"

"No, of course not."

"Oh, good."

"Johnny..." She reached out and touched his arm. "There's been some evidence of gang activity in this school."

Johnny went still. "Yeah? Who says?"

"Mr. Taylor."

Let me tell you something, Battaglia. I'm not going to let your gang buddies recruit anyone from Bayview Heights. If I see any evidence of gang activity—colors, paraphernalia, hand signals—at the high school, I'll take you down so fast, you won't have time to blink.

Cassie was covering for the cop. Interesting.

"What's going on?" he said, carefully keeping his tone neutral. Fear hovered at the corners of his heart, and he had to forcefully keep it out.

"A couple of the kids wearing the same colors, a complicated handshake and a few other signals alerted the administration."

Johnny swallowed hard. "Who is it?"

"I can't tell you that."

She didn't have to. *Hey, Battaglia, tell me more about your pal Zorro...he's definitely mongo.* Johnny had asked DeFazio why he wanted to know. *No special reason, man.*

Johnny had also noticed DeFazio's new haircut. And he'd been wearing red and black a lot.

"Johnny, what are you thinking?"

"Nothing."

"Do you know something you want to tell me?" He shook his head. Clamping down on the emotions that threatened, he stared at the woman whose faith and trust he needed too much. Who could be turned against him, too easily.

"You don't know anything? Or you don't want to tell me anything?"

Years ago, Cassie had said to him, *Promise me just one thing. You won't ever lie to me. Tell me to mind my own business, or you don't want to talk about something, but never lie to me.*

"I don't want to tell you."

She nodded. "All right. In any case, because of what he's noticed, Mr. Taylor is coming out publicly barring any gang activity at Bayview."

"Like?"

"The wearing of gang colors. Any other paraphernalia."

"Like my jacket."

"You don't wear that to school."

"No."

"Why do you still have it, anyway?"

It's my security blanket. Johnny stood abruptly and stuck his hands in his jeans pockets. "It's my last connection to Zorro. He's the only thing in my life that no one can take away from me."

"I don't think that's true."

"Name something else. And don't use yourself. You could leave Bayview anytime. You could get married and your husband could hate me."

"Johnny, that's stupid."

"No, that's reality."

If possible, her eyes got bleaker. He'd never seen her cry, but her eyes were bright today, and bloodshot. She was agitated too, unsettled. "Listen, this isn't about me," she finally said. "All I wanted was to tell you what's in the works. I didn't want to surprise you.''

''I haven't brought the gang into the school, Cassie.''

''I know you haven't. They don't think you have, either.''

''They?''

''Um, Mr. Taylor.''

''Do *you* think all this is necessary?''

She bit her lip.

''The truth, Cassie.''

''I'm not sure. I do know I'm terrified you'll go back into the Blisters. You know that. If they infiltrate the school, you'd be at a greater risk. And of course, I don't want to see anyone else sucked in.''

''But?''

''I'm not sure they're going about it the right way.'' She raked hair out of her eyes. ''But it doesn't matter now. It's a done deal. I just wanted you to know.''

Johnny studied her for a minute. ''Fine, you've told me. I know.''

''How do you feel about it?''

''Like shit.''

She didn't say anything.

''Sorry. I know you hate that kind of talk. I feel bad about them starting this. Like the last time you guys made a *policy* that really screwed up my life.'' He remembered vividly when they'd said kids couldn't leave school early to work. Instead of telling them he and his mother wouldn't eat if he didn't work, he'd up and quit school altogether. And spent six months doing things he was ashamed of now.

''I'm sorry. It isn't aimed at you.''

"Neither was the last one. Or so you said. Does anybody remember that they were wrong about sweeping policies then? I thought you'd all smartened up. Why can't you take one case at a time, evaluate it and make decisions from there? Like you do about the work thing now?" He shook his head, stood and shrugged into his jacket.

She watched the gesture. "What are you going to do?"

"I'm going to work."

"You'll be here tomorrow, right? We're starting a new unit."

You've got yourself a job...but the catch is, you gotta stay in school and not cut out when you get pissed off at somebody.

"Yeah. I'll be here tomorrow. I don't really have a choice." He took one last look at her before he left. Her usually pink cheeks were pale as snow. Something was wrong. *Was* it just worry over him? He started for the door, but the thought that he'd caused her sadness made him stop and turn around. She was sitting with her hand over her eyes, her face down. "Cassie?"

Her head snapped up. "Yes?"

"Get some sleep tonight. I'm pissed off about this, and I think it's the good Captain's doing. But I'll be here tomorrow."

She angled her chin. "That's not enough, Johnny. You've got to stay away from Zorro. From the Blisters."

"You guys do what you have to to keep the Blisters out of Bayview. I can take care of myself."

Cassie stared at him. "Like I said, that's not enough."

"It'll have to be, Teach."

CASSIE ENTERED the library meeting room at precisely two-fifteen, ten minutes after Johnny left. She should feel good about the fact that he'd been reasonable, that he hadn't stormed out on her. All things considered, their meeting had gone well. But she felt rotten. Forgoing the coffee and cookies Seth provided at faculty meetings, Cassie took a seat on the far left side of the room, away from everyone else. Let them do their thing. She'd deal with it, and so would Johnny.

Summoning some of the *cool* the kids seemed to admire about her, she watched Seth standing at the podium. She listened as he made a few announcements, after which he told the staff the purpose of the meeting. Immediately, a buzz filtered through the group. He let it go a minute, then called again for everyone's attention. "I've asked Mitch Lansing to address this issue with you, so I'll let him get to it. Mitch."

The principal left the podium and crossed directly to Cassie. He sat down next to her, gave her a half smile and squeezed her arm. She smiled as best she could, then looked up front.

Mitch strode to the podium, all masculine grace and athletic poise. Cassie stared at the shoulders she'd grasped when he touched her only a week ago in her living room. She watched the lips that had trailed down her neck just three days ago. She took in the broad expanse of chest she'd laid her head against, hearing his heart thumping in reaction to her nearness.

And she felt an incredible sense of loss.

He reached for the laptop computer on the table. Without a word, the lights dimmed and four young boys appeared on the movie screen connected to the computer. They were dressed in red and black, sporting Mohawk haircuts and sneering mouths. One had a scar on his face. Their hands were raised, their fingers splayed like pitchforks. Underneath the picture was a caption, "Coming Soon To A Neighborhood Near You."

Several gasps were audible from the staff.

With perfect timing, Mitch let the scene sink in. Then his rich baritone came over the microphone. "I'm going to give you all a test. Use the pads and pencils you found on your seats."

On the screen flashed several words. "First, translate these terms." They were: *gang bang, mushrooms, copper, kingpin, home boys, gangsta, jumping in, drop the flag, violated.*

Interested, Cassie defined the words. Briefly, she reflected that Mitch had learned his teaching lessons well—he'd immediately gotten the staff's attention and then had them actively participate. She glanced around. Almost everyone was involved. A few here or there weren't writing—Jerry Bosco, of course, was not—but Mitch had grabbed at least ninety-eight percent of the audience. And that was tough to do with veteran teachers on a Monday afternoon.

After a few minutes, Mitch explained the terminology. Murmurs went through the crowd. When he asked if anyone had gotten them all right, no one had.

Then he instructed the staff to write down their definition of a gang. She was so proud of him—how he was validating the knowledge the teachers already had before he presumed they knew nothing. Asking for definitions, he praised a few good ones, then put one on the screen. "I hope everyone can see it. I know adults don't like to be read to."

"We've got a lot of old eyes in this room, Mitch," Bill Carlson called out from the back.

"That's what we keep telling you on the volleyball court," a young social studies teacher retorted.

"Why don't you read it, Mitch," Seth suggested, amid the good-natured chuckles.

"All right. A 1991 law defines a criminal gang as 'any on-going organization, association or group of three or more persons whether formal or informal, that has as one of its primary activities the commission of criminal offenses, has a common name or common identifying sign or symbol and includes members who individually or collectively engage in or have engaged in a pattern of criminal activity.'"

Mitch waited a moment, and then said, "I believe your school is in danger of encroachment by a gang from the city called the Blisters."

Silence. The fluorescent lights hummed above.

"I'd like to tell you a little bit about why kids join gangs, who's vulnerable, and how to prevent gangs from infiltrating Bayview Heights High School. I don't have all the answers, but I do have information that can be useful to you. No need to take notes. Seth has an outline of the pertinent details for you after the meeting. I'll stop for questions after each section."

"I have a question now, Captain."

Cassie watched as Mitch faced down Jerry Bosco. Mitch leaned back on his heels and stuck his hands in his pockets. "Okay, shoot."

"Who's suspected of gang activity here?" He looked around until he spotted Cassie. "The At-Risk kids?"

Seth stood to address Bosco and the rest of the teachers. "We've talked to three boys and their parents. I'm keeping their names confidential for now."

Bosco sat down but said in a booming voice so everyone could hear, "Well, you know one has to be Battaglia."

"As a matter of fact, Jerry, one wasn't Battaglia," Seth said evenly. "And I'd be careful if I were you. Lawsuits can be filed in delicate cases like these, which is one of the reasons I'm not announcing any names."

Bosco turned red-faced, and Seth sat back down. Cassie saw the principal's hands clench, the muscles in his jaw bunch. He looked over at her. She smiled at him, grateful for his public defense of Johnny.

Mitch said from the podium, "What you really need to know is not names, but why *any* kids are susceptible to gangs, what the lure is. Anyone have an idea?"

A health teacher raised her hand. "The breakdown of the family."

"Right."

Zoe added, "Kids who are isolated in school."

"They're called 'throwaway' kids," Mitch said. "And the gangs are called 'orphan institutions,' which take kids in when other institutions let them down."

Again, Jerry Bosco blurted out, "So this is the school's fault, like everything else. We aren't social workers, you know."

Gripping the podium, Mitch looked like he was

counting to ten. "No, Mr. Bosco, you aren't. But do you know the single most important factor in keeping kids straight is success at school?"

Bosco murmured something under his breath. Mitch turned to the screen and flashed up several more indicators that made kids vulnerable: kids who feel they have no control or power in their own lives; kids whose homes are places of conflict; kids with no prospect of a job or a future; kids who are failing, are suspended, or who are routinely embarrassed at school.

A few more questions were asked. Finally, one teacher asked, "What can be done, Mitch?"

Cassie glanced her way.

The attractive young French teacher smiled up at him. "Can you help us help these kids?"

"Yes, Sarah, I think I can."

Sarah? Mitch knew the French teacher's name. How? A sudden stab of jealousy hit Cassie, battering the already weak defenses she'd kept in place since he'd walked out of her house on Friday night.

A list of ten antigang measures came up on the screen. Mitch highlighted the first in yellow. "The first important step is admitting there's a potential for this problem at your school." He hesitated a moment. "I know it's not an easy thing to do. I respect Seth for acknowledging the danger."

Next, Mitch explained how teachers and all staff members needed to get smart and become aware of the gang symbols and paraphernalia. At this point, he stepped aside from the podium and called Seth up front. They demonstrated an elaborate handshake. With a self-effacing smile, Mitch looked at the group. "Don't think we don't feel stupid doing this.'' The teachers laughed. Seth sat back down, and Mitch said, "In all seriousness, that's the handshake that they use now, but any suspicious hand signals should be noted."

"What do we do if we see it?" another teacher asked.

"Bring the student immediately to the office. Or report him or her and the administration will track it down."

Mitch talked about identifying student leaders and getting them on the school's side, which Bosco applauded as a great idea, of course. Then Mitch said, "Another thing you've done well is to identify at-risk students and provide for them so they have an equal chance of success. I've been participating in your program for five weeks now, and it's one of the most effective ones I've seen."

He looked over at Cassie. Her breath caught in her throat at the meaningful glance. "A fourth point deals with my being here, too. The police department needs to work closely with the school. To give information, like this, of course, but even move to develop a positive relationship with the students who are vulnerable to gang activities. Statistics show that kids have more internal conflict at the prospect of joining a gang if they have a good relationship with the local police force." He smiled engagingly and said, "I think it's working, although I'm having trouble keeping up with the homework." Again, the humor broke the considerable tension in the room.

"Another thing you do well is not closing your doors at three o'clock. I've noticed a number of after school activities at Bayview Heights. Even letting kids just hang out in the halls to socialize or shoot the breeze with the staff is a good idea. There's a lot of camaraderie among the faculty and kids here."

No thanks to people like Jerry Bosco, Cassie thought, who'd wanted the building closed to everyone but athletes and kids staying after for clubs and activities. Several teachers had fought to let the kids stay just to socialize. With the help of a teacher committee, Seth had launched a QRS program for after school: any kids could remain in the building as long as they adhered to behavior promoting Quiet, Respect and Safety.

The last five gang-prevention techniques dealt with offering programs for transfer students, educating teachers and parents with inservice courses, finding good community role models and providing counseling for students on the edge. As with the rest of the content, Mitch praised what Bayview Heights High School already had in place and gave suggestions for those they did not.

At four o'clock, when Mitch finished answering one of the many questions fired at him, Seth stood. "It's late," he said to the group. "I can't tell you how much I appreciate your interest. I think you all recognize the gravity of the situation. I'm ending the formal part of the meeting now. If you want to stay around, have a cup of coffee with us and ask Mitch any more questions, please do so. The rest of you drive home carefully. The weather's turned nasty."

Cassie stood up. Her emotions were mixed. She was still afraid for Johnny, and she still felt a more intimate approach would have been better. But professionally, she couldn't deny that Mitch and Seth had done a great job.

Seth grabbed her arm as she started for the door. "Cass?"

She faced him.

"You okay?"

Tilting her chin, she said, "Yes, of course I am." She looked at Mitch, who was surrounded by several teachers. "He did a good job."

"He told me you helped him learn how to give a good presentation."

"Ironic, huh?"

Seth smiled. "Did you talk to Johnny?"

"Yes. He's okay with it."

"Good. I'm glad."

"Me, too."

Seth glanced toward the podium. "You going to stay and talk to Mitch?"

Cassie shook her head. "No, I don't think so."

"Can I do anything?" he asked.

Again she shook her head. "No. I'm tired. I'm going home."

"No volleyball tonight?"

Volleyball. Mitch. Her house, in front of the fire afterward. She bit her lip. "No. Not tonight. Goodbye, Seth."

Against her will, she took one last look at Mitch. Sarah McKay was handing him a cup of coffee and staring sweetly up at him. It was like rubbing salt in an open wound. To escape the image, Cassie turned and headed for the door.

She didn't see Mitch's gaze follow her as she walked out of the library.

CHAPTER NINE

ON TUESDAY MORNING, Mitch barged through the school entrance tired and irritable. He'd overslept and was late because he'd tossed and turned a good part of the night, trying to escape the sad look on Cassie's face during the faculty meeting. He wasn't ready to see her today, with his defenses lowered by fatigue.

Class was underway when he stepped through the doorway. He froze. All around the room were images straight out of his worst nightmare. He watched as eleven kids in Cassie's class went from object to object—inspecting each one. It took a minute for her voice to penetrate his shocked brain.

"All of this is authentic memorabilia from the Vietnam War. For four weeks we'll be studying the art, literature and music of war, focusing first on Vietnam, because it's probably the most relevant to you."

Still standing in the doorway, Mitch scanned the obscene reminders that decorated her room. A flak jacket, several helmets, maps of Southeast Asia, shells, flags, an M-16. God, she even had a claymore mine. The last time he'd seen the highly explosive weapon, which flung shrapnel in the direction of the enemy, it had gotten turned around and he and his squad were diving for cover. Where the hell had she unearthed these things?

When she finished telling them they had ten minutes to "get a feel" for the stuff, she headed for her desk and saw him. His mind registered that her face looked pale and drawn today, but his eyes strayed to the war artifacts.

"Good morning, Captain," she said coolly.

"Ms. Smith." Shaking off the trance, he came into the room. He was bone-deep cold and shivered as he removed his coat.

She cocked her head, stared at him hard. "Are you all right?"

Taking in a deep breath, he nodded. "You?"

"You mean about the faculty meeting yesterday?"

"Yeah."

"I'm fine." Her words were clipped, her tone short. So this was how it was going to be. Over the weekend, he'd accepted that they were going nowhere, so it didn't come as a surprise. It just seemed a little harder to take this morning, given the ghosts that were staring back at him from all corners of the room.

"How did the kids do with the announcement this morning?"

"All right. Joe DeFazio isn't here today."

"Johnny?"

"He did okay." She glanced over where the boy was examining a map of Vietnam. "Actually, he seems unusually intrigued by this introduction to our new unit."

Mitch swallowed hard. "Where did you get all this stuff?"

"I've been collecting it for years. I always go into a war unit after the alienation unit, and this is the result of ten years of collection from pawn shops, novelty stores, people who've come and talked and left things with us."

He nodded. *People who've come and talked.* Vets fell into two categories: those who couldn't talk about their experiences, and those who had to. Most psychologists agreed that the latter were healthier. It seemed an oxymoron to Mitch—a healthy war veteran. But hell, people had to deal with the demons as best they could.

"Mitch, are you sure you're okay? You look… ill."

"I'm just tired." He had to turn away from the sympathy in her eyes. He was too raw today to begin with, and now, bombarded by his past, he wasn't even sure he could get through the next couple of hours.

Take it one day at a time, Mitch, the VA counselor had advised. Somehow, he'd managed twenty-five years of living with the horror he'd seen, the crimes he himself had perpetrated. As he hung up his coat, he closed his eyes to stop a vision of one of those crimes—the bloodied bodies of the Viet Cong soldiers, piled high, ready for burning. His gun had put too many of them there.

Shaking off the memory, he got his journal from the cabinet and took a seat in the back as Cassie said, "All right, everybody. Today you're going to write on this." She passed out to each of them what Mitch thought was a business card. On the square paper, however, was typed, "Join the Marines.

Travel to exotic lands, meet interesting and exciting new people, and kill them.''

There were nervous chuckles around the room, then the kids quieted. And began to write.

Mitch stared at the blank paper. Journal writing. This aspect of the class had been tough for him. He'd written with the kids each day, but it had been surface stuff. He hadn't gotten into what he was really feeling and he'd never mentioned his war experiences. Hell, he'd only ever talked about them to counselors, and a few times to Kurt when he couldn't deal with the pain alone. Write about it now? Never in a million years.

He hadn't realized Cassie was at his desk. ''Not writing today, Captain?''

''Just thinking.'' He peered up into eyes he'd thought at one time he might want to share the horror of Vietnam with. Not now. He picked up his pen as she walked on to see what Peterson was doing. At the top of his page, Mitch wrote, ''Do not read.'' He scribbled, ''I can't do this. I can't write about the war. I can't even think about it. Except for the nightmares, it's not even a part of me anymore. Maybe I can write about this card. I have a lot of feelings about how kids get sucked in. How they go over there not knowing what the hell's going to happen to them.'' And so it went. For ten minutes he skirted any references to himself and wrote around the issue. But the writing was more personal, with more feeling than anything he'd done so far.

When it was time to share, he moaned. He watched the kids pair up. Mike Youngblood asked to be with Cassie, so Mitch got a break there. Though she was angry and upset with him, he could tell that she'd noticed something more was going on with him than the fight they'd had. He didn't want to give her further evidence of his state of mind.

"Looks like it's you and me left, Captain."

Mitch stared up at Battaglia. Damn!

The boy plunked down on the desk next to him. "Wanna tell me what you think of the card?"

Sitting back, Mitch crossed his arms over his chest, trying to look relaxed. "I think it's true. Recruiters suck young kids in when they have no idea what they'll be doing in war."

Battaglia stared off into space for a minute. "You think so? I can't understand why anybody would join. It'd screw up the rest of his life."

Something in his tone alerted Mitch. There was a concern, a sympathy—something—lacing the boy's words.

"You don't always know at eighteen what's best for you," Mitch answered honestly.

Sharp, suspicious eyes leveled on Mitch. "Yeah, so I've heard today." Battaglia scowled. "You talk to Cassie?"

"Briefly. Why?"

"She…she looks sad. Has looked that way since Friday. I thought maybe you could cheer her up."

"I think you've got a better chance of doing that than I do." He held Battaglia's gaze. "I'm glad to see you here today."

The boy looked around the room at the war stuff. "I'm not so glad I came. Especially today."

Cassie watched Johnny and Mitch out of the corner of her eye. What were they talking about? Both looked so serious. God, she hoped Mitch didn't do anything to push Johnny over the edge. And vice versa. Something was wrong with Mitch. He looked somber. She supposed it could be the tension between them because of the gang issue. She could still hear him whisper, *Reconsider, Cass...please.*

She had...a thousand times since Friday. Only he didn't know it, and never would.

"All right, let's talk about the card as a group." After they'd shared their thoughts, she said, "Vietnam is a war many of us can relate to. How many of you know someone who was in Southeast Asia?"

She let the kids tell their stories. Arga's and Tara's uncles, and Jen's father. Several neighbors. Even Peterson's older step-brother.

"Think anyone would like to come in and talk to us about this?"

"Not my dad," Jen said. "He don't ever talk about it."

"How old is your Dad, Jen?"

"Forty-nine. He was in at the end. Really screwed him up."

"My uncle might." Arga spoke softly. "He told me stories. They're really bad."

"Why don't you ask him if he'd speak to our class? Anyone else have any connection to this war?"

She looked around the room, her gaze falling on Johnny and Mitch. Something about their faces—a similar look about them...

Class ended before she could figure it out.

The kids left, and Mitch gathered his things as the next group filed in. His shoulders were tense, his body ramrod straight.

"Mitch?" Cassie said as he headed for the closet. Continuing past her, he grabbed his coat, shrugged into it and turned to face her—ready to bolt. "Yeah?"

"Are you sure you're okay?"

For a minute, a look of naked pain crossed his face. Then it was gone. "I'm fine, Ms. Smith. Just as always."

With that mysterious comment, he left.

MITCH FOUND HIMSELF at Kurt's clinic on Thursday of that week. He'd endured three days of studying the war, and he couldn't handle the pain alone anymore.

First there had been the music: Billy Joel's "Goodnight Saigon" and George Michael's "Mother's Pride." As he listened to Joel's accurate description of the camaraderie among the soldiers, their dependence on one another in the foreign countryside, Mitch remembered an incident. He was marching through the jungle. He was in the middle of the line, as usual. His buddy, Stillman, had been at the point. Mitch had tackled him from behind, but not in time to dodge the sniper's bullet. Stillman had gone home early, paralyzed from the waist down.

But Michael's song got to Mitch even more. Cassie had made what she called a song scrapbook: pictures she'd drawn or cut out of magazines, representing the lyrics. She'd shown them on an overhead screen while she played the song, asking the kids to jot down the images that were most powerful. Mitch had watched the screen in silence—all those children scarred by war, all those families torn apart. He felt wounds open that he'd thought closed for good. The picture of one small Vietnamese boy tightened the fist around Mitch's heart so much he'd had to get up and leave the room. He'd made a silly excuse when he'd returned just before the end of class....

So he'd sought out his brother. As he came through the door into the entry-reception area of the clinic, a young woman bustled in behind him.

"Hi," she said, looking up at him with wide brown eyes peeking out from under shaggy bangs. She shook her coat off, hung it in a makeshift closet and smiled. "I'm Meg Mancini, a premed student. You're Kurt's brother."

"How do you know me?" Mitch asked.

"Kurt has a picture of you two on his desk."

"Oh."

"And Johnny's talked about you."

"Battaglia?"

She glanced to the far side of the room. "Speak of the devil, as my dad says."

Johnny came out of the clinic's inner door. "Devil? Me? Mary Margaret, how unkind." The teasing drained from his voice when he spotted Mitch. "Hello, Captain Lansing."

"Mr. Battaglia."

"Here to see your brother?"

"Yes."

"He's in with an emergency."

"You can wait in his office, Captain Lansing," said a familiar-looking nurse behind the receptionist desk.

"Thank you." Mitch turned to the young woman next to him. "Nice meeting you, Ms. Mancini." He walked through the door, conscious of two pairs of dark eyes on his back.

Johnny felt a slight hand on his arm. "He doesn't seem like such a monster."

A monster? Johnny remembered the captain's strange behavior this week. Because Johnny didn't want to think about Cassie's class and what they were studying, he looked away from the door. He felt his heart turn over at the tender concern in Ms. Mancini's eyes.

"Looks can be deceiving," he said, winking. "Take me, for instance. I look like a punk. You'd never know I was so smart."

Mary Margaret smiled. "You look like Andy Garcia. My favorite actor."

"Your favorite, huh?"

She rolled her eyes. "Uh-oh. I can see I shouldn't have told you that."

"Why?"

"My mother warned me about guys like you."

"Why, Mary Margaret, are you flirting with me?"

"Maybe."

As she headed into the clinic, he grasped the back of her sweater. "Wait a second. I want to ask you something." He tugged her to the far corner of the entry area. "Let me take you home tonight."

Her brown eyes widened. "I don't think so, Johnny."

"Why?"

"I..." She blushed, and turned half away from him. "I'm not like most other girls...I'm..."

"You're a good girl, I know that. I *like* that."

"You do?"

"Sure, and I'll respect it."

Her smile was million-watt, brightening up the dreary room. "All right. You can take me home."

Johnny stared after her as she left to go to work.

Intending to follow, he poured a cup of coffee first. Just as he was leaving the entry, the front door opened and a figure stumbled through it.

It was Zorro. His face was pale, his eyes glazed. The nurse behind the desk asked, "Are you in need of assistance, sir?"

He shook his head, his eyes locking on Johnny. "I came to see my buddy." Zorro stood erect, toughing out whatever had happened. To anyone else, he looked fairly normal. Johnny could tell he was in pain. "Can we talk someplace?"

Quickly, Johnny dragged his friend back into the clinic to an empty examining room.

"What's going on, man?" Johnny asked when they were alone.

Zorro sank onto a chair. His face was stark white and his hands shook as he unzipped his Blisters jacket and pulled down the sleeve. On his arm, Johnny saw red seeping onto a grungy T-shirt.

"You're hurt."

"Just a little scratch. You gotta fix me up, buddy."

"I'll call the doctor."

"No."

"Why?"

"It's from a gun."

"A gun?"

"Yeah. Had a little encounter with the Fifty-second Street gang that I hadn't planned on. The bastards were armed."

"Zorro, gunshot wounds have to be reported."

"I know, man. That why I came here. You can fix it." He glanced around the room. "You got all the stuff here."

"Zorro, I could lose my job if I take care of you."

"Hey, Tonto, it's me. Your best friend. Ain't nobody else gotta know." Zorro grimaced with pain. "The bullet's out. Just clean it up, patch it back together, and nobody'll know."

That was true. Kurt would be with Mitch for a while. Dr. Sloan wouldn't be here until seven when Kurt got off.

He looked at Zorro's pale face and was transported back to another time Zorro's face had been pale.

Johnny had been thirteen, Zorro a year older. A big lug had tackled Johnny and was pummeling him. Zorro had jumped on the bully's back and had been brutally beaten until two of the Blisters knocked the other guy out....

"Why'd ya do it?" Johnny had asked.

"He was hurtin' my main man," Zorro had told him, with blood oozing from his lips. "I gotta help my bro...."

Now Johnny took in Zorro's chalk white complexion and closed eyes as he battled the pain. Aw, hell, he really didn't have any choice. Not when his buddy needed him.

Slowly, Johnny walked to the supplies cabinet.

ON THURSDAY OF THE following week, Mitch watched Cassie's eyes twinkle as she passed out pictures to each student and to him. Despite the strain she was feeling, her demeanor in class gave no clue to the turmoil inside her.

She's so good at hiding her feelings.

It takes one to know one.

"I want you all to pretend you're five years old."

She grinned and Mitch's stomach clenched. "For some of you, that won't be too hard."

Good-natured boos sounded around the room. From everyone except Battaglia. As the unit progressed, he'd become more and more withdrawn. Today, he wouldn't meet Cassie's eyes; instead, he stared blankly at the picture or the wall or his desk. His posture was ready-to-snap tense.

"I've given you each a toy," she continued. "Think about what you—as a five-year-old—would do with it."

She gave them a minute of thinking time.

"Okay, Tara, you first."

Tara grinned. "I got a gun and holster. I'm gonna strap it on and shoot my boyfriend, Dave, between the eyes for teasing me about my outfit today." She indicated her totally black shoes, stockings, skirt and blouse, accented by black lipstick.

Laughter around the room.

Mitch hadn't looked at his toy.

"Joe?"

DeFazio raised mutinous eyes to her. "I got a tomahawk. I'd like to split somebody's skull open."

Preferably mine, Mitch thought.

Ignoring the innuendo, Cassie moved on. "Johnny?"

"I pass."

Cassie hesitated. "Okay, what's your toy so we can do it, anyway?"

"G.I. Joe."

Arga blurted out, "I know, Ms. Smith. I'll dress Johnny's doll with my camouflage outfit and he can crawl through the jungle shootin' at people."

Mitch twisted the picture in his hands.

Cassie went through an array of toys: a battleship, an army tank, bows and arrows, a machine gun. Then she called on Mitch.

He stared down at the lifelike toy. "A grenade." For a minute, he was somewhere else. It was hot. Humid. Stinking.

The grenade felt heavy in his hand. He grasped it lightly...counted to ten...pulled the pin and threw it fifty feet....

"Captain?"

His throat was dry and his hands clammy. "Ah...I...I'd throw it at the enemy."

Cassie stared at him for a minute. He looked away.

"All right, everybody, what's the point of all this?"

Jen said, "These toys are all war toys."

"There's only one way to play with them, isn't there?" Cassie asked. "How? To do what?"

"To hurt somebody else," said Amy.

Youngblood shook his head. "Yeah, but there ain't no harm in 'em. We all played with these as kids."

"Well, let's see," Cassie answered. "I've got a short movie that takes a stand on that issue. "It's called *Toys*. It's only eight minutes long. Let's watch it and see what you think. Make sure you consider it in the context of our war unit."

She turned the lights off, then started the projector. On the screen appeared several small children—about the age of seven. They were in a store, watching a display of toys that revolved on a turnstile. The kids were oohing and ahhing over the antics of the toys: a lion that roared, a clown that jiggled, Barbies and Kens posed side by side.

After the opening, the children's attention was drawn to another display. Army toys. War toys. G.I. Joes in uniform, tanks, guns, an ambulance, medical equipment, spotlights, helicopters. The kids in the movie stared at them.

Suddenly the action froze. The sound stopped. The lights in the store dimmed to nighttime.

And the toys came alive.

Mitch watched as one Joe, on his belly, inched his way up a hill. Another army doll waved flags for an incoming helicopter, which landed right on the scene. Explosions went off, and the unforgettable sound of discharging guns echoed around them. There was the shriek of a siren. A scream. One Joe was suddenly blown apart by a grenade. Another was stuck in the neck with a toy bayonet. At that point, the students in Cassie's class flinched and a couple groaned.

These are toys, Mitch told himself. Not soldiers. Not real men. Not his buddies. Still, when a chopper flew over the dolls' heads, Mitch grabbed the edge of the desk to keep himself from diving to the floor for cover.

He tried to concentrate on the screen. A blast of machine-gun fire ripped through the air; several toys went down. The camera focused on one plastic body turning over in a puddle. The water would be slimy, Mitch knew. It was tepid. It tasted rank.

He swallowed hard and licked his lips.

A quiet descended, the camera panned the entire, demolished area.

Then it was over.

The camera went back to the kids in the toy store. The music resumed, and the children stared at fully intact toys, exactly as they'd been before the freeze frame. The battle had happened only in the minds of little kids. It had happened only in their imagination.

But to Mitch, the toys' war was as real as if it had happened yesterday.

TWELVE HOURS LATER, the war was even more real. Mitch was on his belly, in the jungle, making his way through five-inch-deep water. He could feel the sweat trickling down his back. Something was biting him in the ankle, but he had to stay calm. Separated from his squad when it had been attacked, he needed to find his way quietly. It was dark. The U.S. had the advantage during the day with their advanced equipment, but the Viet Cong ruled the night. They knew this land in the dark, and he didn't. Gulping for air, he inched along. It was then that he heard it…the unmistakable click of a semiautomatic behind him. Mitch turned and screamed…. *No, No, No…*

He sat up in bed with a start, waking from the nightmare that he'd lived twenty-five years ago in a jungle in Asia. His breath came in gasps and he was dripping with sweat. "No, no, no…" he said aloud several times before it sunk in where he was.

He looked down. His hands were fisted in the sheet. The rest of the bed was a tangled mess. He hadn't had the dream in months. Damn, he thought he had this under control. It was the freakin' war unit in class these two weeks that had gotten to him.

Of all the rotten...why had he ever consented to work with Cassie Smith and her dirty dozen?

He yanked on the sheet. Pulling both hands in opposite directions, it ripped solidly down the middle. He stared at the shreds dangling in his hands.

Cassie would say this was symbolic. And it was. His life had been ripped apart by the war and had been in shreds for years afterward.

And he'd be damned if he let it go back to that.

He was leaving Cassie's class.

For good.

THE NEXT DAY, she handed out the novel *Fallen Angels*.

''You guys will love this book,'' she told them. ''It's from the viewpoint of a kid just like you who enlists and ends up in Nam.''

Taking his copy from Som, Mitch stared down at the picture on the cover and thought he might be sick. As Cassie told the kids about Richie, the main character, Mitch stared at the young, innocent faces of the men on the cover. They could have been his buddies. One looked like Silverstein, one a little like Thomas. The two black guys could have been twins for Markham and Stone. Of his entire squad, only Mitch had returned on two feet. Slowly, he traced the outline of one of the boy's faces. Mitch's chest constricted and his vision blurred. Sweat broke out on his brow. He had to turn the book over. For distraction, he glanced around the room, trying to focus on something else. His gaze landed on Battaglia. The boy was mesmerized by the picture. His hand also traced the face of one of the characters. Mitch stared at Johnny, watching his absorption. Empathizing with it. Why?

"Okay, let's read the first chapter now and then talk about it," Cassie told the kids. She noticed Johnny was absorbed in the book's cover. Just as Mitch had been.

Taking a seat on the floor next to Som, she opened her book and tried to read. What was going on with Mitch and Johnny? It wasn't the gang thing—at least not just that. She decided to talk to both of them. Mitch had told her he wanted to see her after class, anyway, so she'd ask him then.

It took about thirty minutes for everyone to finish the chapter. When they were done, she posed the question, "Why did Richie join the service?"

Mike Youngblood, whom Cassie knew was giving careful thought to joining the marines when he graduated, said, "He didn't have nothing better. He wanted to go to college, but he didn't have no dough. Enlisting gave him food and a place to stay."

"And helped his mama and brother," Som put in.

Cassie listened to the kids, encouraging their discussion. They were seated in a circle on the floor. Mitch had taken the chair in back of them, but hadn't said a word.

"I think he's a sicko. You gotta be crazy to join up." This came from DeFazio, who, since a week ago Monday, had found every possible way to disrupt Cassie's class.

Cassie was about to defuse his hostility when Johnny stood. His hands fisted at his sides and his eyes were black and blazing. "You got it backward, you dumb jerk. They aren't crazy when they join, they're crazy when they come back."

DeFazio stood, too. "Yeah, what makes you such an expert? I'm sick of you, Battaglia. You think you know everything."

Cassie stood between them. "Stop it, you guys, right now. I won't have any name-calling in class. If you have a difference of opinion, you'll have to settle it—"

But Johnny wasn't listening. "I know, you dumb shit," he told DeFazio. "*I* know. You're the one who doesn't know anything." Wildly, he looked around. No one spoke for seconds, then he said, "Screw this," reached down, grabbed his jacket and bolted for the door.

Cassie was about to go after him when she saw Mitch leap from the chair and head out. "Stay where you are. I'll take care of this."

Mitch caught up to Battaglia in the hall just before he reached the exit—almost at the exact spot he'd tackled the kid the night Cassie got locked in the storage room. He grabbed a fistful of Battaglia's shirt and yanked back. "Hold on, Battaglia."

Johnny swore and jerked his shoulders, trying to free himself. "Let me go."

Mitch's fist tightened. "Not yet." His voice was gentle, and his tone must have gotten through.

Johnny stopped struggling. He sagged against the wall face first, his arms braced on the tile. Mitch let go of Johnny's shirt and clapped a firm, fatherly hand on his shoulder. "Who do you know that was there?"

Johnny buried his face deep in his arms and shook his head.

"Who?" Mitch asked implacably.

After a long long time, Johnny muttered, "My father."

"I thought it was something like that." He squeezed the kid's shoulder. "But he couldn't have died over there."

"Not physically. His heart stopped beating when I was ten. It stopped feeling long before that."

Mitch swallowed hard. "I know."

The boy turned around, his black eyes brimming. "Yeah, sure."

"I do."

Battaglia's eyes widened. When Mitch didn't elaborate, Battaglia said, "You don't know shit. You're a phony."

Rage welled in Mitch. All the anger he kept so carefully buried started to surface. It was what happened every time he tried to talk about his time in Vietnam, which was why he had to keep everything in control. "I know," he said, "because I was there, too."

Battaglia just stared at him.

"I almost lost it when I got back, too. I was just luckier than your father."

The boy sank against the wall. His eyes never left Mitch's face. Neither man moved for seconds. Then, slowly, Battaglia reached out and laid his hand on Mitch's arm.

Something inside of Mitch snapped. The constricting band around his emotions, tightened year after year by self-imposed loneliness, finally loosened. He reached out his own hand and slid it around the kid's shoulders. "Come on, Johnny," he said hoarsely. "Let me buy you a cup of coffee."

CHAPTER TEN

WHEN MITCH AND JOHNNY walked into Pepper's at ten on a Thursday morning, the old man's eyebrows almost skyrocketed off his face.

Though the tension in Mitch's neck knotted his muscles, inside he was calm. He choose a booth in an isolated corner, out of view from the restaurant. Mitch could see the doorway and counter, but Johnny could not.

Pepper approached them. "What'll ya have, gentlemen?"

"Coffee." Mitch looked at Johnny.

"The same." They were the first words the boy had spoken since his revelation. Mitch respected his privacy; he knew the boy needed time to get back some of his control.

After they were served, Mitch circled his mug with his hands, blew on the coffee and sipped. Johnny still stared out the window.

"How old were you when he died?"

"Ten."

"It was bad?"

Johnny nodded.

"You ever tell anybody about this?"

"No."

"Not even Cassie?"

He shook his head.

"She wouldn't have done this unit if she'd known."

Johnny looked at him then. "About you, either."

"What?"

"If she'd known about you being in Vietnam, she wouldn't have done the unit."

That gave Mitch food for thought. He filed the idea away to digest later. "What'd he do?"

"In the war?"

"Okay, start with that."

"He was a pilot. Mostly helicopters. Later, at home, when he got drunk, he'd talk. I remember a little. He said he was the most hated and appreciated man in Nam."

"Hated, because the birds brought us to the fighting. Appreciated, because they picked us up and took us out."

"What'd you do?"

"I was a paratrooper."

"No shit? You jumped from those planes?"

"Yep."

Johnny sipped his coffee. "You drafted?"

Mitch shook his head. "My number in the lottery was high, so I didn't *have* to go. You know what the lottery was?"

"Yeah, when they drew birthdays to see who went into the army first."

"I enlisted," Mitch said. "What about your father?"

"His number was two."

Mitch stared at his coffee, searching for answers in the dark, bitter liquid. He raised his eyes when Johnny spoke.

"What'd you mean when you said you were luckier than my father?"

"I take it he was messed up when he came back."

"My mother says that. All I remember is the..." Johnny looked back out the window.

Mitch held his tongue. Disclosure was hard.

When the boy faced him again, his cheeks were ashen and his eyes were moist. "Most of the time he kept to himself. But sometimes, he got mad at nothing. He...hit us. I was too little to protect my mother, but I tried."

Mitch ached for the young boy Johnny had been. "Did he ever get help?"

"Like counseling?" Mitch nodded. "Not that I know of." Johnny's gaze leveled on Mitch. "Did you?"

Thinking of the only sane decision he'd made in the first few years he was back, Mitch said, "My brother pushed it. Relentlessly. I went at first because..." God, the memory hurt.

"Because?"

"I beat the crap out of him one time when he was on me about getting my act together."

Johnny's brows rose.

"Abuse happens."

"Why?"

"A few reasons, I'd guess. First, you're trained to be violent. And you do it. You do all of it. Unspeakable things."

Johnny just stared at him.

"Then you see it done by others all the time. Or worse, you experience it firsthand."

"You ever get captured?"

"No. Did your father?"

"Yeah. For six months."

"I'm sure it was hell, Johnny. When you have that kind of experience, your mind snaps. Mine did when…"

"When?"

Mitch shook his head. "There are some things I still can't talk about."

Johnny watched him for a minute. A reluctant grin tugged at his lips. "Yeah, then don't let Cassie know that. She'll dog you until you tell her."

Mitch smiled at how well Johnny knew her. "That why you never told her about your father?"

He nodded. "Like you said, it's tough to talk about."

"Anyway, the violence doesn't go away as soon as you return to the world. It's always there, barely controlled. I couldn't have conquered it unless I'd had help. And sometimes, I go back when I feel my control slipping."

Johnny sipped his coffee and drummed restless fingertips on the table. "My…my dad? You think, if he'd had help, he would've been better?"

A secret and silly wish that he had been this boy's father washed over Mitch with the force of a monsoon. He reached across and squeezed Johnny's arm. "I think he would have. Maybe you need to hold on to that."

The door to Pepper's blew open before Johnny could respond. In walked three guys—all wearing Blisters jackets. They paid no attention to the few late morning patrons in the restaurant.

Mitch saw Pepper stiffen when he turned from the counter and spotted them.

"Hey, old man."

Pepper said nothing.

"Get us some Cokes."

"Or some coke." They laughed at the pun.

"I told you guys I don't want you hanging out here."

"Yeah, well Zorro sent us to give you a message."

The boy whipped out a can of spray paint from his jacket pocket and shook it up and down. "Know what this is, dirtbag?"

Pepper stepped back.

Mitch sprang out of the booth and strode to the counter.

"What's going on here?"

Heads swiveled toward him. "What the hell—"

"I'm a police officer." He whipped out his star and looked pointedly at the can of paint. "You got something for Pepper?"

The boys stood stock-still.

Then the spokesperson said, "No, man. We just came in for somethin' to drink."

"What's that for?"

Holding up the can, the boy shrugged. "This? Oh, this is for a school project. Art class."

The others laughed. "Yeah. We doin' some paintin'."

Mitch stared down the gang members. "Get out of here. If I catch you in Pepper's again, I'll take you in."

"What for?"

Mitch lurched forward and grabbed the wise guy by the collar. "Loitering. Being a menace to society." He yanked hard. "Got it, kid?"

The gang member swallowed hard but said nothing.

Mitch tightened his grip. "I said, *Got it?*"

"Got it."

He let go. With belligerent looks, the trio sauntered out of Pepper's.

Mitch turned to see Johnny, leaning against a booth, staring at him.

ON FRIDAY MORNING, Cassie wrote in her journal that she was worried about Johnny. And about Mitch. When she started to get into painful areas concerning Captain Lansing, she put her pen down and sat back to wait for the kids to finish up. Glancing around the room, she noted that no one was absent but Joe DeFazio—who had come to school with glazed eyes and reeking of marijuana. Cassie had immediately called the nurse and Carolyn Spearman, one of the vice principals, who came and escorted the boy out. DeFazio's absence lightened the classroom atmosphere considerably; his hostility over the last two weeks had affected everyone.

She watched Johnny. He'd propped himself up against the wall, knees bent, writing furiously. She had no idea what had happened yesterday when he'd stormed out of her room. Zoe told her that Mitch had returned to school at noon with Johnny in tow, taken Johnny to Zoe and explained—in vague terms—why he'd missed her class. Mitch left without seeing Cassie at all. Johnny had stopped by after lunch to apologize for disrupting her class. When she'd asked what happened, he didn't want to talk about it. He looked totally drained, so she didn't press it.

Now Mitch was settled in one of the beanbag chairs, writing also. For the first time in school, he was dressed casually in a navy blue sweater. He still wore dress slacks, but had on loafers. He looked so good Cassie wanted to curl up on his lap and cuddle into him.

Shaking herself from the mood, she glanced at the clock. "All right," she said. "Who'd like to share first?"

She waited.

And waited.

Finally, Nikki Parelli raised her head and said, "I will." Cassie was shocked to see tears in the girl's hazel eyes. She read from her journal. "Everybody's talked about their experiences with the war but me. Because I'm ashamed. My father was in Vietnam, too." Nikki stopped reading to swipe at her cheeks. Mitch, who was sitting behind her, put a hand on her shoulder, squeezed it gently and gave her a handkerchief.

Wiping her eyes, Nikki continued, "He came back messed up. He's...he's still messed up. I don't know how to deal with him, especially now that he doesn't live with us. He smokes dope and drinks all the time. He..."

Then she started to cry hard. Cassie started to get up to go to the girl, but before she could, Johnny reached Nikki. Putting his arm around her, he said, "You want me to read the rest?"

Nikki nodded and handed him her journal.

Johnny read, "He used to hit me and my little brother, which is why my mother finally kicked him out. Why would he do that?"

Slowly Johnny lowered the book and lifted his

eyes to Mitch. Something passed between the two men that Cassie didn't understand.

"Nikki," Johnny said. "Not everybody came clean. I...my father was there, too."

Cassie was taken aback. She'd had no idea. But the look on Mitch's face revealed that he had known.

"He came back messed up, too," Johnny continued. "And he hit me, too."

Nikki stared at Johnny with soulful eyes. "Why? Why do they do that? We didn't do anything to them. I don't understand."

Johnny looked up at Mitch again. This time Mitch's expression was strained. His jaw was clenched and his brow furrowed. One hand gripped his journal and the other fisted at his side. After a few seconds, he said quietly, "*They* don't understand why they do those things either, Nikki."

Frowning, the young girl circled around to face him. "What do you mean?"

"Vietnam messed a lot of people up. Some vets came back crazy and did crazy things in the world." He drew in a deep breath. "We don't always know why we do them."

The room went still. Soft laughter came from across the hall, and somebody's heels clicked loudly on the linoleum tile outside their door. But there wasn't a sound in room 401.

Jen Diaz finally said, "We?"

Mitch nodded. "I was in Vietnam."

Cassie sank back on her knees. Again, she hadn't a clue. Again, she could see Johnny had known. Yesterday fell into place.

After a prolonged silence, Austyn Jones said, "Can we ask you some questions?"

"I don't think that's a good—" Cassie began but Mitch cut her off.

"No, it's okay, Cassie." He gave her a long look and turned to Austyn. "You can ask me questions, but I might not answer some of them."

Again no one moved.

Mitch smiled. "And start with the easy ones, would you?"

Jones grinned. "How long you there?"

"Just a little under two years. I was among the last wave sent."

"You drafted?"

Mitch shook his head. "I enlisted." He held up the book. "Just like Richie…"

"Why?" Mike Youngblood asked.

Mitch stared at him. "Because I really believed it was the right thing to do." He glanced around and took another deep breath. "It wasn't."

Again no one spoke. Then Tara asked, "Why, Captain?"

"Because fifty-eight thousand men came back in body bags in ten years. I'm not sure anything can justify that."

Brenda Uter said, "But we had to protect them from communism, didn't we?"

Mitch shook his head. "We moved in on a bunch of farmers who just wanted to farm. We had no right to do it, and in the end, we lost, anyway."

"Captain, you ever get wounded?" Arga wanted to know.

"Yeah, twice."

"How?"

Mitch reached up and rubbed his shoulder. "A cherry didn't follow orders?"

"A cherry?"

Mitch reddened. "Ah, a new guy. A rookie who'd just gotten there."

"Hey," Arga said. "Did they call 'em cherries because they were virg—"

"Yes, that's why." Mitch smiled. "Anyway, we were laying low in the field, waiting out Charlie. It was dusk. There was a noise fifty yards away—the VC did that intentionally to draw us out—and the new guy opened fire. He gave away our position and several men were wounded. I was evac'd out for a shoulder injury and came back in a month."

"Hey, meet any bad women in the hospital?" Don Peterson, the lady's man, asked.

Mitch smiled weakly at Peterson. "Yeah, a few pretty nurses."

The tension eased somewhat at the joking, though Cassie was still holding her breath.

"How about the other time?" Tara asked.

"I got some bad burns."

"How?"

Mitch rolled his eyes. "Because I was stupid."

"What happened?" Amy asked.

All the kids had straightened up and were hanging on to Mitch's words.

"We were burning brush with gasoline. I was in charge. Again, a new guy couldn't get it to catch, so I got p— I got mad and took a can of gasoline, wet down the area. Just as I did, I spied a spark out of the corner of my eye. I dived out, but it was too late."

Cassie listened in awe and in horror as Mitch told

about the extensive burns he'd gotten as a result of the blowup, which eventually sent him home. "Japan was the burn center for all of Southeast Asia. They bandaged me up in the field. But by the time we got to Japan, the bandages had stuck to what was left of my skin. The doctor told me he'd remove them, or I could do it myself. It took four hours for me to get them off in the shower. By the end of it, I was literally banging my head against the wall. I wanted to die."

Cassie shivered. Somehow people back home now only thought about the mental and emotional ramifications of that era. She looked at his hands. "Did you get skin grafts?"

"No. The skin grew back."

"You ever kill anybody?" Jen asked.

He nodded.

"How many?"

"Too many."

"You ever save anybody?" Nikki looked at him with youthful hope and optimism in her eyes.

It was the first time Mitch smiled. "Yeah."

"What happened?"

"It was October '74. We were crossing a two-foot-high, dried-up rice paddy. The VC open fired on us, and my whole squad dived back for the jungle. All but five of us made it. The Captain asked for volunteers to go out into the paddy to see where the missing men were, if they were alive."

"Why didn't you guys just run?" Som asked. She'd been withdrawn and quiet during a lot of this unit. Cassie had discussed her feelings about Vietnam before the unit started, and Som had seemed okay with it, but Cassie worried about her.

"We didn't leave our buddies."

"Oh."

"Anyway, I volunteered to go. I crawled out on my belly with an M-16 on my back and a revolver in my boot. I found the men two-thirds of the way out in a small ravine."

"Anybody dead?" Youngblood asked.

"No, all five were alive. But the oddest thing had happened. One guy had his helmet on and a stray bullet had hit the helmet, circled around inside the lining on the rim and came out the other side."

"Nah, that ain't true," Arga said.

"It is. I wouldn't have believed it if I hadn't seen it with my own eyes."

"Finish the story, Mitch," Cassie said, anxious to hear something good. "What happened with the rescue?"

"The guys were alive, but two had sunken chest wounds, which are the worst you can get—it means the lungs are collapsed. I crawled back to the squad to tell the captain. While he called for a chopper, I got temporary medical supplies and went back out. I doctored 'em up as much as I could, then came back, waited for the rescue team to arrive and led them out to get the men."

Peterson shook his head. "You went out and back three times?"

"Yeah."

"Under fire?"

"Uh-huh."

"You nuts?"

Brenda said, "No, stupid. He's a hero."

Mitch shook his head. "No, Brenda, I'm not. I did horrible things."

Again the silence. And the stillness. No one asked him what *horrible things* he'd done.

"You get any medals?" Amy Anderson asked, breaking the tension.

"I got the Silver Star for that rescue."

"Any others?"

"A Purple Heart for the first injury."

"Captain?" Jen asked. "Would you bring them in so we could see 'em?"

"I, ah, don't have them. Once, in a fit of rage, I threw them in the garbage. My brother tried to salvage them. I stopped him."

Eleven faces studied Mitch.

"But back to Nikki's dad," he said. "He probably had these experiences, too."

Nikki nodded. "He has a Purple Heart and a Bronze Star Medal."

"So he did good things over there. Coming back, though, it was different. Sometimes it was impossible to live with the horror you'd seen—or done."

"How do you live with it?" Cassie asked.

Mitch started to speak when the door from Zoe's classroom opened. "Sorry, Cassie, this mod has been over for five minutes. Your students are supposed to come to me for science and you get my tenth-graders now."

"No fair."

"We wanna stay."

"I wanna know more."

All the kids voiced their disapproval.

Cassie stood. "Sorry guys, it's time to go. Besides, I think Captain Lansing could use a break."

"You be back next week?" Som asked.

"Yeah, I will."

Jones went over and held out his hand. "Good to know you, Captain," he said.

Mitch smiled and shook hands. A couple of other boys followed suit.

Nikki was the last to face him. In her quiet, soft way, she looked up at him and touched his arm. Mitch smiled back and squeezed her shoulder. Cassie's eyes stung.

When the class was gone and the tenth-graders were writing in their journals, she walked Mitch out into the hall. "Wow," she said, peering up at him. There were lines of pain and fatigue etched on his forehead and bracketing his mouth. "That's quite a secret you've been keeping."

Mitch leaned against the wall. "Johnny, too."

"Yeah. All these years, I never knew."

"He's a complicated kid."

"And you're a complicated man." She reached up and laid her palm on his cheek. "A special one."

He leaned into it for a minute. "I'll let you go."

"Mitch, I—"

He put his fingers to her lips. "Sh, don't say anything now. I...just don't." He reached over and smoothed back her hair. "I'm all right."

With that, he was gone.

FRIDAY NIGHT, CASSIE stood on the doorstep of Mitch's town house. She shifted the package she carried and managed to ring the bell. Nervous, she remembered that last Friday night, she'd rejected him outright. Would he do the same to her tonight? It didn't matter. She couldn't stay away.

After the fifth ring, she turned on the stoop and saw him jogging up the walk. "Mitch."

He was dressed in a nylon sweat suit, and his hair was disheveled, his cheeks ruddy. His eyes were bleak. He stopped a foot away from her. "What are you doing here?"

"I brought you supper," she said, holding up the bag.

"I'm not hungry."

"Have you eaten today?"

"I don't want to eat."

She scanned his tense, uncompromising stance. "It's too cold to be running outside."

"What are you? My mother?"

Startled at his tone, her eyes widened.

He ran a restless hand through his hair. "Look, I didn't mean to snap at you. But I don't want company."

He circled around her, went to his door, unlocked and opened it. Uninvited, she followed him in and closed the door.

Pivoting in the large foyer, he said, "Cassie, this isn't a good time for me. I don't want you here. I don't want anybody here." She didn't budge. "Besides, I'm going to work out."

Stubbornly, she set the heavy bag on a table next to the staircase. "Go ahead, work out. I'll get supper ready." She smiled. "It's homemade spaghetti sauce, salad and garlic bread."

Mitch's frown turned into a scowl. *"I don't want you here."*

Placing her hands on her hips, she said, "Why not?"

"Because I'm always like this after I..." He jammed his hands in his pockets. "After I talk about it. Leave now, Cassie."

"You're always like what?"

He raised his eyes to the ceiling. "Morose. Seething. Volatile."

"You need a friend. Let me stay and be your friend."

As quick and as potent as summer lightning, he grabbed her shoulders and backed her up against the wall. "Friends? You and I aren't friends, Cassie." Yanking hard, he pulled open the buttons of her long wool coat and grasped her waist tightly, his hands flexing on her flannel shirt. His whole body aligned with hers, he lowered his head. The kiss was full of savagery.

But Cassie wasn't scared. Nor was she offended. Instead, she felt a dark spark of excitement. He pressed her into the wall, grinding his mouth against hers. She could take this honest, uncensored reaction and give him back hers. When she opened her mouth to him, he broke off the kiss abruptly and pulled back. "What's wrong with you?"

She smiled. "Not a thing. I don't scare easily, Mitch. You can't get rid of me this way. I'm staying."

He backed up another step. "Suit yourself." Turning, he started down the hall.

When he was out of sight, she exhaled heavily. Then she headed down the hall in the direction Mitch had gone. The back of the town house was long and wide. To the right was a kitchen with glossy white appliances, a black-and-white-tiled floor and blond oak cabinets. To the left was a den and another room from which she could hear the clanking of exercise machinery.

Determined, she went into the kitchen and began to unpack the meal. The sauce was heating, the water boiling, and she was assembling the garlic bread when Mitch came out of the adjacent room wiping his neck with a towel. His face lined with exhaustion, he simply stared at her for long seconds.

Cassie stared back. Mitch Lansing didn't know whom he was messing with. "You've got ten minutes if you want to shower before dinner," she said sweetly.

His eyes narrowed on her. Without a word, he left the room. She heard his footsteps on the hardwood floors as he strode upstairs.

When he came down, Cassie tried to ignore his worn, low-slung navy sweatpants and white T-shirt that outlined every beautiful pectoral muscle. "Would you like something to drink? I brought some wine, too."

Again, the silence. Finally, he said, "Wine sounds good."

Relieved, she poured the Chianti. As she brought it to him and handed him the glass, she smiled.

He didn't—but he took the wine and lifted his other hand to her mouth. Gently, he brushed it with his fingertips. "Your lips are swollen. I'm sorry. I was out of line."

"Don't worry, I'm pretty tough."

"Yeah," he said with a half grin. "I noticed."

"Well, sit down while I get this on the table."

He sat and watched her as she brought the dinner

to the table. After she sat down and served the food, he asked, "How's Johnny? Have you talked to him?"

"Yes, this afternoon." She could still see Johnny's black eyes, shining with unshed tears as he told her about his father.

"How is he?"

"Very sad."

"It's probably best that he got it out."

Reaching over, Cassie placed her hand in Mitch's. "For you, too."

Sucking in a deep breath, Mitch held on to her hand so tightly it hurt. "I'm not sure. This is…it's so hard to talk about it. Then, and after, it's rough."

"Have you ever talked to anyone about it?"

"Kurt." He sipped his wine. "And counselors."

"What did they say?"

"That I should get it out. I guess I was ready, too."

Cassie twined her fingers with his. "Mitch, you can talk to me about your experiences anytime. I promise, I won't judge. I've done some things I'm not proud of, too. I'll just be a friend and let you get it out."

"There are some things I've never told anyone."

"Me, too."

He smiled. "All right. I'll remember that." Then he looked at the table and said, "Let's eat."

They devoured the food in companionable silence, broken occasionally by talk about school. When they were done, Cassie insisted he go into the den and relax while she did the dishes. He agreed easily, telling her he had to call Kurt. They were taking advantage of the school's four-day winter break to go skiing.

She cleaned up while he made his call, then brought a tray with dessert and coffee into the den. Mitch was stretched out on a large leather sofa. His eyes were closed and his arm was thrown over his head. A ripple of arousal went through her at how sexy he looked. When she set the tray on the low oak table, he opened his eyes and sat up.

"I've got *cannolis* and coffee," she told him.

"Smells great, but I think I'll pass on the coffee."

"It's decaf."

"Oh, then I'll have some."

"You haven't been sleeping?" Cassie asked as she bit into the creamy dessert.

He watched her mouth. "Ah...sleeping? Um, no, not for a couple of nights."

"I'm sorry. Maybe tonight."

"Maybe." He leaned over and wiped something off her lips. Then he put his finger to his mouth and licked.

Cassie's stomach somersaulted.

His eyes locked with hers, he murmured, "Mmm, tastes good."

Cassie swallowed hard.

When he reached over to take a pastry, he winced.

"What's wrong?"

"My shoulder. When I'm not careful with the bench press, or if I do too much weight, I wrench it."

"Which did you do tonight?"

''Both.''

''Listen, I'm pretty good at back rubs. Why don't I put this stuff away, give you a quick massage, and then get out of here. You're probably leaving early for your ski trip.''

Lazily, he chewed his dessert and watched her. ''A back rub, huh? You're a woman of many talents.''

Ignoring the innuendo, she finished eating, then stood, gathered the dessert remains together and went to the kitchen. She stored what was left in the fridge and returned to the den.

He was stretched out on his back again, looking at her with anything but friendship in his eyes. ''Come here, woman.'' His voice was low and sexy and drew her to the couch.

''Woman?'' she said, peering down at him. ''Pretty macho language, Captain.''

He tugged on her arm and she tumbled down on top of him. ''Well, Cassandra, you make me feel very...male.'' Then he frowned.

''What's wrong?''

''You also make me feel all sorts of soft and tender things.'' He threaded his hands through her hair and fluffed it around her shoulders. ''You wore it down.'' She nodded. ''For me.''

''Mitch, I didn't come here for this.''

His hands trailed down her back, leaving hot coals of desire every place he touched. He stopped at her bottom, where he squeezed her gently. ''No? What did you come for?''

''To be your friend.''

He stared at her hard. "All right. You can be my friend. You can give me a back rub, and then go on home—after a kiss." His eyes dropped to her lips. "I want your mouth."

Cassie's breath hitched. It left her altogether when he said, "Give me something else to dream about, Cass."

Her senses spinning, she lowered her mouth. Butterfly soft, she brushed her lips against his. Then she bit the lower one gently and soothed it with her tongue.

"Oh, God," Mitch said, his hands clenching her bottom.

She covered his mouth again, increasing the pressure in minuscule degrees. His breath started to come fast, too, and he arched into her.

The kiss went on a long time.

Before it got irrevocable, she pulled back. "Sweet dreams, Mitch," she mumbled just as she scrambled off him.

He gave her a searing look and reached for her.

She shook her head. "Not tonight. No decisions tonight. Come on, turn over."

After a last, long look, he flipped over. And moaned.

"Your shoulder hurt?"

"Among other things," he mumbled into the pillow.

Cassie pretended not to hear him.

"Think you can get this shirt off?"

"Oh, I could get it off, all right."

She giggled. His answering chuckle warmed her.

Whipping off the shirt, he lay back down and buried his face in the pillow. And—miraculously, Cassie thought—let her take care of him. She kneaded his shoulder, dug her palm into his spine, his lower back, then up to the deltoid muscles. He moaned, and sighed—and relaxed. Ten minutes later, he was sound asleep.

Cassie moved off of him, leaned over and kissed him on the cheek. She grabbed the big Indian-print blanket from the couch and covered him. Then she left Mitch's house, praying his slumber was restful. After the life he'd lived, he deserved it.

CHAPTER ELEVEN

JOHNNY TOOK THE RICKETY stairs two at a time down into the Den—the underground hangout of the Blisters. It was located in the basement of a strip joint on Twenty-second Street belonging to Sam "Batman" Jolsen's uncle. The guy was a sleaze—always on the fringes of the law—so he didn't mind the gang using the cellar for their hangout. His nephew had been arrested twice—once for larceny, once for sexual assault.

Squinting, Johnny came through the door. Like rats, these guys dwelled in dim surroundings; it took his eyes a minute to adjust. It took his nose a little longer. A haze of marijuana smoke hung in the outer room, underscored by the odor of unwashed bodies. Some of the Blisters bunked here when they were on the run or crashing. In the background were the suggestive rock lyrics of a group aptly named Scumbag. Johnny shook his head, suddenly aware of how seedy the place was. This was real gang life—it had little resemblance to *West Side Story*.

Six of the Blisters were there now. Two of them were new—Johnny didn't know their names. One of the veterans, Rocco Palatti, had been at Pepper's the morning Johnny had been there with Mitch. All of them were flamed up—dressed in the gang colors—which meant something was on for tonight.

Johnny glanced at his watch. He'd signed up to work at the clinic on these two days he had off from school; he had just enough time to see Zorro and get back before his dinner hour was up.

"Tonto. Hey, man, this is really twisted. You goin' with us tonight?" The question came from Wimp, a quasimember, who was the gofer, the butt of jokes, the wanna-be of the group. Every gang had one, though Johnny couldn't understand why anybody would put up with the torment the guys dished out to him.

"Hey, Wimp. No, I came to see Zorro." Johnny scanned the Den. "He here?"

"Yeah, he's in the back with a chick."

"He oughtta be done," Batman put in. "They been back there twenty whole minutes."

The group laughed.

Palatti uncurled himself from a chair and stood up. "Saw you the other day, Battaglia."

Johnny straightened and looked the punk right in the eye. "Did you? I don't recall."

"At Pepper's. With a pig."

"Minding my business now, Palatti? Ain't got nothin' better to do?" Johnny winced inwardly as he fell into the gang speech pattern.

Before Palatti could answer, the door to the other room flew open. Out walked a girl. She was about fifteen; her long hair was dyed a gaudy shade of red and she wore more makeup than KISS. She strutted to the bar and picked up a beer. Johnny turned from her, disgusted, thinking of Meg—whose hair was just as long, but clean and a pretty shade of dark brown. Meg's huge eyes needed no cosmetic help—they were deep chocolate and fringed with thick natural lashes.

She was one of the reasons Johnny was here.

My Dad will want to know everything about you, if you come in and meet him, Johnny.

He could just see Mr. Mancini finding out about the Blisters.

Johnny walked into the back room.

It smelled like sex. Zorro was lounging on a dirty cot, smoking a joint, dressed only in unsnapped jeans. On his upper arm was a small bandage that covered the almost-healed wound Johnny had illegally tended.

Zorro's eyes widened when he saw Johnny. "Tonto. Good to see you." He smiled smugly. "Want me to call Melanie back in here? We could share—just like old times."

The thought turned Johnny's stomach. "I'm not after a quick lay, Zorro."

Half stoned on sex and dope, Zorro's expression was lazy. "Yeah, what you after? Action? We've got some scheduled tonight."

"I guessed as much."

Coming farther into the room, Johnny stood over his buddy.

"I got something I want to talk to you about."

"Sit."

Johnny pulled a straight chair over to the cot and straddled it. "I want a favor. Two, really."

Zorro took a long drag on his joint. When he blew out a puff, the smoke stung Johnny's eyes. "I'd do anything for ya, Tonto. Name it."

Unbidden, and unwanted, a memory surfaced at Zorro's remark. *I'd do anything for you.*

After Johnny's father died, he and his mother had little money, but each month they managed to scrape five hundred dollars together for their rent. Once, though, Betty Battaglia had let one of her boyfriends "borrow" the rent money and they'd never seen him again. Johnny was panicky that they were going to get evicted....

"What's eatin' you?" Zorro had asked him right after Johnny discovered what his mother had done.

Embarrassed, Johnny had said, "Nothin'."

"I'm your best buddy, Johnny, you can tell me."

As his face flushed red, Johnny confessed his mother's stupidity and his own fears.

"I'll get the money," Zorro said matter-of-factly. A day later, he'd thrown a wad of bills on Johnny's kitchen table.

"Where'd you get this?" Johnny asked.

Zorro smirked. "A rich uncle died."

"I can't take money from you," Johnny told him. "Especially this much."

Zorro's black eyes narrowed on him. "Wouldn't you do the same for me?"

Immediately, Johnny nodded. "Of course I'd do anything for you, Zorro."

"Then take the dough...."

"So what do you need, Tonto?" Zorro's voice brought Johnny back to the present. He drew in a deep breath and thought about changing his mind. Zorro had always been there for him. Could he survive without Zorro? Johnny thought of Cassie, and Mitch and Meg—and his new life. He looked Zorro in the eye and said, as gently as he could, "I want you to stay away from Pepper's and out of Bayview Heights High School."

All at once, Zorro's posture tensed. His sleepy eyes cleared and he looked like a different man. "Why would you want that?"

"I have my reasons."

"Why do you care?"

Johnny chose his words carefully. He knew this wasn't going to be easy. "I like the school out there. And I don't want you causing me problems with it."

Quickly, lethally, Zorro sprang off the cot. He circled the chair, pacing in big, solid strides. Johnny knew not to move, that like a wild bear, if Zorro sensed fear, he'd attack.

"Ya know, buddy, funny things been happenin'. First, you start hangin' out with that teacher chick, and raggin' on me about her. Then you're spotted in Pepper's with a pig. Now you here wantin' us to curtail our activities. You turnin' on your brothers, man?"

Slowly, Johnny stood and faced Zorro. *Go forward, not back,* Cassie had said.

"I'm not turning on you, Zorro. I...I love you like a brother. But I'm out of the Blisters."

"Who you kiddin', man? You been pretendin' to be out for months, but you keep comin' back." Naked emotion suffused Zorro's face. "We family. Those other people, they drop you as soon as the goin' gets rough." He lifted his chin. "I never have."

"This has nothing to do with them. I want to go to college, Zorro. I want to be a doctor." Johnny straightened, and saw Mary Margaret smiling at him when he put on a lab coat. *Looks good on you, Johnny. I think you were meant to wear one.* "I'm going to make it, Zorro."

"And leave me behind."

"I...I have to choose."

At the bald statement, Zorro exploded. His eyes bulged and the scar on his face stood out white in stark relief against his dark skin. He didn't go near Johnny. Instead, he faced the small table behind him and shoved it over. The thud brought several Blisters to the doorway. Then Zorro picked up a chair and hurled it against the wall. The sound of wood splintering echoed in the underground silence. He upturned a crate, filled with chains, knives, baseball bats and a few handguns—all instruments of violence. They clattered to the floor.

Then he rounded on Johnny. "It'll never work, Battaglia."

Johnny didn't miss the menacing use of his surname. He started for the door. "I think it will."

As Johnny reached the exit, Zorro called, "They usin' you."

That stopped him. He pivoted to face his old friend. "What do you mean?"

"The cop. And the teacher. They gonna take from you, use you, get what they need, then leave you in the dust."

Johnny shook his head.

"You go now, I won't be here to pick up the pieces."

Summoning every ounce of willpower he had, Johnny turned his back on Zorro. Of anything the other man could have said or done, those words were the hardest to ignore.

So Johnny deliberately called up Meg's innocent face as she gave him a chaste peck on the cheek. He pictured Mitch Lansing reaching out to squeeze his arm. He recalled Cassie hugging him hard after he told her the whole story about his father.

The images helped him keep walking.

"You need me," Zorro shouted from behind him.

Meg...Mitch...Cassie. He had them. No, he didn't need Zorro and the Blisters.

At least, he hoped to God he didn't.

MITCH SAT COMFORTABLY on the thick rug, leaning against a chair. He chuckled as he looked down at his tan corduroy chinos and dark green sweater. Things had really changed in the eight weeks he'd been at Bayview Heights High School. Friday was dress-down day, and though he still couldn't manage the red T-shirt and jeans, he'd compromised, even if it had been tough letting down like this.

But it felt good, too. A lot of things did these days. As he scanned the room, he looked carefully at each student, no longer threatened by the fact that he cared about them. He watched Johnny writing in his journal. Some of them he'd come to care about more than others.

Cassie joined them.

Cassie.

He had to consciously quell his physical reaction to her. It was class time, he told himself. He couldn't afford to remember what her nimble hands had done to his back a week ago, or what her feminine curves had felt like sprawled across him on his couch.

Memories of that night had all but ruined his skiing trip with Kurt. Mitch grinned as he recalled his brother's teasing. *Man, I beat you down the slope four times. Where are you?* For most of the four days, Mitch had been back on that couch with Cassie. Only his commitment to Kurt had kept him from returning early.

As it was, he hadn't been able to see her since he'd gotten back—he'd had an engagement Wednesday with the police department and she'd been busy last night. But they had a date tonight.

The classes, too, had gone easier than he'd expected. The kids were curious during the discussion of the book, but respectful of his feelings and didn't push.

They'd asked how real the book was....

"Other than the lack of swearing, the book is very real. Especially its emphasis on the bugs, the heat and the wetness."

Fascinated, the kids listened intently when he'd told them about the snakes. "There were thirty-two varieties in Nam. Thirty were poisonous, especially the two-steppers."

"Two-steppers?" they'd asked.

"Yeah. If one bit you, you only got to take two steps before you keeled over and died."

"Hey, man," Youngblood had yelled. "Think we can plant one in Bosco's room?"

"Okay, everyone, let's put the journals away and get out *Fallen Angels*."

Mitch picked up the book.

"Today we're going to read a really gruesome part of the story. Anybody who thinks they can't handle it can go into Ms. Caufield's room, skip these few pages and read ahead."

Of course, no one volunteered to leave. Though she was serious about excusing them, her caveat was the best way to keep them glued to their seats.

"Open to page one sixty-eight." They did, and

Cassie began to read aloud. She got through two pages before Mitch started to sweat. This couldn't be...how could anyone know...he breathed in and closed his eyes. He could block out the printed words but not Cassie's voice as she read the account of a child who, when an American soldier had picked him up, had exploded in the man's arms. The boy had been mined by his brainwashed mother.

Bile rose in Mitch's throat. He hadn't realized he'd moaned until he noted the silence. When he opened his eyes, Cassie knelt before him. "Mitch, are you okay?"

He stared at her.

"You look sick. You're sweating badly."

He opened his mouth to speak, but couldn't. Twelve pairs of eyes were on him. He took several shallow breaths to calm himself.

He had to get out of here. Of all the atrocities he'd experience in Nam, this was the worst. What she'd just read aloud...

"Mitch, is it the story? Did..." She hesitated when he covered his face with his hands. "Look," she said to the class, "I'm going to take Captain Lansing out in the hall. You can read by yourselves. Johnny, go get—"

"No." Mitch's sharply uttered word stopped Cassie and any action that had begun in the room. "No!"

"But Mitch, you're obviously upset."

He looked up at her, then at the kids. His vision blurred a bit when it landed on Som. The Vietnamese girl. He'd seen those eyes...those eyes had...

"I..." He stuttered out the words. "I saw this." No one moved.

Finally, Cassie clutched his arm and said, "I'm so sorry."

And then it tumbled out. A story he'd never told anyone, not Kurt, not the counselors...no one.

"I'd been in Nam a year when some new staff was hired at the hooch. They were all South Vietnamese. The government thought it good PR to let the natives we were defending make some money off us." He looked at Som again. "There was a young boy there...he was fourteen. He was quiet, unassuming, like all of them.

"One day, I came back to my bunk and saw him looking at a radio Kurt had sent me. I'd left it on my bed, stupidly, because everything got stolen over there. Anyway, Tam..." Mitch stumbled over the name he hadn't spoken in twenty-seven years. "That was his name, Tam. He was smiling. I'd never seen the kid smile. I thought of Kurt—and me—and the TVs we had in our rooms, the stereos we took for granted. I gave Tam the radio. Slowly, he began to talk to me. He was orphaned, his immediate family wiped out by a raid on his village. He lived with his uncle." Mitch looked around the room, his eyes landing on Johnny. "He was so bright, like you Johnny. And he had the same dream of becoming a doctor. After several months of talking to him, I began to think I could help him. My father was a doctor, Kurt wanted to be a doctor and had the road paved for him. Why couldn't Tam?"

Mitch drew in a deep breath. "I began to make some inquiries about how I could get the boy back to the States. My parents would be able to sponsor him, would be able to help. Apparently, I was overheard—I think it was a phone call I'd made to the embassy. Anyway, it got back to his village—his uncle, we later found out, was anti-American. He hated us, as a lot of Vietnamese civilians did.''

Mitch looked down at the book, feeling his throat closing up. He couldn't finish—yet he had to. Now that he'd started, he had to get it out. ''One beautiful sunny morning, on Tam's day off, I went into the village with the good news. I'd found a way to get Tam home. I decided not to wait until I was discharged, because it looked like the war was ending and I thought I'd have a better chance of getting him out while we were still there. As it turned out, I was right. The U.S. pulled out five months later and no natives were able to get out of Nam for a long time.''

Cassie asked, ''What happened to Tam?''

''They…'' Mitch's vision blurred. ''I'd told him I'd be there in the morning. They knew…they knew what I'd come to tell him. He was standing by a hut. I remember wondering why he seemed so sad. When he looked up and saw me, he started to run in the opposite direction. I didn't know why then. He got about ten feet when…'' Unable to get the words out, Mitch drew in a deep breath. ''He…he blew up…right before my eyes. His little body flew all over in pieces.'' Mitch buried his face in his hands. ''In pieces…'' he heard himself sob out.

He felt Cassie's strong hands on his shoulder, squeezing him. After a long time, he opened his eyes. He saw her eyes brimming with tears. The oddness of that registered somewhere in his muddled brain. Then he looked beyond her. All the kids had gotten up and formed a half circle around him. Not one was dry-eyed. Mitch was the first to speak.

"I haven't been honest with you guys," he said. "I didn't want to work with you because you reminded me of him." His gaze rested on the teary eyes of Som, then on the bright eyes of Johnny. "Especially a few of you."

They stared back.

"And, about me saving those five men. It wasn't bravery. It wasn't heroism. Truthfully, I didn't care if I died."

More aware now, he heard Nikki sobbing. "I'm not saying that to upset you. But it's what happens, Nikki. It's what I was trying to tell you. I went crazy after I saw what they did to Tam. Four soldiers had to hold me down—I was going for my gun, I wanted to shoot whoever had done this to that child. Eventually they had to sedate me. But I found a way to cope with it."

No one asked him how.

He raised his chin. "I shut down. I didn't let anyone in. Unlike your dads, Johnny, Nikki, I was more successful—I could do it most of the time."

"Until you started working with us," Johnny said.

Mitch smiled at Johnny's insight. "Yeah, you guys have a way of breaking down walls." He rubbed the moisture from his cheeks and took in a deep breath. A few of the boys turned away, self-consciously hiding their reaction. Some of the females—including Cassie—were still crying. Huge fat tears were coursing down her cheeks.

Mitch became aware of a commotion in the hall. Class had ended. Cassie noticed it, too, because she stood and went to her desk. She returned with tissues; by then some of the kids had circled closer.

Som leaned over and hugged him. He closed his eyes, willing himself not to cry more. "I'm sorry, Captain," she said before she backed away.

In turns each of the kids made contact—a grave look, a thank you, a squeeze on the arm. Johnny's face was haggard. He came up on his knees and hugged Mitch, too. Over the boy's shoulder, Mitch saw Cassie openly sobbing.

Nikki was the last one. After a meaningful hug, she said, "Thanks, Captain, for telling us this." She drew back and smiled at him. "You got us now, you know, even though you don't have Tam anymore."

Mitch's throat felt tight. He couldn't respond, but squeezed her hand before she left.

The room was mercifully still when the kids were gone. Mitch was dimly aware that this must be one of the days when the tenth-graders went to gym. Drained, he let out a sigh and looked at Cassie on the other side of the room.

Her face tear-stained, she managed to say, "I'm so sorry."

"It's okay. It was a long time ago."

She held up *Fallen Angels*. "This was a bad idea."

He shook his head. "No, I don't think so. I've never told anyone that story. I needed to get it out."

"Maybe."

"And—you know—I didn't even realize until today, that at the time I saved those men, I didn't care whether I lived or died."

Cassie just stared at him. "What can I do?"

He stood and stretched. "Nothing. I'll find a way to cope. Maybe I'll go back to the counselor."

"You're still coming over tonight, aren't you?"

"No. I'll be...worse tonight."

Her eyes filled again. "Please, Mitch, come over tonight."

He shook his head.

Her chin jutted out. "I won't take no for an answer."

Crossing to her, he touched the wetness on her cheek. "I've never seen you cry. How long has it been?"

"More than twenty years."

Gently, he brushed his thumb over her mouth. "I've got to go."

"I'll wait for you tonight, Mitch."

"Don't. I'm not coming."

The last vision he had was of her standing in the middle of her room, her face tilted up, her cheeks wet, saying, "I'll wait."

AT FIVE O'CLOCK that afternoon, Cassie was no longer crying—but she was still upset. She'd raced right home after school, hoping Mitch would come over early. To busy herself, she cooked. She put together homemade chicken soup, baked bread from dough she'd had frozen and made chocolate chip cookies—all food to soothe the soul. When that was done, she built a fire and alternately prowled in front of it or snuggled in an afghan on the couch.

At six-thirty, when the doorbell rang, she flew to it.

Seth Taylor stood on the porch. Behind him a blanket of snow covered her lawn and sidewalk, and big fat flakes filtered down from the sky. "Hi. Can I come in?"

She nodded and struggled to keep her disappointment at bay.

"It's nasty out there," he said, shaking the snow off his boots and shrugging out of his coat. "A real winter storm."

"Oh." Cassie led him into the living room.

"I heard what happened today," he said, when they were settled on the couch. "Are you all right?"

"Who told you?"

"The kids were buzzing about it. And Zoe came to see me after she'd talked to you. She's worried, but she'd already made plans to leave town for the weekend."

Cassie gave him a weak grin. "You're both good friends."

Reaching out, Seth squeezed her arm. "Big news, that Ms. Smith cried. Even when you were a kid, I never once saw the tears."

"It was awful, Seth."

"I bet it was. I know a lot of veterans. Since my lottery number was high, I wasn't drafted. But some of my friends were."

Cassie stared out the ice-encrusted window. "I'm so worried about him. We had a date, but he said he wasn't coming."

Seth angled his head. "A date? I suspected something was going on between you two."

"Why?"

"Let's just say he was very protective of you."

"I wonder where he is."

"Have you tried to reach him?"

She nodded. "I called his house twice. You think I should try again?"

"Yeah."

At her principal's urging, Cassie telephoned Mitch's home. No answer. Next she called the police station. Hal Stonehouse said Mitch had left work about four. He'd seemed unusually quiet today, Hal told her. Was anything wrong?

Finally, she called Kurt. She sipped the coffee Seth had retrieved from the kitchen as she waited for Mitch's brother to come on the line.

"Lansing."

"Kurt, this is Cassie Smith. We've never met, but I'm a friend of your brother's."

"Yes, Cassie. I've...heard your name." There was amusement in his voice, before awareness dawned. "Has something happened to Mitch?"

"No, no, I don't mean to alarm you. I was looking for him...." She stumbled when she started to tell him what had happened in class. Her eyes stung. Somehow she got out a brief version.

"I haven't seen him. But I'll make a few calls and get back to you." He took her number and hung up.

Cassie turned to find Seth donning his coat. "I'm going to drive around town and look for Mitch. I've got a commitment at eight with my son, but I'll call or stop back."

"Thanks. I'd go out, but I think I should stay here in case he changes his mind and shows up."

Smiling, Seth said, "You're not in this alone, Cassie. Neither is he. I'll be in touch."

An hour later, Seth called. He hadn't found Mitch. Promising to call back, he told her everything would be all right.

Cassie sank onto the couch, unable to block out the horror revealed that morning. She took in deep breaths, trying to get a grip. The child blown apart before his eyes...Mitch going wild...his stone-faced reluctance to get involved. No wonder he was so controlled, so in need of rules and regimens.

The bell rang again, startling her out of her ruminations. Again she flew to the door, dragging it open hopefully.

And there he stood. His face was wind-whipped, his eyes wide and wild. He stared at her, his hands stuck in the pockets of his bomber jacket. "I couldn't stay away. I tried. I drove all over, then it got too bad on the roads. I was heading home...." He scanned her house. "I ended up here instead."

Heaving a sigh of relief, she drew him inside and closed the door on the bitter, frigid air. She turned and watched him, thanking God he'd come.

He paced. "I shouldn't have come. I...don't know why I did...." He stopped abruptly and faced her. "I want, I need...something..."

Slowly, Cassie crossed to him; she encircled his neck with her arms and pulled him close. He was cold and tense and, she knew, hurting, so she molded her body to him. "I'll give you whatever you need, Mitch."

Stiffening, he pushed her away. "No, no, don't say that. I..." Then he yanked her back to him and buried his lips in her hair. "I don't know what I'm doing. What I'm saying. I—"

The phone rang. Cassie whispered, "I've got to answer that." She told him about calling Kurt, and how Seth was looking for him. He followed her into the living room while she answered it; Cassie assured Seth that Mitch was all right and thanked him for his help. All the while, Mitch paced in front of the fireplace. She phoned Kurt, too, and told him Mitch was with her. Holding her hand over the mouthpiece, she said, "Do you want to talk to him?"

Mitch shook his head, then said, "I'd better." He took the phone from her. "Yeah, I'm all right.... No, no, you don't have to do that. It's rotten weather, anyway." He turned and studied Cassie. "Yes, I'll stay here." She saw him grip the receiver. "Yeah, I love you, too." He barely got the last words out.

Setting the phone down, he said, "I shouldn't be here."

"You told Kurt you'd stay."

"He's worried."

"A lot of people care about you."

"I shouldn't be here," he repeated.

"Why?"

"I have nothing to give you, Cassie."

"Then let me give to you."

His emotions flared, skidding out of control again. "I won't be satisfied with a back rub tonight."

Her eyes never left his. "All right." Unbuttoning her sweater with steady hands, she crossed to him. By the time she reached him, the front was undone, her lacy bra peeking out.

His eyes riveted on it, then locked on hers. "I don't want a mercy f—."

She pressed two fingers against his lips to preclude the offending comment. "That's the stupidest thing I've ever heard."

He frowned.

"I've wanted this for weeks," she told him, molding her lower body against him. "So have you. We've been dancing around it because we're both wary.'' She reached up and twined her arms around him again. ''I'm sick of the caution.'' She brushed her lips against his. ''Make love to me, Mitch.''

His hands went to her waist. They flexed several times there. They pulled her close. ''If I do...I'm going to want you all night, Cassie.''

She shivered involuntarily, then whispered in his ear, ''I've never been wanted all night before.''

Holding her close, he plunged his hand in her hair. He kissed her deeply, then led her toward the fire.

Snagging the afghan from the couch, he tossed it on the floor. Two big, fat pillows followed it. Kicking off his shoes, he stepped onto the afghan and pulled her with him. The firelight flickered on his face, softening the harsh planes of his jaw. Reaching up, she ran her palm over it. It was sandpapery.

''My beard's rough. I'll hurt you.''

''You can't hurt me that easily.''

His eyes on hers, he smoothed his hands down her arms, then rubbed his knuckles up and down in the opening of the sweater. They scraped the skin of her stomach and chest.

''So soft, yet so tough. You are a study in contradictions.''

Her hands gripped his shoulders, and she closed her eyes to savor his touch and his words. Dizzying currents of pleasure shot through her at the simple caress. ''I love it when you touch me.''

His hand clenched on her waist. ''Cass, don't say that kind of thing. I'm trying to control myself.''

On her tiptoes, she breathed into his ear, ''I want your uncensored response.''

He held her even tighter. "You don't. I can be an animal."

"I don't care. All of it makes you the special man you are. I want all of you, Mitch."

His arms banded around her with stunning force. He dragged the sweater off her shoulders. Drawing back, looking down at the black, demi-cup bra she wore, he said, "Oh, God."

She looked down too. His big hands closing over her breasts made her breath catch in her throat.

"Hurt?"

"No. It feels wonderful."

Slowly, she inched her hand down to his waist. His breath hitched. "These chinos look so sexy on you." She pressed her palm against his fly. "I want to feel you, see you. I want you inside me."

Suddenly, he closed his eyes. "Oh, damn. I don't have anything with me. Any protection."

She chuckled. "Forty-six-year-old men don't carry rubbers in their wallets or their glove compartments?"

"Not this forty-six-year-old man," he said against her hair. She could smell the outdoors mixed with his clean male scent. "There are other ways, of course, but I wanted..." His hand stroking up and down her back almost robbed her of thought.

"It's okay," she finally said. She slipped out of his arms, darted across the room, down the hall, into the bathroom. She returned with a box of condoms.

He scowled. "I'm not sure I like your having these on hand."

She chuckled again. "Zoe bought them for me."

"Zoe?"

"She teaches a health class to the At-Risk kids.

She's vigilant about taking precautions—she watches over me." Feeling suddenly shy, she dropped the box onto the floor and burrowed back into his arms. "I haven't used that many, Mitch. I haven't needed them."

His heartbeat picked up speed. "I haven't needed many, either. And I'm sorry about jumping to conclusions. I'm feeling so raw right now, I'm not thinking straight."

"If it helps, I'm feeling pretty raw myself."

He planted a wet kiss on her shoulder. "It helps."

He fondled her backside through her jeans, then gripped her tightly. Tension came into his body— but it was tension of another kind. "No more talk," he said, caressing her. He slid his hands around and pulled hard at the snap on her jeans. As he brushed them down her legs, he bent on one knee, disposing of her jeans and her socks. He stayed down and buried his face in her stomach, just above the lacy top of her panties. He outlined their black band with little kisses. When he finished, he pulled the panties off with more haste. Giving her bare middle one last kiss, he stood and fumbled with her bra, his hands unsteady. She laid her face against his chest. His heart thrummed. Reaching down, she pulled at the hem of his sweater and drew it over his head. Her own heartbeat quickening, she yanked at the buttons on his shirt. He helped her with shaky hands. She licked the hair-roughened skin of his chest, his nipples, ran her palms—somewhat frantically—all over him. His breathing became very fast. When she slid her fingertips inside the waistband of his pants, his body jolted forward.

"Take them off," he said harshly.

Cassie smiled against his chest and caressed his buttocks.

He drew back. Blazing eyes watched her as he tore at the snap and kicked off his socks, pants and underwear. He pulled her close before she got to look her fill, then dragged her down to the floor and covered her body with his. "I won't be able to wait long," he said in between kisses on her neck and shoulder. His mouth moved down to cover an aching nipple. Cassie sucked in her breath and arched into him. He slid his hand between their bodies, tangling his fingers in her wet curls. "Mmm, Cass..."

"I don't want to wait, either."

He fumbled on the blanket, drawing back to rip open a packet and roll on the condom. Then he covered her again and reclaimed her mouth. "You feel so good...too good."

"Mitch..." He suckled her again, placed his hand between her thighs and palmed her. "Mitch..."

"Wrap your legs around me."

Blindly, she did as he instructed.

He positioned himself and tried to ease into her. Her hips bucked and his restraint broke. His thrust was hard and strong and forceful.

"Oh...Cass...you feel so...oh, God."

"Mitch."

He stroked her, grazed her all over inside, then thrust mindlessly, recklessly. It started fast for her and was upon her in an instant. Lights burst beneath her closed lids. Every muscle strained toward him, her heart hammering in her chest. She came up slightly off the floor and clutched his shoulders, digging her nails into him. "Oh...oh..." She moaned, groaned into his skin. Then she was flooded with sensation and pleasure and feeling that increased and burst, then increased again and finally exploded. She couldn't breathe in enough air as she cried out his name, over and over and over.

Cassie's explosion snapped the last vestige of Mitch's control. She was so tight and wet. He wanted to prolong the sensation, but he felt himself going over, and he couldn't stop it. Rockets went off in his head, and his body quivered as she spasmed around him. All sensation focused on that one spot where their bodies joined. He felt himself grow harder, bigger, and he pushed and pushed and pushed until he was so deep inside her he couldn't stand it. Then everything went black, except for the burst of lightninglike pleasure that shot to every part of his body at once. He was electrified by her, heedlessly seeking the currents that jolted between them.

Unable to stop himself, he collapsed on her. He knew he outweighed her by more than fifty pounds, but an earthquake couldn't have made him move at that point. Slowly, he became aware of several things about her: her breathing was ragged, her body slick against his. Eventually, when he finally could, he raised himself up on his elbows. Her eyes were closed, her hair wet around her face, which was sheened with sweat. He watched her chest heave. And for one primitive moment, he was overcome with pure masculine power: that he had destroyed this strong, vibrant woman's control, that he had shattered every defense she had. He couldn't remember all of it, but he did know she'd come apart completely and splintered around him.

Then the tenderness came, at odds with the sense of victory he'd felt. With stunning intensity, he wanted to protect her forever, keep all harm from her, shield her from any hurt. The juxtaposition of the two equally potent feelings made his head spin.

He felt her hands in his hair. "Mitch." Her voice was hoarse.

It took courage to look into her eyes. They were shining with unabashed surrender. "I...I never felt like that before. It's such a cliché, but I never realized how I'd held back...in everything," she told him.

"Not with me," he said harshly, feeling displeasure at the implication that any other man had had her.

"No, not with you." She swallowed hard. "It's...scary."

Did she realize what she was doing...what power she was giving him over her? Where had all her armor gone? He wanted to warn her not to give him so much, and at the same time he wanted to get down on his knees and thank her for it. He smiled grimly at the paradox.

"Why are you smiling?"

"Because I feel so gentle and tender toward you one minute, then I want ravish you the next." He

scowled. "I feel more comfortable with the ravish-
ing part."

"I know what you mean. Me, too."

He kissed her nose. "We're a pair."

"Yes, we are."

Easing off her, he rolled to his side and tugged
her close, snapping up half of the quilt to cover
them.

"Want to sleep?" she asked, nestling into his
chest.

"No, just stay close for a minute."

She did. Then she said, "Want to talk?"

"Absolutely not."

"How about eating?"

"Yeah, I am hungry."

"I've got food all ready."

He tightened his grip on her. "Thanks, Cass. For
being here. For luring me here. For this. I
feel...better."

She kissed his breastbone. "*I* feel wonderful."

They snuggled for a few minutes, then untangled
themselves from each other and stood. Cassie bent
down and picked up the green plaid shirt he'd had
on underneath the sweater. She put it on and he felt
his heart constrict. There was something about her,
standing there in the firelight—her hair mussed from
his hands, her mouth swollen from his lips, wearing
his shirt—that elevated the moment from one of raw
passion to one of deep intimacy. He stared at her.

Unaware of what he was feeling, she chatted.
"I'll get the soup reheated. You might want to..."
She looked up. "What?"

He grabbed her and crushed her to his naked body. "I want to stay tonight...all night."

Against his chest, she said, "I want you to."

When the storm of feeling passed, he drew back. "Is there something I can do with my car? I wouldn't want the neighborhood or the kids to see it here in the morning."

She reached up and smoothed her hand down his face with heart-rending tenderness. "Thanks for thinking of that. This is a small town. You can put it in the garage."

Mitch's car stayed in Cassie's garage until Monday morning.

CHAPTER TWELVE

"I DON'T LIKE SURPRISES, Cassie." Mitch sat across from Cassie, sipping coffee in the teacher's lounge on his last morning at the high school.

Innocent gray-blue eyes peered up at him over her own mug. In the week since they'd first made love, he'd seen that look several times. It meant trouble. "All right," she said. "I'll remember that."

"What's going on? You met me at the door and ushered me down here before I could even take my coat off." He glanced at his watch. "We were supposed to be in class fifteen minutes ago."

"I told you. The guidance counselors are with the kids talking about the Scholastic Aptitude Test results for college entrance."

"On my last day? How convenient."

"What do you think is going on?"

He wanted to kiss that smug look off her face. "I'm afraid the kids have planned something to say goodbye to me."

"Would that be so bad?"

"Yes. I..." He stopped as his heart gave the funny little lurch that it did every time he realized he wouldn't see the dirty dozen every day. "I'm going to miss them."

"You've been a wonderful influence on them, Mitch. They'll miss you, too." She reached over for his hand and gave it a brief squeeze. "*I'll* miss seeing you every day."

He arched an insolent brow. "You don't plan to see me every day? I got the definite impression last weekend, and almost every night this week, that you liked seeing...*a lot* of me."

Cassie's eyes turned smoky. "Oh, I like seeing a lot of you, all right."

Her husky retort reminded him of intimacies they'd shared—slow, sensuous massages, the way her nails felt digging into his back, waking up with her wrapped around him. He shifted uncomfortably in his seat. "Good. Because you're gonna see me, sweetheart."

She nodded toward his suit. "Decided to go out like you came in?"

Instead of laughing at her joke, he said somberly, "I want you to know I'll never be the same as I was before I stepped into your classroom, Cassie."

She asked, "Are you glad?"

"Very." The kids had taught him as much as he'd taught them. They'd also come to mean a lot to him. *Too much.*

The woman sitting across from him meant too much, too. And Mitch had never been happier in his life. Cassie had brought him complete sexual fulfillment. Even more important, they grew closer every day—emotionally and, hell, even spiritually. He frowned, wondering what he'd do if he had to let her go.

"What is it?"

"Nothing."

She looked skeptical but glanced at the clock. "Well, we should get back."

"Oh, *guidance* gave you a time frame."

"Yep. Come on, let's go."

As they walked through the corridor, Mitch marveled at how much at home he was at Bayview Heights High School. He thought about the fear he'd experienced the first time he entered this building. As teachers and staff stopped him to say goodbye and tell him what a good job he'd done, he felt a warmth and sense of belonging. The only comparable relationships he'd had were in Nam with his buddies. Four weeks ago he wouldn't have let himself make that comparison.

At the door to the classroom, which was closed for a change, Cassie insisted he go in first. He took a deep breath and opened the door.

"Surprise!"

As he expected, the kids had planned a party. He donned his best stern-cop look and said, "Aren't parties against school rules?"

"Not if Mr. T. okays them." The remark came from Johnny, who stood in the front of the eleven kids lined up around a table.

"He okayed this?"

"Yes, I did." Mitch hadn't seen Seth in the back of the room.

Mitch faced Cassie. "You knew about this?"

"Of course."

"I'll remember that, Ms. Smith." His eyes promised retribution.

He saw Cassie bite her lip and try to keep from blushing.

Nikki Parelli crossed to Mitch and took his hand. He remembered when he first came here how touching a student had bothered him. Today, it was natural to clasp her hand in his. "Come look at the cake," the young girl said.

On the table was a sheet cake big enough to feed an army. In its center was his profile, outlined in black frosting. In one corner was a picture of the book *Fallen Angels*. In another, a badge with BVHPD emblazoned on it, and in the bottom left corner, an outline of the school. To the left of his profile was a quote that read, "To teach is to touch lives." Then the kids had added, "You've touched ours." To the right, they'd written, "Cop of the Year."

Moved by the sentiment, Mitch had to struggle for composure. "This is a work of art. Where did you get it?"

Peterson said, "Amy made it."

Mitch turned to the shy teenage mother. "It's beautiful, Amy. You have a lot of talent."

Amy reddened, but said in a timid voice, "Ms. Smith got the home and careers teacher to help me, but I did most of it myself."

"Thanks. I appreciate the effort."

"I made the punch," Youngblood said.

"Yeah, and he didn't even try and spike it," Arga teased.

Again Mitch assumed the mock-stern look. "He'd better not."

The kids decided to have cake and punch right away. They all crowded around Mitch and chattered at once.

After ten minutes, Seth got him alone and reached out to shake his hand. "Before I leave for a meeting, I want to thank you for all you've done here, Mitch.

I can't express how pleased I am that it worked out."

"You're welcome."

"And," Seth said to Cassie as she joined them, "I'd like to hear Ms. Smith say it."

"Say what?" Cassie asked.

"That I was right about this facet of the Resiliency Program. Come on, let's hear it."

Cassie rolled her eyes. Today she wore jeans and the school T-shirt over a turtleneck sweater; her hair was pulled off her face with a headband. Her outfit and the gesture made her look like one of the kids. "All right, all right. I guess it worked out."

"Say the words, Cassie," Seth demanded. *"Mr. Taylor was right."*

"Mr. Taylor was right."

"Ah, that sounds so good." He turned to Mitch. "I understand I'll see you at the Winter Ball tonight."

Mitch rolled his eyes this time. "Cassie coerced us all into going. Something about class camaraderie and bonding."

"Not all of us will be there," Cassie told him after Seth left. "Joe DeFazio can't attend because he hasn't been in school for a week. And Mike isn't coming, either."

"Youngblood? Why?"

"I don't know."

Mitch scowled. "I'll talk to him before I leave."

"Time for presents," Arga yelled. "Everybody find a seat."

Mitch took a beanbag chair, while most of the kids dropped to the floor around him. Cassie perched on a desk behind the group. When he threw her a questioning look, she shrugged, indicating she didn't know about the presents.

"This one was *my* idea," Jones said as he gave Mitch a long, thin box and watched him unwrap it. Inside was a tasteful paisley tie. "It's to go with those cool suits," Jones told him.

Mitch held it up to his neck, as if to model it, and Jen Diaz snapped his picture.

"Mine's next." Nikki held out a rectangular package. Mitch shook it next to his ear, pretending to guess what it was. Inside, he found a cloth-bound journal. "It's from all of us. We thought you might want to keep writing after you left."

"Yeah, and you won't have to worry about sharing it with anyone," Tara teased.

"Watch it, guys," Cassie warned, but she was smiling broadly when she said it.

Mitch smiled, too. "I'd like to keep writing."

"Open it," Nikki told him.

In the front of the book, Mitch found all the kids' signatures.

"So you won't forget us," Tara said.

Mitch felt his throat close up. "I won't forget you."

"I picked this one out," Arga said, defusing the charged moment.

Mitch unwrapped an extra-extra large red T-shirt like the ones most of the kids wore today. He laughed heartily, stood and shrugged off his suit jacket. He tugged on the shirt and Jen took another picture of him and Arga, arm and arm.

When Mitch sat back down, Som said, "Go on, Johnny."

Mitch noticed Johnny Battaglia held the last gift.

He clutched a square, neatly wrapped package a little too tightly. When Johnny handed it to him, the boy said, "This was my idea." Mitch heard Johnny's silent *I take responsibility for it.*

Ready to joke, Mitch looked up into Johnny's face. Usually filled with cocky self-assurance, his expression was...uneasy.

"Nah, we all agreed," Brenda told him. "We wanted to do this, too."

The hair on the back of Mitch's neck prickled. He glanced over at Cassie. She must have caught the kids' seriousness, because she shook her head, telling him she didn't know what gift they'd chosen.

Mitch tore the paper off and found a plush velvet box—the kind jewelry came in. Slowly, he raised the lid.

His heart skidded to a halt. He closed his eyes briefly, struggling for control. He knew the kids would be hanging on to his reaction.

Inside the box was a Purple Heart and a Silver Star. He swallowed hard as he studied them. He traced the gold rim of the heart and its purple interior with a fingertip, then touched the gold of George Washington's profile mounted in the center. He brushed a thumb over the faded purple-and-white ribbon attached to it. His gaze zeroed in on the star. The outer gold part was a little tarnished, but the inner silver star sparkled off the lights above. Its red, white and blue ribbon had faded, too.

Mitch looked up at the kids. They seemed to be holding their collective breath.

His eyes locked on Johnny. "Where...?"

"Your brother had them. That day when you

made him throw them in the garbage, he fished them out after you left.''

''I never knew.''

''He said he hoped some day you'd heal enough to want them.''

''How did he know you knew about them?'' Mitch asked Johnny.

''I brought it up.''

''I see.''

''Turn it over,'' Johnny said hoarsely.

Mitch did. On the back of the star, it read, ''Sergeant Mitchell Lansing. 1973.'' He pondered the inscription for a moment then cleared his throat. ''This wasn't engraved.''

''I know,'' Johnny confessed. ''I had it done.''

Still on the edge of control, Mitch stared at the reminders of the war...the personal, painful reminders.

Nikki stepped forward next to Johnny. She knelt down in front of Mitch and touched his hand. ''Captain Lansing?''

Mitch raised his eyes to hers.

''Tam would have wanted you to have these. To be proud of these.''

Mitch felt his eyes sting but managed to maintain control. ''You think so, Nikki?''

''I know so, Captain.''

''Well, okay then. I'll keep them.''

''And be proud of them,'' Johnny said.

Mitch looked at Johnny again. ''And be proud of them,'' Mitch repeated.

CASSIE SCANNED the party house where the Bayview Heights High School Winter Ball was held annually and smiled with satisfaction. It had been one of her goals to get the At-Risk kids to attend this year, making them feel more a part of the regular school community. Nine out of twelve had shown up. Of course, DeFazio hadn't come; he'd been in and out of school for the last three weeks and his parents had provided lame excuses about his absences. Seth had scheduled a support services meeting next week to discuss DeFazio's problem.

Amy Anderson was missing, too. She'd called just before Cassie had left to say her baby was sick and she couldn't leave him. She'd sounded sad, and Cassie's heart ached for the young mother. But it was Mike Youngblood's absence that bothered Cassie the most. When she'd asked him why he wasn't coming, he'd shuffled his feet as if he was embarrassed and would only say he didn't want to. Deep down, Cassie suspected he didn't have the appropriate clothing, but when she'd broached the subject, he'd been evasive. Most of the kids had scraped together some kind of jacket and tie or dress, but she thought Youngblood probably couldn't find anything at the group home.

"What's the frown for, Teach?"

Cassie turned to find Johnny—dressed in an immaculate dark suit and white shirt that set off his coloring—with a beautiful young girl on his arm.

"Hi," Cassie said, reaching out to touch his arm. Then she addressed his date. "I'm Cassie Smith."

"Hi, I'm—"

Johnny cut her off with a grin and the words "Mary Margaret Mancini."

The girl shook her head. "I'm Meg. For some

reason, Johnny prefers my whole embarrassing name.''

''It's a pretty name,'' Cassie said. ''Nice to meet you.''

''I love your dress,'' Meg said.

''Thanks.'' Cassie looked down at her new purchase. It had been fun splurging on the peacock blue silk party dress. With cap sleeves, a narrow waist and just-above-the-knee length, it was modest enough to wear to a school event, yet sexy enough to make Mitch notice—if he ever got here.

''Where's the captain?'' Johnny asked with a knowing look. Sometimes that kid seemed to read her mind.

''He said he'd meet us here at nine.''

''Hello.'' She heard Mitch's voice from behind. Just the sound of it made her knees weak.

Cassie turned to find Mitch, dressed in a charcoal gray pin-striped suit that accented his linebacker's shoulders. With it he wore the tie the kids had given him today. Cassie was about to comment on the tie when Mike Youngblood stepped out from behind Mitch.

Wearing a three-piece navy blue suit, a light blue shirt and a tasteful striped tie, Youngblood grinned broadly at her. Even his shoes were spit-shined. The entire outfit was brand new.

Austyn Jones had joined them and whistled when he saw Mike. ''Hey, Youngblood. Where'd ya get those duds?''

''Down at the Hub.''

''Man, how you afford that store?''

Mitch said smoothly, ''I made him a loan. He's

working it off by painting the inside of my town house on weekends.''

Cassie's heart swelled when she realized what had happened. *I'll talk to Youngblood before I leave,* Mitch had said today.

"You look great, Mike," Cassie said, and gave Mitch a sideways glance.

The music switched abruptly to an old Beatles tune, and several of the kids—including Johnny and Meg—hit the dance floor. The rest went in search of punch, leaving Mitch and Cassie alone.

Cassie stared at Mitch knowingly, until he said, "What?"

"Thanks. For what you did for Mike."

Mitch stuck his hands in his pockets and watched the dancers. "I didn't do anything. I told you he's working it off."

"Oh, sure. Painting the brand new walls in your town house."

"Builders use cheap paint. Besides, I'm thinking of doing my bedroom over and thought a couple of black walls might be an interesting change."

Cassie laughed.

"You can give me your opinion later, when you see it."

Then he leaned over and whispered, "You're gonna pay, lady, for wearing that dress."

Her breath hitched at his husky innuendo. "Why, whatever do you mean?"

"It hugs that cute little behind of yours, Cassandra, and you know it." He gave her a searing look. "I can't wait to get my hands on you."

"You'll have to," she said, laughing. "But I'll

make it worth the wait. After all, I never renege on my bribes."

They both chuckled at how she'd gotten him to attend the dance—by agreeing to spend the rest of the weekend at his house.

Some payment, she thought.

They watched the kids for a minute in contented silence.

"Johnny's great out there," Mitch said.

"Yes, I didn't know he could dance like that."

"A skill all hunks should develop."

"Oh, yeah?" Cassie gave him a sexy up-and-down perusal. "I don't see you out there."

Despite the fact that they were in a crowded party house, in front of hundreds of students, Mitch slid his arm around her shoulders and briefly hugged her. "Trying to turn my head with compliments?"

"Maybe."

"You'd better stop flirting with me. That dress and that sparkle in your eyes is enough. Don't stretch my control by turning on the charm, too."

"Okay, I'll just resort to being my old, prickly self."

Again, he laughed. It was then that Cassie realized how unfamiliar his response was—she hadn't heard him laugh this much since she met him.

They socialized with the kids and several staff members for the next half hour.

Then Tara Romig approached them. Dance star that she was, she'd been spinning around the floor since Cassie had arrived. The DJ had just begun "Rock-Around-the-Clock." Tara said breathlessly, "Can you guys jitterbug?"

All the kids joked and made wisecracks. When no

one would dance with her, she shook her head. "What's the matter with you?"

Mitch stepped forward. "They're all young punks, Tara. Let's show them how it's done."

Tara's eyes lit up like twinkling stars. "Really, Captain?"

"Really, Ms. Romig." He held out his hand.

Tara took it and they made their way to the dance floor.

Cassie's mouth fell open as she watched Mitch fall into step with the trained dancer. It was incredible.

His feet moved fast and smoothly. He pulled Tara to him with both hands, then spun her around. As soon as she was sure of his rhythm, she went with him, giving an extra spin, sliding along his arm. Once, he dipped her. She gave herself to it then, reversing her hands so Mitch could spin. He did, then grabbed her around the waist and let her do a complicated turn.

Cassie was so enthralled, she didn't see the kids on the floor moving until they had circled Mitch and Tara. Her own students sidled in so they could see, and Cassie followed suit. For another few minutes, Mitch and Tara tore up the floor. Mitch's cheeks were flushed but his eyes were shining with pleasure.

When the song ended, the kids whistled and clapped. The DJ immediately played another jitterbug tune. Tara and Mitch danced again.

Seth came up to Cassie in the midst of it. "He's a man of many talents."

Unable to tear her eyes away, Cassie nodded and said, "He is."

Seth chuckled, but it turned into a frown when macarena music came on. "Oh, no."

"What?" Cassie asked.

"I told the student government if they got more than eighty per cent of the student body to attend, I'd let them teach me the macarena."

Cassie giggled. "This I've got to see."

The president of the student government made the announcement that Mr. Taylor was going to dance, and asked everyone to join them. Lines formed as Cassie stepped back.

"Oh, no, you don't," Mitch said, coming forward and grabbing her hand. "Get out here."

Cassie retreated farther. "No, no, Mitch, I..."

He was dragging her toward the floor. "Mitch, really." She grabbed his arm. "Mitch!" He stopped. "I can't dance."

"What?"

"I said, I can't dance. It's one of those social things I never learned."

He said, "You mean, my little volleyball jock can't master a few steps?"

She angled her chin.

"My tough cookie who walked the streets of the Village alone is afraid of a little line dancing?"

Her eyes flared. "Oh, shut up. All right, I'll try."

Cassie reached the floor, gripping Mitch's hand. Seth had pretty much mastered the few steps, and Tara took over with Cassie. Mitch, of course, fell right into line, effecting each turn, arm movement and shimmy of his body easily and fluidly.

Damn it, Cassie wasn't giving up.

A long ten minutes later, Mitch pulled her close

when an old Elvis Presley tune came on. "Think you can handle this one?" he teased.

She glided into his arms but tried to keep a respectable distance. "I think I can."

"You did pretty good out there," he said, his breath close to her ear.

"I managed." She looked up at him. He looked younger, more animated than she'd ever seen him. "Where'd you learn to dance like that?"

"In Nam. Some of the guys in my squad said it was pitiful how white guys couldn't dance. They taught us all their moves. Then a couple of the officers decided we all needed to learn the old stuff."

She grinned. "It's sexy."

"Sexy, huh?" He ran his hand down her back, stopping at her waist. "You wanna see sexy, I'll show you sexy...later."

Cassie settled into him and looked around the room. Johnny was glued to Meg, and they were barely moving. Jones was dancing with Tara, and several others had paired up. A few of her students stood on the sidelines, but they were smiling and joking with one another.

Cassie felt a deep and abiding contentment as she rested her head on Mitch's chest and heard his heart thud reassuringly beneath her ear.

NO ONE INSIDE saw the shadowed figure step back away from the window into the snow.

No one inside heard him turn to his companion and say, "Yeah, he's here. They're all here."

MITCH'S MASTER BEDROOM didn't need painting. Huge, furnished in smooth, cool teak, it sported a king-size bed, built-in closets and a glossy wall unit holding books, a television, a VCR and stereo. Recessed lighting gave the room a soft, sensual glow.

Donned in clingy teal silk pajamas, Cassie stepped out of the bathroom onto the plush, off-white carpeting. Mitch was sprawled on top of the bed, his hands linked behind his head. He'd undressed and the dark green top sheet was flipped over his lap. Matching pillows behind his head made his eyes forest green. She was drawn toward him. When she got to the bed, he reached for her. Slowly, she straddled him. Provocatively, she bent over and kissed his naked chest.

"Payback time?" she murmured into his skin.

He slid his hands inside the waistband of her pajamas and cupped her bottom. "No more teasing, love," he told her. "I want you now...."

But there were words after, as they cuddled under the heavy down comforter. Apparently, the earlier, easy camaraderie and then the closeness of sex had made him want to confide in her. About Vietnam.

"I was so disillusioned when I got there," he told her hoarsely. "They faked body counts to make it look like we were winning. And too many U.S. fatalities were friendly fire."

Lying on her side, Cassie crooked her arm, rested her head on her hand and combed the hair off his forehead. "That's horrible."

"It was an atrocity."

She kissed his cheek. "I'm sorry you had to go through it."

His eyes hazy with hurt, he pulled her close and said, "Me, too." They cuddled in spoonlike fashion, and there were no nightmares for Mitch as he held on to her as they slept.

On Saturday afternoon, they lazed by the fire as light, fluffy snow drifted by the window. Mitch was distracting Cassie by tracing a tiny line of freckles from her shoulder to her chest, unbuttoning her sweater along the way. Her skin warmed beneath his fingers.

Gazing at him, she asked, "I know you never married. But you never wanted any kids?"

Mitch felt himself closing down—but her eyes stopped the reflexive action. There was so much trust in them.

"I was too young to think about it before I went to Nam. Then after what I saw, what I did, I could never let anyone close enough. And I didn't want to bring a child into this world."

"I used to feel that way, too," she said, running her palms down his back. "But then I decided I could protect her, and help her in ways I never got helped."

"Her, huh?"

"Yeah. Wouldn't you like your own little bundle of sugar and spice to take care of?"

Mitch hadn't thought he would, but right then, gazing down into Cassie's expressive face, he wanted things he'd never even considered before.

She'd planned to leave Sunday afternoon, but he enticed her into showering with him. They'd soaped most of his body and half of hers when he braced her against the tile wall and took her. He felt full and firm and totally male against her, inside her. Cassie gasped for breath as the water turned cold on her fiery skin....

She wanted to snuggle afterward in bed.

Mitch held her close and kissed her hair. "You said there were things you'd never told anyone before."

"Yes."

"Tell me one."

She shook her head, burying her face in his chest.

"Tell me."

Cassie drew in a deep breath. Dark secrets were meant to be hidden.

"Just one," he pleaded.

She finally said, "One of my mother's boyfriends seduced me when I was sixteen. He was a cop."

Mitch uttered a crude expletive. After a moment, he told her, "That helps to explain your prejudice against the police."

"Uh-huh. But it wasn't all his fault. I was willing. I'd been with boys before." She sighed heavily. "When all the AIDS information came out, I got tested because of what I'd done. I was lucky to get a clean bill of health. I've been ashamed of all of it for a long time."

"You were a kid, Cass."

"Yeah. A really mixed-up kid."

He pulled her closer, entangling his legs with hers. "It's why you've been careful in your adult life, isn't it?"

"Yes. I respect myself more."

"I respect you, too."

Mitch kissed her goodbye at eight o'clock that night, telling her to drive carefully and call him when she got home. Happier than she'd ever been, she left him standing barefoot and sexily mussed in his doorway.

CHAPTER THIRTEEN

LATE THE NEXT DAY, Cassie's throat felt as if someone had stuffed a sock in it. Steeling herself as best she could, she surveyed her living room, focusing on the shambles in the middle of the floor. From behind her, Mitch rested his hand on her shoulder and squeezed it.

"I'm so sorry, love," he said.

Biting her lip, Cassie breathed in deeply and swallowed hard. These were only material things, she told herself. All her life she'd resisted getting attached to "things." Oh, she liked pretty clothes, comfortable furniture, a new car. But ultimately, she'd never let them matter too much to her. So this was okay, she repeated silently, she could handle it.

"Is it all right to touch them now?" she asked Mitch.

"Yes," he told her, his voice strained. "We secured the whole area last night. The forensic team was here early this morning and got whatever prints there were. They took pictures, too."

Cassie sank to her knees. Gingerly, she reached to the top of the pile. Her chest tightened.

"What is it?" Mitch asked, squatting down next to her.

"A yearbook." She stared at it before tossing it aside, then waded through more of the heap.

"They're all here. All my yearbooks. For every year I taught. Every single one is either torn apart or covered with the paint." Her voice caught on the last words.

"Honey, maybe you should let me and some of the guys clean this up."

"No." The word was sharper than she intended. She reached for his hand and squeezed it in apology. "I told you last night I wanted to do it. Something may be salvageable."

"I don't think so, Cass."

"I want to see for myself."

"All right." Mitch stood. "I'll be back here." He indicated the rear of the room. "I want to make sure that window is secured."

Cassie nodded. Turning back to the pile, she sifted through it methodically. Carefully, she examined each of the yearbooks, remembering the kids she'd taught, trying to visualize the faces of all those whose lives she'd touched and who had influenced her. Now their images were covered with red spray paint. She tossed them all into the bins Mitch had provided, cringing at the irrevocable loss.

Underneath the yearbooks was her collection of classic novels and plays. Over the years, she'd found leather-bound editions in the city, out-of-print copies in rare books stores, a few first editions in out-of-the-way places. She smiled as she picked up a copy of *Romeo and Juliet.* She'd gone without new clothes for months so she could afford it. Now pages were ripped out, and globs of red paint stuck the rest of them together. Its dark leather binding had been slashed.

Her poetry collection had met a similar fate.

Mitch came back and knelt down next to her. She looked up, shaking her head, holding one of the mutilated volumes. "Seth gave me the set when I graduated from Geneseo. He and his wife came up for the ceremony. My mother was dead by then. He brought these all wrapped up in pink-and-silver paper. There were twenty volumes." She dropped the book she held and picked another one up, battling back the tears when she recognized the title. "Did you know e.e. cummings is my favorite poet?"

Mitch reached out and ran his knuckles down her cheek. "Now, why doesn't that surprise me?"

"You've read him?"

Mitch nodded. "Yeah. He's a little too avant garde for my taste, but I managed to understand a verse or two."

Cassie smiled, but when the doorbell rang, she startled.

Gently, Mitch soothed his hand down her back. "Shh. It's okay. It's three o'clock. The security guy from Strong's said he'd be here midafternoon."

"Mitch, I don't..."

She didn't finish because Mitch's face darkened. Cassie watched him once again tamp down the rage that had almost erupted last night when she'd driven back to his condo to tell him what she'd found when she'd gotten home: someone had smashed in a first-floor window and broken into her house. Throughout this whole ordeal, he'd kept a rein on his temper, and she appreciated his squelching his own feelings to help her get through it.

Now he took a stand. "Don't say it, Cassie. You need a security system, period. I won't back down on this." He stood and crossed to the foyer.

Two months ago Cassie couldn't have imagined letting anyone impose his will on her like this. But she'd acquiesced on everything. Last night, he'd demanded that she stay with him until her place had been taken care of. This morning, he'd insisted on getting the house wired. Cassie had let him take over. She didn't want to admit to herself what it meant about her feelings for him that she'd allowed him to make these decisions for her.

He opened the front door. From her vantage point on the floor, Cassie could see the security expert greet Mitch. But before the man came in, Johnny materialized in the archway.

Mitch let them both in. As the security man set his gear down, Mitch drew Johnny aside, spoke briefly to him, then went back to discuss the alarm system.

Johnny approached her. "Cassie?"

She looked up at him, suppressing what she felt. "Hi."

Just like Mitch, he reached down and squeezed her shoulder. "This is awful."

"How did you find out?"

"Ms. Caufield told me. But it's all over school. The Connors," he said, referring to her next door neighbors, "saw the police cars last night and their son Jimmy got a peek at the inside of the house before he came to school."

"Well, it was bound to get out."

"I hope it's okay I came. I want to help."

Cassie looked back down at the remains of what had been her only good memories of the past. "I'm glad you came. I was going to do it all myself. I thought I could salvage some things. But it's all destroyed. I..." She looked at Johnny and her voice trailed off.

He'd knelt down and picked up a ruined book. A glob of red paint caked on his fingers.

"Be careful," she said, falling easily into the teacher role. "You'll get messy."

Before Johnny could respond, Mitch joined them. "The security guy is going through the house now."

Cassie watched Johnny. The boy was frozen, staring at the red paint, slowly rubbing his fingers it. Without a word, he looked up at Mitch.

Mitch said, "You want to tell her, or should I?"

Soberly, Johnny said, "I will." He faced Cassie. "I...I'm sorry, Cassie. The Blisters..." He glanced back down at the red paint again. "This is their trademark."

SOMETHING HARD SLAPPED across Johnny's mouth. His eyes flew open. It was dark in his bedroom, but he could see a figure looming over him. He felt something cold and sharp against his neck. Every one of his muscles constricted. He could be dead in an instant.

"It's me."

Johnny's body sagged with relief.

After a moment, he shook his head, trying to dislodge Zorro's hand. Zorro dropped his right arm from Johnny's mouth, but kept the knife strategically positioned at Johnny's jugular.

"What do you want?" Johnny asked.

"We gotta talk, home boy."

Home boy? So Zorro hadn't given up on him yet.

"Why the blade?"

"So you'll listen."

Then it came flooding back. Cassie's sad eyes and drawn features as she threw her most precious belongings in the garbage.

Heedless of the danger, Johnny spat out, "You bastard."

"I didn't do it."

"Yeah, sure. Red paint is the Blisters's trademark."

"I didn't do it," he repeated. "It's one of the reasons I'm here." Slowly, Zorro pulled back his stiletto. Flipping it in, he reached down and stuck it in his boot. Then he pulled up a chair and switched on a light on the bedside table.

Johnny leaned back against the pillows. "Tell me you know nothin' about it."

"I know somethin'," Zorro said. "Doesn't mean I had anything to do with it."

"You hate her."

"She's a bitch."

Johnny stiffened.

"Ease up, man," Zorro said with a shrug. "DeFazio jumped in today."

Johnny expelled a heavy breath. "He's a jerk. Why you want him?"

"Gotta keep up our numbers, Tonto. Besides," Zorro said, his eyes slitting with anger, "I need a new sidekick, now that you ditched us."

"So you pick a dopehead?"

"My business." Zorro stared at him. "Just came here to tell you we didn't know he'd go after the teacher." Zorro smiled silkily. "You know he had to do somethin' heavy to jump in. Just to start out right with us."

Johnny couldn't believe he'd once been a part of

this—done these things, made others do them. "So why tell me?"

"I didn't want you to come after me for it."

Johnny looked at his friend carefully and, despite all that had happened, felt a tug of regret at losing him. "Why do you care? You're done with me, remember?"

Zorro leaned forward on the straight chair and linked his hands between his knees. "Yeah, well, I been doin' some reevaluatin'."

"Why?"

Zorro looked up at Johnny with the eyes of the old friend he'd always been. "'Cause she's gonna turn on you, man."

"So you said before."

"And I changed my mind about you and me. Since we got history together. I'll be here when she does it."

"Don't hold your breath."

"She's gettin' chummy with the cop."

Johnny tensed, remembering his conversation with Mitch.

She okay? Johnny had asked.

Yeah.

You didn't let her stay here last night, did you?

Ah…no, she's staying at my place for a few days.

Her closeness with Lansing had felt okay then. "So?"

Zorro shook his head, as if Johnny had said something incredibly stupid. "Push comes to shove, she'll pick him over you any day."

"What do you mean?"

"The pig's after somethin' from you, Tonto. Why else he want anything to do with you?"

For a moment, Johnny saw his father, standing over him, a belt in his hand. *You good-for-nothing brat.*

"You don't know what you're talkin' about."

"Wait. It'll happen just like I say. They'll use you. And my guess is, it'll be to get at me. At the Blisters. When it happens, you come back to your family, man. We be there for you."

And as stealthily as he'd come, Zorro disappeared into the night.

"I DON'T CARE what you have to do," Mitch barked into the phone. "I want the results by noon." He slammed the receiver down and clenched his fists to keep from throwing the whole instrument across his office. Consciously, he leaned back in his chair. Just as the counselors had taught him, he closed his eyes and willed every muscle in his body to relax one at a time. It worked better this morning than it had two nights ago.

Seeing Cassie's fear when she'd returned to his place...watching the realization sink in...witnessing her suffering as she threw out the pieces of her past. He'd wanted to howl with rage—and tear somebody apart.

Preferably the Blisters.

Instead, he'd promised himself he'd stop this gang, no matter what. He'd end their threat to Cassie—and to Johnny, the boy who had also come to mean so much to him.

It had enraged him to see Johnny's pain as he told Cassie the red spray paint was a calling card of the Blisters, that they had done this to her.

And amid her very real suffering, she'd comforted

Johnny. She'd told him it didn't matter. That the books were only material things. She'd made him promise to let Mitch take care of this and not get involved.

It was in that completely selfless moment that Mitch had realized he was in love with Cassie Smith. He didn't know what he was going to do with the knowledge, but it was there, in a corner of his heart, for safekeeping.

A movement across the room drew him from his reflection.

Mitch's jaw dropped when he saw Joe DeFazio's father in the doorway to his office.

"Mr. DeFazio."

"Captain." The man's voice was hoarse. And he looked different from the brash, arrogant bully who'd told Mitch five weeks ago to leave his son alone. DeFazio's shoulders were hunched and his eyes bloodshot, as if from lack of sleep.

"What can I do for you?"

DeFazio inched into the room.

"Sit down."

The man perched on the edge of a seat in front of Mitch's desk. His eyes darted around the office. Mitch waited.

"It's my boy."

"Joe."

"He's...he's gone."

"What do you mean?"

"He hasn't been home since last weekend."

"Why haven't you notified us?"

"Because...he called his ma. Told her he was staying with friends. Says he's quitting school."

"How old is he?"

"Eighteen."

Legal age to make the decision. "Do you know where he is?"

"He wouldn't say. But we called a buddy of his. Youngblood. The kid told us he thinks Joey's hanging out with a gang in the city. They tried to get Youngblood to go with 'm, but he said no." DeFazio looked up at Mitch. "My boy said yes. Why'd he say yes, Captain?"

For a brief moment, Mitch took pleasure in the fact that Youngblood was able to resist the lure of the gang. But it was quickly overshadowed by the fact that DeFazio had been sucked in. "Your boy said yes for a thousand reasons, Mr. DeFazio."

"Can you help me?"

"I'll try," Mitch said.

IT WAS A MISTAKE. Mitch could see it as soon as he put the question to Johnny. Mitch had gone to Kurt's clinic, to find the boy, to ask for his help, over Cassie's objections....

"I don't think it's a good idea to involve Johnny." Cassie had stared at Mitch over her desk when he'd come to school to tell her about DeFazio.

"Cassie, he can help us. I need to know where the Blisters hang out."

"Get the New York City police involved. They should know something."

"Time is important. Besides, Johnny's strong enough. He'll be able to handle this."

"I'm not sure. Insecurities like his are hard to overcome. I know."

"I think you're wrong...."

But she'd been right. Mitch knew it as soon as

he'd broached the subject with Johnny. The boy had stiffened first, then shut down right before Mitch's eyes. "What do you mean, I could help? I'm not part of them anymore."

Mitch tried to backtrack when he pegged Johnny's reaction. "It's okay. I'm worried about the DeFazio boy. I figured if you knew how to contact him, we might be able to do some type of intervention."

"You want me to tell you where the Blisters hang out, don't you?"

"Look, Johnny, I'm not making myself clear here. I just thought—"

"Cassie know about this?"

"Cassie?"

"Yeah. Does she know you're here?"

"Yes, but—"

And before Mitch could explain, Kurt burst in on them. "I need Johnny and all available staff members. Stat."

The emergency had taken two hours. Mitch had stuck around, but by the time he got to see Johnny again, the kid had his mask back in place. "Sure, it's cool. I understand."

Mitch suspected Johnny didn't.

JOHNNY WAITED FOR DEFAZIO in the back room at Pepper's. It wasn't very private, but it was where DeFazio had wanted to meet.

Closing his eyes, Johnny leaned back against the rough plaster wall and tried to stop the anger. First Lansing, now DeFazio. Why was everybody wanting to talk to him? Shit, he just wanted to be left alone.

They'll use you...they want something from you...my guess is, it'll be to get at me. At the Blisters.

Johnny tried to banish Zorro's claim, but it had taken root and grown in the twenty-four hours since Lansing had approached him. Johnny had finally gotten the nerve to talk to Cassie about it. She'd been evasive, tiptoeing around her feelings about him helping the cops out. It had made Johnny more nervous.

There was a loud rap on the outside door. Johnny unlocked it to find DeFazio shivering in the alley. He stumbled in. Enraged at what this punk had done to Cassie, Johnny grabbed DeFazio by the collar and raised his fist. But he halted when he saw the kid's face.

"You look like shit."

"I feel like shit."

Bruises covered DeFazio's forehead and cheeks. His nose and one eye were swollen. The bruises hadn't yellowed yet. It had only been four days since his initiation. He looked grotesque.

"What you want from me?" Johnny asked, releasing him. He couldn't make himself pound the punk's already battered face.

DeFazio sagged against the wall, his eyes darting around the small room. "This safe?"

"What? You got national secrets?"

"I got information. Bad information."

Johnny scowled. "About?"

"They kill, Johnny."

"Who?"

"The Blisters."

Johnny shook his head. He'd never seen the gang

kill anyone, but there had been talk. Which Zorro had denied, so Johnny had ignored.

"You don't know what you're sayin'."

"I do. They...that...you know, that guy who..." DeFazio sank onto a chair and put his hands over his face.

Johnny waited.

"They killed that cop last year. He was only twenty-four. He had a pregnant wife." DeFazio looked up at Johnny. "Geez, I didn't know they killed people."

"How do you know this now?"

"I overheard Zorro and Hulk talking."

Johnny digested that.

"What should I do, Johnny?"

Johnny sank into a chair. "I don't know."

The door that led to the pool room opened. Pepper stood in the archway, his wrinkled features accented by a frown. "What are you guys doing back here?"

"You eavesdropping, old man?" Johnny asked.

Pepper straightened. "This is my place, kid. Not yours."

Johnny remembered talking to Cassie once. *You ask Pepper to keep an eye on me, Teach?*

Yes, Johnny, I did. I'll do anything to keep you straight.

Just then, one of the workers called back, "Pepper, phone call."

"I'll be right back," Pepper said, and left.

Johnny turned to DeFazio and swore.

"What are we gonna do now, Johnny?"

They're gonna use you....

"Let's get out of here," Johnny said.

MITCH LOOKED UP from the desk where he sat in Cassie's classroom. There was a new poster on the wall. It was titled A Teenager's Bill of Rights. His gaze lit on number nine. ''A teenager has the right to adult guidance in his life, even if he doesn't know he needs it.''

A good omen, Mitch thought. At least, he hoped it was.

Restless, Mitch stood and glanced at the clock. Cassie should be back any minute. She'd agreed to meet him at three o'clock, but Zoe told him Cassie had unexpectedly gotten called to Seth's office. Mitch needed to talk to her before she saw Johnny at four o'clock.

After wandering around the room, Mitch found himself standing before the bookcase, staring at the books, portfolios and journals. Cassie was worried because Johnny had written furiously in his journal all week, but had marked the entries Private, Do Not Read. Now Mitch knew why. This morning, Pepper had come to see him and told him what he'd overheard two days ago.

Johnny hadn't told Mitch.

And it hurt.

He thought he'd gained the boy's trust.

Leafing through the stack of journals, Mitch stopped at Johnny's. He could read it, get some insight into what was going on in the boy's mind.

A teenager has the right to adult guidance.

He picked up Johnny's black-and-white notebook.

A teenager has the right to privacy.

A rustle at the door distracted him. Mitch turned to stare into the angry face of Johnny Battaglia.

Arms crossed over his chest, the collar of his

leather jacket turned up, Johnny's black eyes were accusing. "I might have known."

"Known what, son?"

"Don't call me that."

Mitch held up the journal. "I didn't read it."

"And I believe in Santa Claus."

"I'd like you to believe in me."

Fierce emotion flickered in Johnny's eyes. He glanced around the room. "Where's Cassie?"

"Right here," she said from behind Johnny.

Stepping away from the door as Cassie came into the room, Johnny jammed his hands in his pockets. Cassie stopped when she saw the journal in Mitch's hand. Mitch held his breath. She gave him a puzzled look, but not an accusatory one. *Thank God.*

Johnny was watching her carefully. He frowned at what he saw—at her trust in Mitch.

Putting the notebook back, Mitch gestured to the table in the corner. "Let's sit down."

"I don't want to sit down," Johnny said.

"What *do* you want, Johnny?" Cassie's voice was concerned. "You asked to see me at four o'clock. You're more than a half hour early."

"I got called into work but...I wanted to talk to you."

Mitch caught the uncertainty in Johnny's tone. *Teenagers have a right to guidance....*

"Do you have something you want to tell us, Johnny?" he asked. "Something about what happened at Pepper's?"

Johnny's eyes widened, but he said nothing. Then he looked at Cassie. "You set me up with him?"

"What do you mean? I didn't know Mitch was

going to be here when you and I talked." Then she turned to Mitch. "What happened at Pepper's?"

"Tell her, Johnny."

Johnny glared at him and remained silent.

"Two nights ago, DeFazio met Johnny there," Mitch began. "He told Johnny the Blisters were responsible for killing the young police officer, Gifford, last year." Cassie gasped. "Pepper overheard Johnny and DeFazio and came to me this morning." Mitch looked at Johnny. "Pepper didn't come to see me until today because he was afraid of the Blisters and didn't want to report it. He thought you might."

Johnny's gaze never left Mitch's, but Johnny's heart felt like it had been stabbed with Zorro's blade. "You want me to help you get to them, don't you?"

They gonna use you, man...to get at the Blisters.

"I want to help *you*."

"Yeah, sure." He turned to Cassie. "You want this, too?"

"I want what's best for you, Johnny. I always have."

Mitch said, "We *both* want what's best for you."

Johnny glanced at Mitch, then back to Cassie. "You want what's best for him."

"No, Johnny, that's not true," Mitch protested.

Needing to believe him, Johnny thought about all the adults in his life. His mother, who drank throughout the day. His father, who hit him. Teachers like Bosco. Had any of them really wanted what was best for him? He looked hard at Cassie and Mitch. After a lifetime of disappointments, believing in these two was too great a risk to take. "Leave me alone. Both of you."

Cassie said, "No, Johnny." She came up behind

him and touched his shoulder. Because he wanted her comfort so badly, he shook her off violently. "Why are you so angry?" she asked.

Because anger's easier. I know anger. And it was better to be mad than to feel the crushing hurt that pushed at his insides—because Zorro had been right. They were using him to get to the gang. He'd just witnessed the proof.

Mitch came closer, too. "Get something straight, Johnny. Cassie's not at fault here. If you're angry, take it out on me."

Push comes to shove, she'll pick him over you any day.

Johnny whirled on them. "I got things straight, Captain. First you wanna know where DeFazio is. Now you want help proving my friends killed somebody."

Mitch angled his chin. "I want the Blisters to get what they deserve. And yes, I'd like you to help me. I want you to help DeFazio and all the other kids who could get sucked in like he did. I'm not ashamed of wanting that. But—"

Johnny looked from the cop to his teacher. "You agree with him, don't you?"

Cassie said, "Johnny, I don't know exactly what's going on here. But if you can help Mitch stop them, maybe you should—"

Johnny turned his back on her again, shutting out her words. Other voices sounded in her head. *I'm afraid he'll turn you against me...the cop and the teacher...no one will ever care about you but me, Johnny.*

Johnny took in a deep breath, unable to stop the messages. He said, "I'm outta here."

As he reached the door, Cassie bounded after him. She latched onto the edge of his jacket in the hall. "Johnny, please, don't go. Talk to me."

"Go talk to *him.*" Johnny shrugged off her grip and raced down the hall and out the door.

CHAPTER FOURTEEN

EVERYONE HAD ALWAYS SAID how smart Johnny Battaglia was. And they were right. He was so smart he knew exactly how to get what he wanted. And he set about getting it methodically.

First, he returned to school the morning after his confrontation with the good captain. But he skipped Cassie's class. He wandered the halls until a corridor supervisor caught him.

"Where are you supposed to be, young man?" Johnny pivoted to look at the ugly face of Jerry Bosco. Just perfect.

"Take a guess."

Even Bosco's balding head reddened. "I asked you a question. Either answer it or you're coming with me."

"Screw you," Johnny said, and turned his back on the man.

Bosco made the mistake of grabbing his arm. "Now, just hold on, kiddo."

Johnny whirled on him. "Don't touch me, you bastard." Johnny's head began to swim with the hurt and rage that had been boiling inside him since three o'clock yesterday afternoon. Because of it, he edged Bosco back against a locker. "Touch me again, creep, and you'll be sorry."

From behind, a hand clasped his shoulder. "Johnny."

Stepping back from Bosco, Johnny turned.

Mr. Taylor stood a foot away. Johnny had always liked and respected the principal.

"Come with me, Johnny."

"He's nothing but a worthless punk," Bosco scoffed. "He should be taken out of here in handcuffs."

Johnny whirled back around and lunged for Bosco. Strong arms came around him from behind again. "You won't hit him, Johnny. There'll be no fighting. Calm down." Taylor kept up the soothing refrain with his arms immobilizing Johnny until some of Johnny's anger abated.

He didn't remember exactly how he got to the principal's office. But he was seated in front of Taylor ten minutes later.

"I know what happened," Mr. Taylor said.

"Bosco's an asshole."

"Not with Mr. Bosco. I know what happened with Ms. Smith and Captain Lansing. But I can't let you disrupt the school like this because of your problems with them. I'm giving you in-school suspension for a week and mandating counseling with Ms. Sherman starting right now." He reached for the phone to call the school psychologist.

"No."

The principal's brow arched. "No?"

"I won't go. To either."

"Then I'll have to suspend you."

Johnny stood. "Don't waste your time. I'm not coming back, anyway."

"Sit down, Johnny, we need to talk."

"I'm done talking," he said, bounding out of the office before Taylor could circle his desk and try to stop him.

Four hours later, Johnny walked into the Forty-second Street clinic. He'd drunk half a bottle of bourbon and smoked two joints in the intervening time. Unsteadily, he made his way back to Kurt's office.

Kurt looked up from his desk. "Johnny? It's a little early for you to be here, isn't it?"

Johnny hadn't noticed before how Kurt's eyes were the exact color of his brother's. The reminder made this easier. "Five weeks ago, I treated a gunshot wound on a friend in this clinic."

Kurt frowned and dropped his pen on the desk. "Gunshot wounds have to be reported to the police."

"I know."

"Why didn't you tell me about this then?"

Geez, they were so alike. Playing so goddamn altruistic. So phony. "I'm tellin' you now."

"All right. Why are you telling me now? You know I'll have to take some action."

Johnny just stared at him.

Kurt came out from behind the desk. He crossed to Johnny. "Johnny, I had faith in you. I was thinking about offering you some kind of scholarship to college and med school in return for your working here. Why are you doing this?"

Johnny's throat closed up. In that moment, he saw all his dreams fade away.

What's a punk like you doing with those kinds of dreams, anyway?

"I don't believe you. You're no more interested in me than your brother is."

Before Kurt could respond, Johnny left the office.

But he returned to the clinic at ten that night when Mary Margaret got off work. Having drunk more bourbon and smoked more dope by then, he was flying high. He intercepted her as she walked out the front door.

"Oh, Johnny, thank God you're here. I was so worried."

He put his arm around her and edged his nose into her hair. Her clean scent filled him. "How worried, baby?"

She pulled away. "You smell like a distillery."

"Just had a little drink."

"Are you driving?"

He looked at her. She was blurry, but he could still see that her eyes were clouded with concern. "I got my car. Come sit in it with me for a minute."

"I won't drive with you if you're drinking. I won't let *you* drive."

He dragged the keys out of his pocket. "Here. I just wanna be with you a minute."

Meg took the keys and followed him to the car.

As soon as they got inside, he was all over her. He'd never come after her with a man's passion before, but that didn't mean he didn't know how.

At first she giggled when he touched her. He kissed her deeply. For a minute, she responded.

But when his hand went to her blouse, she shrank back from him. "Johnny, what are you doing?"

"For a smart girl, that's a dumb question."

He yanked at one of her buttons.

"Johnny, stop." He didn't. "Johnny, please."

Despite the booze and pot, her plea momentarily got to him. But a voice nagged at him from inside, *Finish this. Finish with all of them.*

"You said you respected me." Meg's voice was strained.

He gave her a disgusted roll of the eyes. "I do respect you, baby. But I'm human. I got needs, Mary Margaret." Reaching out, he took her hand and brought it to his crotch. "You gonna meet them or should I go somewhere else?"

"Why are you doing this?"

He wished people would stop asking him that. "I told you, I got needs."

She tilted her head like she did when she was trying to figure out a complicated calculus problem. "You're doing this on purpose, aren't you. To alienate me."

"Baby, I don't wanna alienate you. I wanna screw you."

Even *her* courage couldn't withstand that. Tears welled in her big brown eyes. "I thought, some day, we might make love, Johnny." She threw her head back proudly. "But you'll never, ever *screw* me."

She yanked open the door and tumbled out.

Johnny lay his head back on the seat and closed his eyes. It was done now.

Mary Margaret was gone.

Kurt and the clinic were gone.

Lansing was gone.

School and Cassie—especially Cassie—were gone.

He reached for the ignition before he realized Meg had taken off with his keys. It didn't matter. Where he was going wasn't far from here.

CASSIE SANK TO THE FLOOR in her living room and dragged out a box from underneath a table. Pulling back the cardboard flaps, she dug through the tissue paper. It rustled gently, but the sound seemed loud in the still semidarkness just after midnight.

Carefully, she took out a leather-bound book and ran her fingers over the title, *The History of Medicine.* She'd begun collecting the volumes when Johnny had chosen the topic of medical history for his senior research paper. She'd found the first book while exploring her favorite Manhattan used-book store. After checking around, Cassie had discovered there were ten volumes in all. Over the last six months, she'd managed to locate three. They were expensive, but she was going to give them to Johnny for his birthday—today—and for graduation.

Sighing deeply, she doubted she'd see him today. And it looked as if he wasn't going to graduate from high school, either.

Cassie swallowed hard to stop the despair that threatened to engulf her. Johnny had been suspended from school for an incident that Seth suspected the boy had purposely instigated. Cassie had been unable to get in touch with Johnny at home. The most she could do was hope he'd calm down and come back to school at the end of the suspension. Then, when she'd talked to Kurt about Johnny quitting the clinic, she'd become alarmed. But it was the phone call from Meg Mancini that had edged Cassie into all-out panic. The girl had told Cassie directly and without embarrassment how Johnny had treated her in the clinic parking lot. Meg seemed to realize Johnny was trying to alienate her, and after a few days, she had decided to call Cassie. Though Meg's voice betrayed the hurt Johnny had inflicted, she was obviously more concerned about his welfare.

"Cass? What are you doing down here in the dark?"

Cassie turned to see Mitch silhouetted in the moonlight. He looked big and strong and safe, and Cassie wanted to bury her head in that safety. As he stepped farther into the room, she noticed he wore the dark green terry robe she'd bought for him to keep at her place.

Something had changed between them when Johnny had stormed out two days ago. Mitch had been distant, though he'd stuck around and tried to talk about how to get Johnny back. It hadn't been the time to discuss their feelings for each other, but Cassie worried about what was happening to them.

Mitch came close enough to see what she held. "Honey, what are you doing?"

"Just looking at the present I bought Johnny for his birthday." She stared up at Mitch. "I couldn't sleep. I'm sorry I woke you. You need the rest."

"No more than you." He sat down on the floor next to her.

"Are you kidding?" she said, reaching out and rubbing her hand over his jaw. It was rough and raspy. "For the past week, you've been working day and night with the New York City police to ferret out the Blisters and find Johnny."

"A lot of good it did."

"Well, we got Joe DeFazio into the Crisis Intervention Network your friend runs in the city."

"Yeah, thanks to your testimony at the hearing that he needed help and not punishment."

"He got community service, too."

Mitch was silent, then said, "There's been no sign of Johnny."

When they'd found Joe DeFazio hiding out at Johnny's house, he'd told them about the Den. Cassie had hoped they were on their way to locating Johnny. But the hangout had been abandoned, and the anti-gang specialists from New York said the group had gone underground to avoid being found.

"Today's his birthday."

"I know."

Cassie showed Mitch the books. "I've been collecting these."

Slowly, Mitch ran his fingers over the embossed cover of the one she held. "He'll love them." Mitch grasped Cassie's hand. "I'm going to find him, Cass. I promise."

The determination in Mitch's voice reflected his behavior for the last seven days. He'd worked feverishly all day, then come to her at night and made love to her with a desperation that frightened her. She welcomed him, though; they both needed the solace. They'd grown closer, sharing their despair, seeking respite from it.

Still, neither had spoken of the future.

She tried to tell herself it didn't matter—that this wasn't the time for promises. That they should be concentrating on getting Johnny back.

But it did matter. Because she felt the two were connected.

Deep in her heart, Cassie knew Mitch cared for her. And she'd never experienced such passion in a man before. But his reticence to talk about his feelings for her was connected to Johnny.

"What are you thinking?" he asked her.

She held his gaze. "Things you don't want to hear."

He ran his knuckles over her cheek. "You know how much you mean to me."

"Mitch, what happens when we find Johnny?"

"What do you mean?"

"Are you sticking around? For us both?"

He drew back his hand. "I've ruined things between you two."

"No, you haven't."

He stood, distancing her physically and emotionally. "Yes. In twenty minutes, I destroyed years of work you did with him."

"Are you saying you were wrong to ask him for help with the gang?"

"No, I don't think I had a choice. Too many young lives are at stake. But maybe somebody else could have handled it better. I feel as if I've ruined Johnny's life." After a pause, he finished, "Just like Tam's."

Cassie felt herself go cold. "No, Mitch, the situation with Johnny has nothing to do with Tam. And you weren't to blame for Tam, anyway. Cold-blooded killers murdered that young boy."

Mitch tossed back his head and closed his eyes. "It seems as if my actions with kids always end up causing them harm in some way. Sometimes I think I was right to keep to myself...not to get involved." He looked directly at her then. "With anyone."

Panic skittered down her spine. "With me, too?"

"Maybe."

Cassie stood and looked into his eyes. Raising her chin, she said, "I love you, Mitch. Can you just let me go, knowing that?"

A muscle leaped in his jaw. He swallowed hard. After a moment, he pressed his fingers against her mouth. "Shh...no declarations now. No questions. Let's just concentrate on getting Johnny back. We'll decide what to do then." He reached for her hand. "Come back to bed now."

She knew him so well, she thought as she placed her hand in his. The stubborn set of his chin. The tilt of his head. The bleakness in his beloved green eyes.

Cassie had her answer, even if Mitch didn't know he'd given it to her.

"HAPPY BIRTHDAY, BRO," Zorro said, passing a joint to Johnny.

Johnny took a long drag and let the drug anesthetize him. It was taking more and more these days to block out the memories, more and more to quell the doubts. He'd spent the week in a haze of alcohol and marijuana, and it still wasn't enough to forget who he used to be. To forget the dreams he'd abandoned.

"Thanks, Zor."

Johnny's best friend stood and crossed to the battered bureau on the other side of the room. They'd crashed at Zorro's place at four this morning and had just awakened in the late afternoon.

A drawer creaked when Zorro opened it. From inside, he pulled out a package. "For you."

Ludicrously, Johnny noticed that it was wasn't wrapped. It was in a plain brown paper bag. Out of nowhere, a memory hit him....

"Isn't this a little frilly for me?" Johnny had

asked Cassie after she'd handed him a brightly wrapped present on his last birthday.

Cassie had laughed and ruffled his hair. "What a sexist statement for a liberated guy like you...."

"Open it," Zorro said.

Viciously, Johnny banished the memory. Cassie was dead to him. They all were. From the bag, Johnny drew out his present.

He stared at it, feeling a surge of panic so great his hand started to shake. His gut told him to drop it and run like hell. His mind reinforced what he knew to be true. *They gonna use you, man....*

Zorro was watching him intently when Johnny looked up.

"Like it?" Zorro asked.

"I don't carry a blade, Zorro. Why'd ya give this to me?"

Zorro sat down on a straight chair facing Johnny. "Time to make the tie, Tonto."

"The tie?"

"Yeah. I been coddlin' ya for months now. And this last week, I been lettin' ya coast. But it's time you prove you're with us."

Johnny's heart slammed into his rib cage. "How?"

Zorro leaned back. "Well, I thought seein' this was your eighteenth birthday, that you oughtta 'come of age,' so to speak." Black eyes narrowed on Johnny, losing all of their warmth. "We got some action on for tonight. At eleven. We gonna e-lim-i-nate one of our enemies. The way I figure it, you get to use this blade like you always wanted. You know, in your future. You gonna perform a little surgery."

"Who is it?"

"A friend of yours, Tonto."

Johnny steeled himself. "Who?"

"You gotta make a commitment, buddy. You wanna stay with us, you got to prove it. Tonight."

Johnny simply stared at him.

"You one of us or not, Tonto? Tell me now."

CHAPTER FIFTEEN

"TWELVE." MITCH CURLED his arm, pulling the barbell toward his body, expelling a heavy breath. With excruciating slowness, he lowered it, then dropped the weight to the floor. Sweat poured down his forehead and he wiped it with a towel. He winced and rubbed his shoulder.

I'm great at back rubs. Let me give you one, then I'll get out of here.

Despite his black mood, he smiled at the memory of Cassie coming to comfort him the night she'd found out about Vietnam. She was such a treasure—defying him, forcing him to let her help him. How could he ever give her up when the time came? Did he have to? What would be best for Johnny? For Cassie? He thought about how he'd blown his relationship with Johnny. He thought of how he'd hurt Cassie with his need for rules, and her need for flexibility. She'd gone along with his plan to eliminate gang activity at Bayview, but she'd hated his method. Would they ever be able to compromise? The thoughts only added to his frustration, already too close to the explosion point.

He looked around his exercise room. He'd come here at nine tonight when he'd finished work, instead of going directly to her house. Oh, he'd go to her. He wasn't strong enough to resist her yet. But he had to rid himself of some of his rage before he saw her. She'd come to know him well. Too well. She'd see right away how desperate he was tonight.

There was no sign of Johnny anywhere. Mitch had personally scoured all the known hangouts of the Blisters. He'd made every street contact in New York he could think of, and had coerced the city cops to do the same. He'd called in a hundred favors. But there was still no trace of the boy.

The irony of his situation didn't escape Mitch. Leaning back against the weight bench, he told himself once again that if he found the kid—no, *when* he found the kid—he should let Cassie go. That would be the unselfish thing to do. Johnny needed her more than Mitch did.

Yeah, and if you believe that, I got a bridge to sell you.

Flinging the towel aside, swearing vilely, he stood and kicked the gym bag he'd left on the floor. ''All right,'' he said aloud. ''I need her as much as Johnny does.''

Torn by the conflicting emotions, he jammed his hand through his hair. Cassie had said he wasn't thinking straight because he felt guilty about Johnny going back to the gang. Was that true?

Maybe, but it wasn't just that. He *should* give her up. He *should* sacrifice his own need for the boy.

Like a father would do for his son.

Mitch closed his eyes, swamped by what he felt for both Johnny and Cassie.

Then he heard the crash.

Instantly, his cop's instincts kicked in. His whole body tensed as he identified the noise and its location.

A broken window. In the back of the house.

Without making a sound, he reached down into the gym bag and fished out his nine-millimeter. Straightening, he picked his way to the door of the exercise room. He'd left no other lights on in the house, and the exercise room couldn't be seen from the back door. Tiptoeing down the hall, he held his breath.

He heard more sounds. Shuffling. Then a groan when the intruder knocked into something. His back to the wall, Mitch felt his way down the corridor and stopped just where it met the kitchen. In the splash of moonlight, he could see a figure. Tall. Broad-shouldered. The collar of his jacket turned up.

When the intruder reached the apex of the kitchen and hallway, Mitch sprang out. He knocked the guy to the floor and pinned his hands behind his back in seconds.

"Mitch, it's me. Johnny."

Stunned, Mitch let go of Johnny's arms and eased off him. Just as Mitch set down his gun, he realized how stupid the move was. The kid had broken into his house. The kid hated him. The kid could do him harm. And now, Mitch was vulnerable to him—and to whomever Johnny had brought along. Remaining perfectly still, Mitch was sickened by the thought of Johnny planning to hurt him.

"I had to see you," Johnny said. He'd righted himself and was sitting across from Mitch.

"Why?"

"Look, could we turn on some lights?"

"Tell me first why you broke in."

"I didn't think you were here. There weren't any

lights on in the back of the house. I was gonna wait for you.''

Was this a trap?

''You could have called me.''

''There wasn't time.''

''What do you mean?''

''Geez, Mitch, turn some lights on so I can see you.''

And do what?

''Tell me why you're here first.''

''Okay. You gotta help me stop 'm. The gang's going after Pepper tonight. They're gonna use him as an example.''

''What are they going to do?''

''Kill him.'' Mitch could hear the strain in Johnny's voice. He sounded very young. ''They want *me* to kill him, Mitch, as proof that I'm really one of them.''

Mitch's heart leapfrogged in his chest. Slowly, he stood and switched on a lamp. It cast Johnny in a mellow light, but the glow didn't soften the ravages of his face. His cheeks were sunken and he hadn't shaved for days. His eyes were hollow.

''Johnny…''

The boy stood, too. ''Look, I'm not going to do it. But *they* will. They're gonna be there at eleven when Pepper closes the pool hall. I made some excuse about seeing my mother on my birthday and said I'd meet them there later.'' He grabbed Mitch's arm. ''But I came here, instead. You gotta help me, Mitch. You gotta stop them from hurting anybody else.''

Mitch reached out and grasped Johnny's shoulders. ''I will.'' Impulsively, he pulled the boy into a bear hug. "Thank God you came to me." Then he let Johnny go. "All right, tell me everything you know."

THE ALLEY BEHIND Pepper's pool hall smelled like garbage day in New York City. It was dark, too, but thankfully the cold front had abated.

Mitch had told the backup officers he'd called to park the black-and-whites out of sight and to meet him at the pool hall on foot. Pepper had been hurried out a side door, and the few patrons had left. Six officers had surrounded the building by ten-thirty, and they were all in place.

At exactly eleven o'clock, a car rolled to a stop at the end of the alley, its lights off. The driver left the engine running and six guys piled out. Mitch was huddled behind a protruding wall at the back entrance where Zorro had told Johnny to meet them. Two other officers hid behind the trash cans across from Mitch. Three more were around the corner.

The gang members strode down the alley. Mitch could barely make out the red on the front of their jackets. Just before they reached the door, Mitch and three officers stepped out from their hiding places, guns cocked, arms out straight in firing position. "Stop where you are," Mitch said loud and clear. "This is the police."

Pandemonium broke out. The last three gang members turned and ran. Two of the others dived toward the officers behind the trash cans. The first one lunged for Mitch. The maneuver of his attacker and the darkness unbalanced Mitch, and the gun flew from his hand. The punk plowed into him.

Mitch was slammed back into the brick building.

His head spun dizzily. On reflex, he raised his arm and grabbed the wrist of the attacker. He threw his weight forward. The man fell back. Then he tripped. Mitch didn't let go. They fell to the ground together. Bone crunched on the gravel, but the attacker kept hold of Mitch. He was smaller but strong. And determined. Mitch parried a thrust of the guy's knee. In doing so, he lost some of his advantage. It was enough to let the guy roll over. He pinned Mitch to the ground.

On his back now, Mitch could only see a silhouette above him. Mitch's grip loosened and the guy raised his arm. Mitch saw the blade gleam in the moonlight just before it came down at him. With one adrenaline-induced surge, Mitch thrust his whole body to the side. The guy fell forward. Mitch pounced on him and heard a heavy groan. The man went still.

Behind him, Mitch heard a scuffle.

He turned around in time to see another gang member come at him with a knife.

A shot rang out and the world went black.

CASSIE WAS STARTLED out of a fitful sleep by a noise. When she heard it again, she realized the doorbell was ringing. She glanced at the clock over the television. It was 2:00 a.m. She'd fallen asleep on the couch waiting for Mitch to come to her tonight. Awake now, her heart picked up speed as she wondered why he was so late. She hurried to the door and pulled it open. On the porch was Johnny Battaglia. His messy hair, unshaven face and disheveled clothes registered briefly before he threw himself into her arms.

"Oh, God, I'm so glad to see you," she said, holding the boy close.

He held on tight for a minute. "You won't be glad."

Tugging him inside, she didn't let go of his arm. "Why wouldn't I be?" She hugged him again. "I've been so worried about you."

He drew back. "Mitch is in trouble, Cassie."

"Mitch?"

"Yeah. I got him into trouble."

"What do you mean?"

Standing in the middle of the foyer, in halting and self-deprecating words, Johnny told her about the gang's two-fold plan to kill Pepper and cement Johnny to them.

Cassie squeezed his hand and summoned the strength she needed for him. "You did the right thing by going to Mitch, Johnny."

"Did I?"

"Absolutely."

"I don't know anymore." He clutched at her arm. "Where is he now? I waited at his house for hours, like he told me to. I didn't answer the phone, like he said. When it got so late, I tried to call the police station, but the guy at the desk wouldn't tell me anything. Just that Mitch wasn't there. So I came here."

The bleakness in Johnny's eyes touched her heart. She quelled the panic that threatened to surge through her. "He'll be fine, Johnny. He's a good cop. He can take care of himself."

"Zorro hates him," Johnny said distractedly. "And you. He'll go after Mitch. I know he will. I shouldn't have asked Mitch for help."

Cassie drew in a deep breath. "Come into the living room. We'll wait here together. Everything will be all right."

She hoped her voice was calm. Although she meant what she told Johnny about Mitch's skill, the thought of him being involved in a gang fight chilled her. For an hour, she sat with Johnny, holding his hand, reassuring him and praying.

At 3:00 a.m. the bell rang again. Cassie dashed to the foyer, but Johnny hung back in the living room. She threw open the door—and once again, Mitch stood on the porch.

Mitch groaned as Cassie flung herself at him and pain lanced from his shoulder through his entire body. She drew back, her eyes dropping to his shoulder, which was confined in a tight-fitting sling. "Oh, my God, you're hurt."

"I'm all right."

"You're in pain." She stepped back. "Come on in."

He came fully into the foyer and studied her. Her hair was half in a braid and half out. Her face was pale and drawn. Her clothes were wrinkled. But she'd never looked better to him. Without a word, he held out his good arm to her. She came back to him gingerly. He circled her neck with his hand.

Though he saw Johnny hovering in the living room, he tugged Cassie close for a minute. He'd had a flash of insight in the moments before he was stabbed—something to do with grabbing onto any happiness you can and making the most of the time you have in this life. In her ear, he whispered, "I love you."

Her body trembled and he knew she was crying.

He held her tightly against the uninjured half of his chest, relishing the feel of her, needing her to know he'd never let her go now, no matter what.

When she pulled back slightly, her watery eyes returned the declaration before she whispered, "I love you, too."

"Everything's going to be fine now. I'm alive and I'm not leaving you. Ever."

"Thank God." It took a few moments for her to regain her composure. But, just as always, she pulled it together and smiled at him. Then she turned to look at Johnny.

Mitch followed her gaze. Johnny stood alone next to the couch, his shoulders hunched, his posture stiff. The desolation on his youthful face made Mitch's heart go out to him. Striding into the room, Mitch reached the boy and grasped his arm. "You did the right thing in the end, Johnny. Hang on to that when all this starts crashing down on you."

Johnny nodded. "I'm just glad you're all right."

"I am." He looked at Cassie. "Let's sit down. I'm fine, but my shoulder hurts like hell, and I'm tired."

When they were seated, Cassie asked, "What happened?"

Briefly, Mitch explained the chain of events in the alley behind Pepper's.

"What happened to your shoulder?" Johnny asked.

"A knife wound. They treated it in Emergency." He didn't tell them he'd been brought in almost unconscious but had refused to stay in the hospital. He knew he had to see both Cassie and Johnny face-to-face to convince them he was all right.

White-faced, Cassie seemed to struggle for control. "What happened to everyone else?"

Mitch's expression was somber. "Two of the officers have superficial knife wounds."

Cassie glanced at Johnny, then back to Mitch. "The Blisters?"

"Most of them were arrested."

Johnny spoke up. "Most of them?"

"Zorro was badly hurt."

Johnny blanched.

"You have to know, Johnny," Mitch told him honestly. "I tangled with Zorro. He fell on the knife he attacked me with."

Cassie said, "How badly is he hurt?"

"He's in critical condition. After they treated me, I stayed around the hospital to see how he made out. Finally, the doctor came out of surgery. The knife wound was close to Zorro's heart. I left this number to be called when there's any word on him." He turned to the boy. "Johnny, they don't know if he'll live."

Cassie got up and went to Johnny. She knelt in front of him and squeezed his hand. "We'll face this together, Johnny. No matter—"

Just then, the phone rang. Reluctantly, Cassie stood and answered it. Her face paled even more when she turned to Mitch. "It's the hospital. They want to talk to you."

With grim resignation, Mitch rose and took the receiver.

"Captain Lansing?" a voice on the other end asked.

"Yes."

"This is Dr. Hanson. You wanted to know about

the boy who was brought in. Zorro, they called him.''

''Yes.''

''I'm sorry. His heart just gave out.''

Immobilized, Mitch gripped the receiver. Finally, he managed to say, ''Oh. Well, thank you for calling.'' After he hung up, he turned to find Johnny still seated and Cassie behind him with her hands on his shoulders.

Mitch walked over and squatted before Johnny. He took his hand. ''I'm sorry, Johnny. Zorro's gone.'' Mitch tightened his grip on Johnny, and Cassie squeezed his shoulder.

Johnny froze for a moment. Then he shook them both off and stood.

Mitch was forced back but he rose, too, and reached out quickly. He got the back of Johnny's shirt and held on tight as Johnny started for the door. ''No, Johnny, don't leave. I'm sorry Zorro's dead. But don't run away.'' He yanked on the flannel with his good arm. ''Stay here with us. We'll help you through this.''

Johnny turned and faced them, tears running down his cheeks. He stared at Mitch, then glanced at Cassie, his face a study in torment. ''I...I...''

''We're your family now,'' Cassie said.

Johnny still looked torn.

''Yes, son, we are,'' Mitch told him.

At those words, Johnny's whole body sagged into Mitch. Careful of his injury, Mitch pulled the boy to his chest. Johnny sobbed as he burrowed into Mitch. ''It's okay, John, I'm here for you. We're both here for you.'' Looking over Johnny's head, Mitch locked his gaze on Cassie. ''For good,'' he said hoarsely. ''We're both here for good.''

EPILOGUE

Johnny's Journal

WELL, LIFE SURE HAS BEEN interesting the last few days. I just got back from Cassie and Mitch's wedding. I'm still in my tuxedo—Mary Margaret said I looked sexy in it. Kurt said I'll need one when I get to be a big-shot doctor.

I was the usher at their wedding. Can you believe it? After all that I did two months ago, they still want me in their lives. Mitch says I have to care about myself to believe I deserve to have people care about me. I'm trying.

I still miss Zorro. Cassie says that's okay. He was like a brother to me, and just because he went bad doesn't mean my feelings for him disappeared. Sometimes I just can't believe he's dead. When I get down, I try to talk to somebody…Mary Margaret, Kurt, Mitch or Cassie. They even put me in touch with the anti-gang specialist in New York, and he helps me to see why I got involved with the Blisters to begin with.

Mostly, I'm just grateful for another chance. Cassie says she got one when she was my age, too, and look how cool she turned out. I still feel guilty about all the trouble I caused them. She says that's okay, she feels guilty, too, sometimes, about the things she did in her past. It keeps her honest. Mitch says Cassie and I are a lot alike, but Cassie says I'm really more like him. I consider both comparisons compliments.

Two letters came today: a scholarship notification and a letter from Columbia University. I always knew I was smart, but now the tests prove it out. A National Merit Finalist. That means I'll get money to go to Columbia, which of course had the good sense to accept me. I'll be working at the clinic because Kurt's footing some of the bills, too.

Not bad for a punk like me, huh?

Mitch's Journal

I'LL NEVER FORGET what she looked like coming down the aisle on Seth's arm. Her face glowed, and her smile was just for me. I pushed for the church wedding. She'd wanted to elope, but I wouldn't hear of it. I insisted on a traditional wedding, with all the trimmings. She wore an ivory lacy dress that couldn't hide her curves but made her look young and innocent. In keeping with tradition—she says it just shows how much I like rules—I provided something old, something new, something borrowed and something blue. I gave her the sexiest light blue undies you ever saw and told her to wear them beneath her gown. Her engagement ring was old—it had been my mother's—and it looked right on her hand. Her wedding band, of course, was new. The borrowed part gave me pause and I fudged a bit on that. I *borrowed* a saying from one of her posters, and had it engraved on a bracelet for her. It read, "Teaching Someone To Love Is The Greatest Gift."

The ceremony was a real tearjerker. At the altar, Seth handed her over to me and said, "Take care of her for me, Mitch."

Of course, Cassie's eyes filled, then she took my hand and said, "Ready, big guy?"

"I'm ready, love," I told her, and we took our places next to Kurt and Zoe.

Johnny was at the altar, too, right where he should be.

Cass and I are still fighting over her name. I want her to have mine—that's the *right* way—but the most she'll give in to is to hyphenate it, Smith-Lansing.

We can't agree on where to live, so we've still got two houses.

But we both want a baby soon. How did she put it that day—our own little bundle of sugar and spice? We planned the wedding right before spring break so we can work on that in the Caribbean.

All in all, I'm a pretty lucky guy.

Cassie's Journal

THE WEDDING WAS LOVELY, even if I did initially fight against having it in a church. Yeah, I said church. Can you imagine? I got married in a church. In front of God and half of Bayview Heights High School. But Mitch wanted it, and ever since he was almost killed, it seems I can't say no to him about anything. Of course, he takes advantage of it every chance he gets. And God, he looked so sexy in his tuxedo, I wanted to rip his clothes off right there at the altar.

Almost all the At-Risk kids came, including Joe

DeFazio. He's back in school, and even though he won't graduate with his class, I think he's going to make it. He tells me he's saving up to replace some of my books, but I told him it's not necessary. His coming back is enough.

Johnny's doing great. He was bursting with pride to be an usher for Mitch—they're pretty tight these days. Meg was at the service, too, and all three of them conspired to get me to dance at the reception.

Mitch came to my house two hours before the wedding, even though it's bad luck to see the bride on the day of the ceremony. He insisted on every other damn tradition, I'm surprised he broke this one. But I was glad he did. He kicked Zoe out. Then he made the sweetest love to me ever. It brought tears to my eyes. When I asked him what that was all about, he said it was insurance so I didn't jilt him at the altar.

Fat chance. I may have made some stupid decisions in my life and done some dumb things, but I'm not about to let go of the best thing that ever happened to me.

I'm so lucky. I've got so much. Mitch. Johnny. Friends like Zoe and Seth. When I was fifteen, I never thought my life would end up like this.

I guess it just goes to show you, "If you want the rainbow, you have to put up with the rain."

*   *   *   *   *

Be sure to watch out for Seth Taylor's story.
Kathryn Shay's next
Harlequin Superromance will be out in
December 1998.

**Make a Valentine's date
for the premiere of**

◆ HARLEQUIN® **Movies**

starting February 14, 1998 with

Debbie Macomber's

This Matter of
Marriage

on **the movie channel** tmc

Just tune in to **The Movie Channel** the **second Saturday night** of every month at 9:00 p.m. EST to join us, and be swept away by the sheer thrill of romance brought to life. Watch for details of upcoming movies—in books, in your television viewing guide and in stores.

If you are not currently a subscriber to The Movie Channel, simply call your local cable or satellite provider for more details. Call today, and don't miss out on the romance!

the movie channel tmc

*100% pure movies.
100% pure fun.*

◆ HARLEQUIN™
Makes any time special.™

DEBBIE MACOMBER

invites you to the

HEART OF TEXAS

Join Debbie Macomber as she brings you the lives
and loves of the folks in the ranching community
of Promise, Texas.

If you loved Midnight Sons—don't miss
Heart of Texas! A brand-new six-book series
from Debbie Macomber.

Available in February 1998
at your favorite retail store.

Heart of Texas by Debbie Macomber

Lonesome Cowboy	February '98
Texas Two-Step	March '98
Caroline's Child	April '98
Dr. Texas	May '98
Nell's Cowboy	June '98
Lone Star Baby	July '98

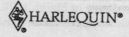

HARLEQUIN®

BESTSELLING AUTHORS
IN THE SPOTLIGHT

.WE'RE SHINING THE SPOTLIGHT ON SIX OF OUR STARS!

Harlequin and Silhouette have selected stories from several of their bestselling authors to give you six sensational reads. These star-powered romances are bound to please!

THERE'S A PRICE TO PAY FOR STARDOM... AND IT'S LOW

$1.99 U.S.
$2.50 CAN.
Special Offer

As a special offer, these six outstanding books are available from Harlequin and Silhouette for only $1.99 in the U.S. and $2.50 in Canada. Watch for these titles:

At the Midnight Hour—**Alicia Scott**
Joshua and the Cowgirl—**Sherryl Woods**
Another Whirlwind Courtship—**Barbara Boswell**
Madeleine's Cowboy—**Kristine Rolofson**
Her Sister's Baby—**Janice Kay Johnson**
One and One Makes Three—**Muriel Jensen**

Available in March 1998
at your favorite retail outlet.

THE WEST TEXANS

**Welcome back to West Texas—
and the Parker Ranch!**

TEXAS LAWMAN
by Ginger Chambers

*Long before the War between the States,
Parker sons and daughters ranched Parker land.
Eighty-eight-year-old Mae Parker aims
to keep things that way.*

*But there's a rebel in every family—
including the Parkers.*

Jodie Parker has been a thorn in
Sheriff Tate Connelly's side for years—she's
wild and rebellious and beautiful. Now Tate's
got two choices: he can arrest her for aiding and
abetting a wanted man—who just happens to be
her ex-lover. *Or* he can help her prove the man's
innocence. On one condition. That Jodie settle
down once and for all. In the arms of the law!

Available March 1998
wherever Harlequin Superromance® books are sold.

HSRWT778

Don't miss these Harlequin favorites by some of our top-selling authors!

HT#25733	THE GETAWAY BRIDE	$3.50 U.S.	☐
	by Gina Wilkins	$3.99 CAN.	☐
HP#11849	A KISS TO REMEMBER	$3.50 U.S.	☐
	by Miranda Lee	$3.99 CAN.	☐
HR#03431	BRINGING UP BABIES	$3.25 U.S.	☐
	by Emma Goldrick	$3.75 CAN.	☐
HS#70723	SIDE EFFECTS	$3.99 U.S.	☐
	by Bobby Hutchinson	$4.50 CAN.	☐
HI#22377	CISCO'S WOMAN	$3.75 U.S.	☐
	by Aimée Thurlo	$4.25 CAN.	☐
HAR#16666	ELISE & THE HOTSHOT LAWYER	$3.75 U.S.	☐
	by Emily Dalton	$4.25 CAN.	☐
HH#28949	RAVEN'S VOW	$4.99 U.S.	☐
	by Gayle Wilson	$5.99 CAN.	☐

(limited quantities available on certain titles)

AMOUNT	$ _____
POSTAGE & HANDLING	$ _____
($1.00 for one book, 50¢ for each additional)	
APPLICABLE TAXES*	$ _____
TOTAL PAYABLE	$ _____

(check or money order—please do not send cash)

To order, complete this form and send it, along with a check or money order for the total above, payable to Harlequin Books, to: **In the U.S.:** 3010 Walden Avenue, P.O. Box 9047, Buffalo, NY 14269-9047; **In Canada:** P.O. Box 613, Fort Erie, Ontario, L2A 5X3.

Name: _____

Address: _____ City: _____

State/Prov.: _____ Zip/Postal Code: _____

Account Number (if applicable): _____

*New York residents remit applicable sales taxes.
Canadian residents remit applicable GST and provincial taxes.

Look us up on-line at: http://www.romance.net

075-CSAS

HBLJM98